GODDESS COMPLEX

Praise for *Goddess Complex: A Novel*

"Inventive … *Goddess Complex* is astute about the repetitiveness of misery, and how pain can accrete like an enclosing wall, rising to block out the rest of the world … [The book] takes a sharp, unexpected turn as Sanjana flies to India, where she intends to finalize her divorce but ends up at a remote resort run by her doppelgänger, Sanjena, instead. It is here that Sanjana's focus on her alternate lives turns literal, the novel swerving into a more frenzied chronicle involving elaborate deceptions, a cultish pregnancy influencer and a lot of blood … Haunting and hilarious, *Goddess Complex* is at once a satire, a Gothic tale, a novel of ideas, a character study. Like any individual life, the book bristles with possibilities."

—R.O. Kwon, *The New York Times Book Review*

"Sathian [*Gold Diggers*] wraps a whip-smart satire of Millennial womanhood around an arresting story of mistaken identity … a dazzling *Operation Shylock*–esque hall of mirrors … Sathian's social commentary is riotous … and she finds intriguing new angles on the doppelgänger theme … This is incandescent."

—*Publishers Weekly* (starred review)

"With its piercing exploration of the unrelenting pressure on women to have children, Sathian's witty and wise novel will resonate with readers on either side of the debate and everyone in between."

—*Booklist* (starred review)

"Suspenseful to the very end … this well-crafted, mysterious novel with some dystopian twists is a worthwhile read. Fans of Margaret Atwood's *The Handmaid's Tale* will devour it."

—*Library Journal* (starred review)

"Sathian unspools a wide-ranging, at times hallucinatory, yarn that encompasses her protagonist's frustrations with rigid rules about femininity, motherhood, Indian American social norms, and more … Not for nothing does the novel feature an epigraph from the Gothic classic *Rebecca*; the novel is rife with doppelgängers, gaslighting, hidden histories, and more, all to the purpose of questioning the behavioral expectations placed on women like Sanjana … It's a noble goal, with fine set pieces that are both funny and melancholy."

—*Kirkus*

"Buckle up, readers: *Goddess Complex*, an heir to the best of Kafka or Roth in both its savage comic brilliance and its depth of meaning, is the wildest of rides. I can't remember the last time I read a book that was simultaneously so serious in its ambition—this is a novel, ultimately, about female power and agency—and such a perfectly plotted page-turner. I could not put it down."

—Vauhini Vara, author of the Pulitzer Prize finalist *The Immortal King Rao* and *This Is Salvaged*

"*Goddess Complex* is hilarious, astute, and thoroughly enjoyable."

—Ayşegül Savaş, author of *The Anthropologists*

"*Goddess Complex* is the most interesting, illuminating, and bold contemporary novel of ideas I've read in years. Sanjena Sathian has given us a world that's split—between India and America, between acid and ache, between the longing to reproduce and the longing to remain inviolate, between comedy and horror—in a way that affords us that rarest of opportunities: a space to truly think."

—Sarah Thankam Mathews, author of the National Book Award finalist *All This Could Be Different*

"Sanjena Sathian has written a novel of great wit and daring, a phantasmagoric journey that dazzles at every turn. It's surreal, it's funny, it's raw, and it glimmers, sentence upon sentence, with brilliance."

—Elizabeth McKenzie, author of *The Dog of the North*

"Sanjena Sathian's *Goddess Complex* is brilliant, audacious, and funny as hell. In a voice reminiscent of Phoebe Waller-Bridge and Miranda July, Sathian writes about young adulthood with wit, heart, and aching precision. This isn't a novel about a character stuck between two worlds, but a woman stuck between the world and herself. And that's why I loved it."

—Neel Patel, author of *Tell Me How to Be*

"*Goddess Complex* has the rare quality of being both raucously funny and deeply affecting. Sanjena Sathian explores many topics in her second novel, from the surreal world of the pregnancy industrial complex to big questions of identity and self-creation. But it never loses sight of a simple, human concern: how to preserve our individuality in a world that seeks to degrade it. In one beautiful sentence after another, she shows us the absurd expectations of our modern moment, and the result is nothing less than spellbinding."

—Lee Cole, author of *Groundskeeping*

"Sanjena Sathian has written a whip-smart millennial mystery that charts a satirical course through the absurd cultural landscape of female identity. Funny, searching, and delectably rebellious."

—Lexi Freiman, author of *The Book of Ayn*

"Sanjena Sathian's remarkable new novel is as clever as it is unsettling, at once horrifying and hilarious—*Rosemary's Baby*, if Rosemary could freeze her eggs. An utterly contemporary psychological thriller about motherhood, identity, and doubles, *Goddess Complex* establishes Sathian as an indispensable writer of our generation."

—Andrew Ridker, author of *Hope* and *The Altruists*

GODDESS COMPLEX

A NOVEL

SANJENA SATHIAN

HarperCollins *Publishers* India

First published in the US by Penguin Press 2025
An imprint of Penguin Random House LLC

Published in India by HarperCollins *Publishers* 2025
HarperCollins *Publishers* India, Cyber City,
Building 10-A, Gurugram, Haryana – 122002, India
www.harpercollins.co.in

2 4 6 8 10 9 7 5 3 1

P-ISBN: 978-93-6569-353-9
E-ISBN: 978-93-6569-590-8

Typeset in 11.5/15.2 Adobe Caslon Pro
by HarperCollins *Publishers* India Pvt. Ltd

Printed and bound at
Manipal Technologies Limited, Manipal

MIX
Paper | Supporting responsible forestry
FSC™ C043100

This book is produced from independently certified FSC® paper to ensure responsible forest management.

HarperCollins *Publishers*, Macken House, 39/40 Mayor Street Upper, Dublin 1, D01 C9W8, Ireland

For Bill, of course

Contents

Part Two

Part One

The past is still too close to us. The things we have tried to forget and put behind us would stir again, and that sense of fear, of furtive unrest … might in some manner unforeseen become a living companion, as it had been before.

—Daphne du Maurier,
Rebecca

I

Expectations

It began innocuously enough, with a text message from an unknown number that arrived while I was soaping my armpits in the ladies' room of the New Haven train station.

So you and K are back in town

I presumed that the sender had seen me lugging a forlorn expression around campus recently, where I was, in fact, *back* after a long spell away. Possibly we had even brushed past each other on the train platform moments earlier. I glanced over my shoulder, quickly, as if some figure might materialize from one of the Pepto Bismol–pink toilet stalls. Then I stood, very still, for perhaps half a minute. All was silent. I became suddenly aware of the foolishness of my posture, the way I was leaning toward the mirror, lit by the sickly fluorescence, my true eyes fixed on my reflected eyes, like a cat tensing up at its likeness in a windowpane. I shook off the chill that had run down my neck at the sight of the initial, *K.*

There had been nasty, disjointed flashes like this all year, as acquaintances whose names I could not remember, whose faces I failed to place, crossed streets or cafés to say hello and, inevitably, ask about Killian. He was, after all, still legally my husband. I usually just said, "Oh, he's out of town," because I could not bring myself to explain the limbo of our situation. I had ghosted him last summer, and we had not spoken in nearly a year. I was something between a wife and an ex-wife, between who I had been and who I would be next.

I pocketed my phone and returned to the task at hand: dabbing my smelly underarms with a damp paper towel. I had stopped shaving (out of laziness rather than self-empowerment) and the more forested my pits grew, the more they seemed to become their own ecological zones. On top of that, I had lost my deodorant, and I could not bathe, as I could not go home: it was commencement weekend on campus, and in order to escape the celebratory crowds of smug families and promising graduates who would emphasize, by contrast, my own pompless circumstances, I'd Airbnb'd my place to some undergrad's parents and fled to my friend Lia's, in Brooklyn. My stay had begun pleasantly, until, after I'd poured the four-dollar wine I'd brought as my keep, Lia coyly pushed her glass aside and announced that she was *expecting*.

"Expecting what?" I asked, absently, thinking of a piece of mail, or another guest.

"*Expecting* expecting."

Her beam matched the sheen of her stainless-steel appliances. Lia and her husband Gor had recently bought a two-bedroom condo in a new-construction high rise in Dumbo. All the appliances seemed straight out of plastic wrap. I felt like a mannequin in a showroom. In college, Lia had passed one barefoot, braless summer volunteering on a dairy farm, sleeping on alpaca rugs, extolling Diva Cups. More recently, she and Gor, both attorneys at white-shoe law firms, had been featured in a *New York* magazine piece about millennials' home-buying "journeys." I was still unaccustomed to this new Lia, who had found serenity in her renunciation of renunciation.

My throat clogged, and instead of congratulating her on having become successfully inseminated, I said, "Who the fuck says *expecting* instead of pregnant?"

Her doll-like features immediately contorted into an expression of utmost sympathy. I grasped that she thought I was jealous.

It was true that my life was increasingly becoming the warped inverse of hers. I'd left Killian the month she and Gor celebrated their two-year wedding anniversary; signed a lease on a dank studio weeks before they closed on the condo. And there was something else, too: unbeknownst to Lia, I had terminated a pregnancy last August. The pregnancy had transformed what had once been my ambivalence about childbearing into a certainty. I could only think: I do not want it in me; I cannot be split.

For weeks after the procedure, I cramped and bled. The doctor said the bleeding went on too long; my womb, she deadpanned, had "relaxed too much."

So, no, I did not envy Lia's forthcoming rascal.

If I coveted anything about her life, it was the glow of comprehensibility that surrounded her. Once, I, too, had made sense, but of late, I was becoming less defined. I seemed to have abdicated my birthright citizenship to the nation of marriage and mortgage and motherhood, and beyond its borders lay uncharted terrain. I did mourn *something* after the procedure—not a specifically rendered unborn child, some slo-mo picture of a dark-haired creature soaring higher and higher on a bright red swing. (I had not contracted Killian's childhood Catholicism.) Rather, I grieved the loss of a version of me who was more fathomable to the world.

Had I told Lia about the abortion, she would no doubt have glanced, pro forma, at the pink I'M WITH HER mug on her trinket shelf, assuring me (assuring *herself*) that she bore no judgment. But I feared that everyone I knew had suddenly inherited a capacity for love that I lacked, and I was certain *they* believed that I was missing out on the Fundamental Mystery of Humankind. So, I kept my *choice* to myself.

I tried again: "Wow!" I said. "Your baby will be so cute."

Lia bit her lip.

I asked whether she and Gor planned to hyphenate Wojciechowski-Grigoryan.

Her palm flattened against the gleaming black countertop like she was massacring a large bug. "I guess I never told you. I took his name."

She stood abruptly and went to dump her wine in the sink. With her back to me, she began to loop a lock of her blond hair around her index finger, turning the knuckle paper-white, cutting off circulation. She was nervous.

"No. Or, yes," I agreed. "You never told me."

"I knew what you would say." Her vast blue eyes narrowed warningly, puddles shrinking in the sun. "And before you say it, there are a lot of reasons people change their names." Lia enumerated them: being closer, forming a clear family unit. Anyway, what was feminist about being forced to choose between her shitty father's unpronounceable surname and her very nice husband's?

I pointed out that my name is Sanjana *Satyananda* and Killian's is Killian *Bane*, but I had not become Sanjana *Bane* in order to assimilate into an easier identity. Plus, I added, she was blond. She asked what that had to do with anything, and I said it meant she didn't get to complain about her ethnic last name.

Things escalated from there, and in the end, discovering that my dearest, oldest friend had remade her legal identity without informing me led me to snark something half-baked about the ethics of reproducing in the face of climate change. Lia burst into tears, which, while not unheard of in our eighteen years of friendship, made me seem especially cruel now that she was crying for two. Gor soon appeared in the doorway and suggested I leave.

I am an anthropologist, so I know: spinsters make good demons. We infiltrate the bodies and minds of the happily married, sowing discord. We steal babies, kill babies, eat babies. You have to banish us. Out in the field, I knew a female healer who specialized in exorcisms for infertile women. Her instrument of choice was the broomstick, with which she beat barren wives. The wives themselves sought this treatment. Often, they came to the healer knowing exactly what, or who, was to blame for their empty wombs, and they'd tell the healer: My sister, my neighbor, my enemy, she died unfulfilled (which could only mean sonless) and cursed me with this brutal bequest. Then the healer would lift her broom and get to work delivering the blessing of progeny.

Having finished armpit dabbing, I exited the bathroom into the vestibule of the train station. Its high vaulted ceiling, a miniature of Grand Central, reminded me of the ersatz quality of life around this campus. Like the imitation Oxbridge architecture, the station was a snow globe synecdoche of a vaster, more authentic reality. Filmmakers sometimes shot scenes here to pass off as Manhattan at rush hour—students, a blur of navy and black suits, playing the bankers and consultants commuting from suburbia whom they would, in time, become.

I sat on a bench to text Max the Harm Reducer, the twenty-four-year-old altruist with JV soccer good looks I'd been seeing. Perhaps he could lend shelter after my expulsion from Lia's. Just as

I'd sent Max my SOS, though, a second message arrived from my unknown correspondent. Below the oddly hollow declaration—So you and K are back in town— it read:

I hear some big things are happening 💓

I typed:

whos this

My thumb hovered over the send button.

Then, Max's name flashed up and my phone began to buzz.

He apologized in his sweet, nasal voice: he was busy tonight. He sounded like he was in a restaurant. Glasses clinked and voices swelled behind him.

"Are you on a date?" I asked. I meant it to come out flirty, but it sounded accusatory, clingy. I had no right to those feelings, as I was the one who'd insisted on our being nonexclusive so fervently that I'd cast myself as nearly ethically nonmonogamous, even a little turned on by the prospect of belonging to a harem. In actuality I desire neither; I was merely trying to move more weightlessly through the world. "Why would you call me if you're on a date?"

"I, uh. Thought it was an emergency."

I tried what my ex-therapist, Dharma Matheson, LMFT, MSW, had once suggested would *root me to the present in times of agitation*. I closed my eyes and did a Kegel.

I opened my eyes. A South Asian woman about my mother's age was scrutinizing me across the antechamber from behind the counter of a Dunkin' Donuts. I smiled. She did not smile back. When I encountered my own kind in the wild, it could go either way. Sometimes they mistook me for one of them. Nice Daughter, Sweet Sister. Other times I failed to pass, and they intuited the real me: a thirty-two-year-old soon-to-be divorcée currently on medical leave from her graduate studies, who had twice overdrawn her bank account in the past year to pay rent. When my mother was my age, she was in a successfully arranged marriage, with two children, an MD, and an expectation that the next generation would outearn her. Dunkin' Auntie seemed to know all this, sorting me into the category of Bad Brown Girl, like she *knew* I was a married woman currently begging a man to take me in, and that I would have delivered an enthusiastic extramarital blow job in gratitude.

I assured Max that it was not an emergency.

I went outside, Auntie-ji's eyes boring into my back, and waited in the balmy May air for the campus shuttle to pull around. I weighed my options. In better times, I'd have crashed with someone from the anthropology department, but all my friends had either graduated without me—i.e., on time—or defected from the academy for noncontingent jobs with employer-backed health care. My campus ID wasn't working, due to the medical leave, so I couldn't slip into a library to pass out on a couch. I had one choice left. It was not ideal.

I settled into the largely empty bus and glanced back at the blue bubbles on my phone screen. The area code was 408—Northern California. That could be anyone in my world of coastal elites. My whos this lingered, unsent.

I glowered at that second note—I hear some big things are happening—and the stupid throbbing pink heart emoji. Pity, that's what that heart signified. My texter knew my marriage had failed. They did not want to offer me comfort; they wanted to gawk at my fuck-ups.

It's okay to keep others out for a while, Dharma had said.

You're waiting.

(For what?)

To encounter your next *incarnation*, she'd said, as though it were obvious. You just haven't met her yet.

2

Two-Faced

I woke to morning sex: my sister's chunky mutt, humping my thigh to the rhythm of his own constricted panting. I kicked the dog with my free foot. Down the hall, Maneesha and her husband Ajay were rousing themselves. I heard muffled voices, groggy and domestic, then the patter of small socked feet.

"Chikkamma."

My sister's kid Naina, seven and uncanny, like one of those matted-haired children in horror movies, stood in the doorframe, unblinking, wearing navy blue paisley-print pajamas. The dog belly-flopped next to her. She stooped low and brought her face to the animal, the two of them sharing some communion that I'd never seen pass between her and another human.

"Hey, Naina," I said. "Remember, you don't have to call me Chikkamma."

Maneesha had dubbed me Chikkamma without my consent. Given the choice, I would have opted for Aunt, pronounced the American way, *ant*, rather than Auntie, let alone Chikkamma. I loathed the claustrophobic specificity of the title, a name reserved solely for a mother's younger sister. "Small mother." As with so much Indian shit, the family unit was inescapable; you could never opt out of the preordained hierarchy of filial nomenclature.

"I'm not Naina," she said, in a dignified manner. "I'm Rachel Carson. And Amma says you're Chikkamma." There was something pinched and disdainful about the way Naina said *Amma*. It mirrored the way she spoke, full of periods rather than the exclamatory, high-pitched inflections I'd always associated with little kids. She was a miniature Bartleby, her tantrums speechless protests, e.g., lying on the neon Astroturf during kickball in dreamy existential critique of the game. What, after all, was chase? What was ball? She seemed to understand, already, that humans ought to be studied rather than joined. In Naina, my genes unquestionably lived on. All this pained Maneesha. Naina, the refusenik, was not what—not who—she'd expected when she decided she wanted a baby. I thought Maneesha deserved the unwelcome surprise, as did anyone who said they wanted a *baby*, a tabula rasa swaddle of blankets, rather than a full human who might turn out to be a serial killer or a B student.

"Naina, sweetie, what's that?" Maneesha called.

Naina stayed stubbornly silent.

Ajay amended: "Rachel Carson, what's that?"

"Sanjana is here." In my ear, Naina whispered, "I have to go to dance. I hate dance. It hurts my feet."

"Hey!" Maneesha shouted. "You mean Chikkamma is here?"

Ajay hissed, not quietly enough, "Did she mess up the dates?"

The Satyananda-Varma clan was leaving for Greece for the summer. Ajay had a fellowship to study the relationship of management practices to the eurozone collapse. Maneesha was on "sabbatical" from her job at Xerox. (I had no idea what Maneesha did at Xerox. I pictured her office full of lines and lines of copy machines and blank-eyed employees scanning copy after copy of blank A4s, and one brave rogue worker sliding down his slacks, making copy after copy of his ass.) I was to be their sanctioned squatter, caring for the garden, Maneesha's houseplants, and Jerky the sexually frustrated dog. Jerky didn't travel well, prone as he was to airplane panic attacks. (His full name was Beef Jerky because he was beefy and the only nonvegetarian in the house.) In addition to feeding Jerky, I was also expected to post regularly from "his" social media accounts. He had quite a following. Every caption was written in an absurdist, incomprehensible puppy patois; for instance, I ruff my hooman lil sis and doggos borking & mlemming @ new hay hay pupper park 2day day.

It hadn't been straightforward for my sister and brother-in-law to bestow upon me the privilege of house-sitting, but when they announced their summer abroad, they'd clearly felt trapped. I lived a few miles away in a shitty apartment; for them to invite anyone else to stay for free in their manse would have been *rude*, and Maneesha valued the appearance of cordiality. Yet for years I had not really been *of* my family. As a teenager, I'd been what my mother called *two-faced*: at home, I pretended at innocence, while in the world I was cultivating a double life laden with cursing and smoking and drinking and heavy petting. Unfortunately, I was often caught out in my mild rebellion; I left clues: the smell of weed in my hair, the too-loud barfing after a night of secret vodka chugging. In adulthood, the years of discord led me to develop a self-protective flakiness. I ignored phone calls, skipped holidays, refused to babysit. I believed my intentional distance made matters easier on the whole clan—and especially on me. Plenty of brown girls divide themselves in two, as I had, but over time, maintaining both selves takes a toll. Away from my family, I could pretend that I was not two separate people, one insufficiently dutiful and the other insufficiently free, but one nearly coherent being.

Maneesha emerged from the bedroom, wearing pajamas identical to Naina's.

"Are those Mommy-and-me pajamas?"

"Naina likes them." Maneesha nodded encouragingly at her daughter, who did not respond. "Nainu—Rachel Carson—get dressed. Kavita Auntie and Diya are picking you up in thirty minutes."

"I have growing pains." Naina pointed at her ankle. "I can't dance."

"If it hurts, you'll sit with Kavita Auntie and watch the steps so you don't get behind."

"I want to sit with Sanjana," Naina announced. "I want her to come to class."

"*Chikkamma*," Maneesha corrected.

"Sorry, Miss Rachel, I'm busy," I said.

Maneesha glared. Naina's expression dimmed slightly, enough to elicit guilt. I had intended to be someone to Naina. A Maneesha antidote. A cool aunt. But spending time around Naina required me to shift into yet another version of myself—responsible, almost wise, an identity I'd never rehearsed.

In the face of Naina's tiny brutal frown, I had the instinct to ruffle her hair, but she did not like being touched. I offered, "How about some breakfast later?"

"Bear claws," Naina pronounced, and flounced off to change into her salwar kameez.

"Where did she eat bear claws?" I asked Maneesha.

"In their animal unit at school. They're studying the *environment*," Maneesha said, with despair. "She makes me turn off the water all the time. Someone taught her 'If it's yellow, let it mellow.' Urine everywhere, just *stewing*. I flush before I even open the lid. Anyway, I'm *really* worried about this Rachel Carson thing. We gave her an easy name on purpose, but it seems like it's hard to win out over the desire to be white." She raised her eyebrows reprovingly at me, as if to say that this impulse was my fault.

"At least Mother gave you a name people can sound out."

Maneesha said, "Stop saying *Mother*, you sound like a freak."

What was freaky, in my opinion, was that our mother had forced us to keep referring to her as *Mommy* long after the acceptable age to do so. *Mom*, she'd said, was too American; *Amma* made her sound like her mother.

"Sorry-ji, Mummy-ji," I said, namaskar-ing.

"Don't caricature our culture," Maneesha said. "It's rude.

Why are you here, anyway?"

I explained about renting my room, leaving out Lia and Max. Maneesha *hmm*ed, vaguely, rummaging in her kitchen cabinets. I reached for my phone to check the time. Maneesha was saying something, but I missed it.

On my home screen was a new message from last night's unknown correspondent, time-stamped around four a.m.:

👼

"Sanjana! I *said*, do you want coffee?"

"Uh, sure."

My first thought was that the yellow angel-baby emoji resembled Maneesha's old Cabbage Patch doll. The toy, which Maneesha had inventively named Baby, had been a gift from my Raleigh-dwelling aunt and uncle. Before I was born, my family had traveled to a place called BabyLand General Hospital in northern Georgia, where Maneesha plucked Baby from something called the Mother Cabbage tree. She had been invited to raise her right hand and take an Oath of Adoption before receiving Baby's birth certificate. Photos depicting Baby's origin story were framed all over Maneesha's childhood bedroom. Unfortunately, while Maneesha tended to Baby gently, I was more feral, and during a tantrum, I tried to replant Baby in the ground from which she'd come. In the process, I decapitated her.

"Oh, darn it," Maneesha said now, with that cartoon-princess-pure mouth of hers, banging a cabinet closed. "We're out of beans. Can you go get some?"

"Yeah," I said, not looking away from the phone screen, as though if I stopped staring at it, the little angel would dissolve into its gleam.

Surely—just a wrong number. A run-of-the-mill, twenty-first-century mix-up. *K* could be anyone. I knew the rule about unknown texters: never reply. Any stranger could be a spammer trying to bait you into a conversation. Once, Killian decided to engage all wrong numbers for a while, and developed a "friendship" with a call center worker in Gurgaon, who invited him to come "pick up chicks." But then the guy's boss took over and began demanding Apple gift cards and Social Security numbers, same as everyone else.

Maneesha was waving her American Express Black card in my face, pinched between two gel-manicured fingers. No one in my family ever asked me to contribute funds. I provided labor; they, capital. Nonetheless, I knew she would check her statement carefully after I'd left to be sure I hadn't gone rogue on her dime. "Flat white for me, macchiato for Ajay. For the beans: single origin, medium roast. And *please* claim you couldn't find bear claws. I have whole wheat flapjack mix and fruit. We're trying to get Naina to turn her dislike of fruit into an observation that fruit may not be her favorite but it still nourishes us." She shook her head vigorously, like Beef Jerky wagging himself dry. "Okay. I've got to light the lamp."

I was only half listening to her, but that got my attention, because her intonation suddenly sounded a lot like our mother's. "Like, you're praying?"

"Mommy helped me set up a whole mandir room a while ago. You haven't come by in *ages*." She gave a martyred sigh. "Oh, and take Jerky out for a walk and a little potty, will you? There are treats by the leash. He gets one when he potties well."

"How am I supposed to carry all that shit—sorry, *stuff*— and also walk your dog?"

"Sanjana," Maneesha said, stepping into her temple. "Some of us juggle all that *stuff* every day."

Beef Jerky peed everywhere in little spurts. I wasn't sure if this was territorial or if he had a doggy UTI. I pictured myself serving him a dish of cranberry juice. Then he took a runny dump by the fence bordering the university farm. I left the poop there too long, because I was mentally elsewhere. A wrong number—that *was* the easiest explanation. But another possibility crept into my mind. What if Killian had told people about my pregnancy last year, and some peripheral acquaintance was now reaching out to congratulate me?

I couldn't guess *who* he would have told. Just before I'd left Killian last summer, in rural Goa, he'd thrown away his laptop and phone in a burst of asceticism and was threatening a possibly permanent hiatus from his career as an actor. We'd had minimal contact since Goa. He replied to no calls or texts or emails. Neither of us was on social media. Nor had I been in touch with any other element of my life back in India. None of our shared acquaintances in Bombay reached out to me when I disappeared, which stung, but the crowd had always been more *his* people than mine—backup dancers and expat Seekers and carpetbagging do-gooders—which meant they'd surely chosen *his* side in the split.

Our last interaction had come in March, when a piece of snail mail arrived at my New Haven apartment. It was handwritten, in all caps to render legible Killian's usually indecipherable serial killer scrawl, and enclosed in a bright yellow DHL envelope with the return address of our old building—*Bandra West, Mumbai, MH, 400050, India.* The letter's tone was terse and pained. He told me he was in a *private, fragile place* and would be unreachable for several months. He was also moving out of our apartment and could not yet provide me with a new permanent address. *I am sorry,* he said, adding, rather floridly, *but my heart remains broken.* I was ready to be done with our relationship for good—to finalize a divorce—but, after that note, consigned myself to waiting out his hurt and anger. "I was going to be a father," he'd said, shortly before I left. "You *took* that from me." And then he had cried, which was not unusual. He cried almost every day when I was pregnant, like a manipulative, leaky tap.

No. Killian would not have gone around telling people about his dead *baby*. He was wounded, but he had never been cruel. A coincidence, nothing more. I put my phone away and kept walking.

At some point, I realized I'd taken Jerky down Hillhouse and toward campus instead of making for the cafés near East Rock. I had, in fact, walked to the coffee shop across from Max's building.

It occurred to me that if Max really liked me—enough, I mean—he might have ditched his date last night. Perhaps this was a power play. I had not been treating him as sufficiently desirable. Poor Max Nishimura. He was cute in his stringbean way, with luscious black locks and an athletic gait. And he was Good, too, not just benign. He worked in harm reduction, at a needle exchange. We were alien and amusing to each other. As always happened to me at the beginning of an infatuation, I was fascinated. Desire, for me, begins with fixation. I ache to examine another person so closely that I tumble through the film of identity separating us to be devoured by them.

In Max's bedroom, on the second floor, the blinds were down. Something flitted on the other side of the glass—a hasty darting movement. A shadow cast, then hidden.

I needed to get away before a girl emerged from his building with post-fuck hair. As I was trying to puzzle out my escape, Max appeared before me, wearing headphones, mesh basketball shorts, and a purple T-shirt reading *Race Against Cancer*.

He dropped into a squat to scratch Jerky's grouchy jowls. "Hello, sweet friend! What is *your* name?" He spoke in that universal baby-and-pet voice. "When did Sanjana get you?"

"His name is *Jerky*. He's my sister's. She lives up on Prospect Hill."

Max was redolent of pheromones in the late spring heat, all coconutty.

I was still holding the bag of Jerky's "potty." I made to toss the still-wet, still-warm shit. "How was your date?"

"She's just someone I met at my brother's wedding. I mean, *she* asked *me*." He raised two sizable palms, callused from the climbing gym, as though fending off potential anger. "There was an age difference."

"How old was she?"

"Like, thirties." He remembered a moment too late. "Well—not like you. She was very ... focused. It was like a job interview?"

"A Clock Ticker," I said.

"Oof. That seems harsh." Max fidgeted, as though I were trying to trap him into saying something offensive. "I think it's fair for people—for women—to, like. Know what they want."

"My friend Lia was a self-identified Clock Ticker," I said. "She wrote up this manifesto about claiming the term and published it on Medium. Right after she broke up with this guy who called her a Sperm Chaser."

"Jesus," he said. "Men are, well. Wow."

"Men have clocks, too."

"Like, old sperm?"

I had not planned on discussing aging semen. That wasn't even what I'd meant by clock, per se. I was just thinking of Killian thrusting, whispering, *I want to put a baby in you.* Afterward, saying, *It was primal.*

Standing before Max, I felt a visceral stab of pain between my legs. I bit my lip, to keep the past at bay.

Jerky barked a storm at a passing toy dog that looked like a toilet brush. I yanked him back.

"Hey," I said. "Can you hold his leash?"

Max looked delighted.

I went into the café to collect the drinks, beans, and some twice-baked almond croissants that might have been bear claws (I saw no reason to deny Naina), and reemerged to find Jerky licking Max's face in a manner I found unacceptable.

"Here." Max held out Jerky's leash and relieved me of my cornucopia. "Let's swap."

We traipsed back up Hillhouse. In the distance: the crackling of speakers and the sound of someone howling, *How you feeling, class of 2018?* Manic applause and whoops.

"What happened to you last night?"

"I was supposed to be staying with a friend. But we had a fight."

"Why?"

"She's pregnant." As soon as I said it, I felt mortified.

"Whoa," Max said, in a voice so surfer-slacker that he seemed more twenty-four than ever. "Like, on purpose?"

I laughed, which turned into a snort, and then I started coughing so hard that my eyes watered. It felt good. "Yeah," I said, when I was done hacking. "On purpose. Or, at least, it's welcome." Then I decided to try something, maybe because I was thinking about how young he was, how far from the muddle of my stage of life. The stakes were different with him. If I were consumed by him, I might feel cleansed. In the blue aquatic depths of our shared guilelessness, we would swim through life effortlessly.

I said, "I had an abortion."

You were, as a feminist today, supposed to Shout Your Abortion, but this was only the third time I'd told anyone. I'd asked an acquaintance in the sociology department, Hira, to be my ride to and from the clinic. She was kind, unprying, gave me a heating pad. The matter had also inevitably come up with Dharma Matheson, LMFT, MSW. I had not told my adviser, Alisandra. Dharma had instead written a note claiming I was too mentally unwell to continue in grad school and diagnosing me with "adjustment disorder": I was struggling to adjust to adulthood, she wrote—never mind that I had been an adult for fourteen years already. The university expected DSM-approved pathologies to justify medical leave. My nebulous feelings about my abortion could not fit tidily into a box on a form. Neither were they a spiritual scar. They were just slippery and strange and every time I said the word *abortion*, I felt clumsy, like I was laying claim to something heroic and vital that didn't belong to me.

Max took a steadying breath, then spoke in the voice of a professional Harm Reducer. "Thank you for sharing that with me." He avoided my eyes, looking instead at Jerky, who was slumped on the sidewalk, a gray puddle of wrinkles, fur, and fat.

I remembered the feeling of sitting in a stalled autorickshaw one late night in Bombay, and seeing, in the side mirror, that the driver has his penis out and was working it diligently. It was not, of course, the first time I had seen a man masturbating in public; the act occurs along the same spectrum of male entitlement that includes adjusting one's ball sack in plain view. But it was the first time a man had me at close range. Frozen, I stared back in a manner one might have mistaken for brave. My driver went limp.

Maybe having your mark acknowledge you head-on is a boner-kill. I imagine that, as I told Max about the abortion, my face resembled the driver's: relief in the exposure, followed by disappointment. Flashing— shouting—not so thrilling after all.

"But... why did you guys fight?" Max asked. "Is she prolife, or something?"

My distress was not about electoral politics. It was more abstruse than that. For decades, all the ways in which Lia was unlike me had brightened and balanced my world. She had always been benevolent with her social ease, including me in every part of her selfhood. But then she became rich, married the painfully dull Gor, and bought a house, and the Lia I'd long known slowly diminished. I realized that she had been laying away plans to depart our shared universe all along. I was becoming an accessory, an artifact of her past; she was making her own way, going somewhere I could not follow. This—her baby, her new blood family—would calcify the change. Our private subjectivities would diverge. There were so many names for the precise femininity she was already experiencing, now. There were books and blogs and a public fellowship of mothers to which she would soon belong. I was being left behind—a childless divorcée in her thirties—to make a life without a script as she moved ahead into a life with clear milestones, each with its own gift registry.

Dharma had once wrinkled her nose as I described this feeling—not a desire for children, but a fear of the *lack* of children—and asked, "Who are your role models? Who are the childless women you grew up around?" The question had made me laugh aloud. I had one spinster great-aunt. My mother lent Maneesha and me out to her on visits to Mysore; she smelled of cloying rose water and baby powder and spent the hours with us roughly braiding our hair and rubbing Fair and Lovely into my skin and counting everything *she* would do differently with us, if we were *her* granddaughters. There was also a single childless auntie in my family's gaggle of Indian friends in Boston, a divorcée who was gossipy and interfering and frequently borrowed money she never paid back, and my mother liked to use her as a warning to Maneesha and me—Janani Auntie had neglected the natural order and was, therefore, a burden. Dharma's eyebrows had shot up at this recounting: So it was *cultural*, my problem? She had ended the session looking relieved, as though she could persist knowing feminism hadn't failed; only some backward immigrants.

"Up, Beef Jerky," I said. To Max, I added, "I don't need to talk about it. I have therapy tomorrow."

He exhaled audibly.

I couldn't begrudge Max his ineptitude. In my early twenties, I myself had once congratulated a classmate on her "baby" when she told me she was pregnant; she had flinched and told me she planned to get an abortion, and I had stood there with my own gaping trout mouth. After that, I looked up *What to say when someone tells you they're getting an abortion*. The first hit was propaganda from the United States Conference of Catholic Bishops. Planned Parenthood, hit number seven, suggested various sentences that were either a mouthful or completely cold. ("You can make the best decision for yourself!" "Let me know how I can support you!") There was definitionally no public etiquette for a right to privacy. The whole point was that it belonged to you, and you alone.

Max and I walked the rest of the way to my sister's in awkward silence. In the driveway, he said, "I hope you're okay. It doesn't make you a bad person."

"I know it doesn't," I snapped, and he quailed, and then I felt wretched. "I mean, thanks. Sorry. Thank you. Sorry."

He nodded somberly, hesitated, kissed the top of my head, dryly.

I could not remember how to perform intimacy. The last time I'd tried, things had gone horribly wrong. I had followed Killian Bane somewhere I barely escaped. I was in a hurry, when I met him, to become myself. I had been waiting my whole life for my life to begin. He had helped me become me. But I never knew that you could accidentally become the wrong version of you, that you might one day have to escape yourself. How hideous it is to know that there is someone inside you—someone you once trusted, because she *was* you— who steered you straight into disaster. You never know when she will rise up from the depths to possess you once more.

3

New Asian Mommy

Therapy that Monday was not with Dharma, whom I'd dumped, but with Dr. Bonnie Kim, PsyD. This was our fourth session. When I'd come for my intake three weeks earlier, Dr. Kim had leaned back in her chair and asked, with deep implication, if I'd ever had an Asian American therapist before. I admitted I had not. She'd crossed, then recrossed her slender legs, as if settling into the significant position in my life she was about to inhabit: the first person qualified to speak to both my culture and my brain chemistry.

Dr. Kim's calling was ministering to the Asian souls of New Haven, as was clear from the landing page of her website, which read: *Do you feel lonely? Do you feel ill-equipped to manage your emotions as an adult? Is your relationship to your family a little "complicated"? Do you feel trapped between two worlds? That's the case for many Asian Americans. I take an analytical approach to help you work through your minority experience and ethnic identity.* Reading this, I'd initially felt heartened. But as the days ticked by leading to my first appointment, I began to obsess over how I would distinguish myself from others sharing my *minority experience* and *ethnic identity*. The notion of fitting into a template disturbed me.

On that first day, Dr. Kim had asked, "Why do you want to work with an Asian American therapist now?"

Her office, which had no windows, was crowded with large fake plants that she clearly considered comforting. Behind her was a fish tank lit turquoise. "It's not like I want a new Asian mommy," I'd said, too quickly. "It's mostly that I had a white therapist for a year and then one day she said my name and I realized she'd never learned it. She called me *Jenna*."

Dr. Kim said, "Now let me be sure I know how to pronounce your name," and I said, "It's S-A-N-J-A-N-A, pronounced SUN-jun-ah. There's no *e*. I'm not sure how anyone could get 'Jenna.'"

I had sounded out my name for Dharma several times when we first met. I do it instinctively when I introduce myself, but inevitably my name is mangled. My freshman roommate gave up and called me Sunshine for a whole semester. It didn't help that she once saw me ordering a coffee and telling the cashier my name was Sunny.

Trite as it is, over time, these fuck-ups erode your sense of self. I could be more optimistic and consider each iteration of my name—*SAND-jay-nah, sahn-jah-NAY, SOON-jay-nah, sahn-HEY-na, Sonya, Janine, Sunny*—a chance to reincarnate. And yet, though I wish it did not, this name business affects me on some instinctual level.

"SUN-jun-ah," Dr. Kim said, as I made my way out of her office that first day. That was perhaps the only thing she'd done that made me feel understood, but it was sufficient to make me return.

This particular morning, I spent a few minutes railing against Alisandra, my adviser, who had not answered my emails in months. She'd been on research leave all year, but I was afraid that when school restarted in August, I would find her hostile to me. Last May, just before my life turned upside down, I had dropped out of my PhD program and disappeared for several months. Alisandra had shown mercy in taking me back, pending medical leave, largely thanks to the note from Dharma. But I knew how my adviser looked at me now: like a cyst that might turn malignant any day. She didn't want her name on my CV, didn't want someone to call her one day, when I applied for a postdoc or job, to ask what on earth she'd been thinking when she signed off on me.

Dr. Kim asked if my anxieties about Alisandra reminded me of any other relationships in my life.

I batted a faux frond out of the way. It kept flopping into my face.

We were taking a turn toward my mother. Dr. Kim had a thing about my mother. Possibly this was my fault for having uttered the phrase "new Asian mommy" at our first meeting, but all in all, I found it a little 101. There was, I thought, the prospect of more interesting matters at play in my own ego-id-whatever dance, but Dr. Kim was hewing to the same Freudian algorithm laid out in a course book that told her all neuroses were matrilineal. Her view seemed to obscure the possibility that I possessed any particular *me*-ness.

"It makes *me* think of your mother," she said eagerly, not waiting for me to reply. "I'm thinking about the fact that you fear yet another woman with power over you—Alisandra— rejecting you. Like your mother did."

(I heard once that the German word for *academic adviser* translates as something like "doctor mommy" or "doctor daddy." I chose not to offer this catnip to Dr. Kim.)

"That makes it sound like she sniffed me and kicked me out of the pack."

Dr. Kim's lips pressed together as though she were holding in a spit take. "Well. Humans, like other animals, depend on belonging *somewhere*."

It is difficult not to date the conflict with my family to the emergence of my interest in fucking, which arrived when I was fourteen. My mother whiffed something alien in me— desire, a lust to be made new—and it troubled her. She took my metamorphosis personally. The problem, in part, was that Maneesha was the anti-slut—so pure that, even as a Hindu, she joined the Christian kids' abstinence society. My sister was a snitch, too. She once heard that I'd been felt up behind the middle school by Orin Leibowitz and told our mother, who grounded me. In Maneesha, my mother had proof that not all desi girls were easy because they were, as she put it, "trying to prove their cool-girl whatnot to these white people"—a surprisingly astute assessment of the motivations behind my early promiscuity.

As I got older, I heard stories of immigrant mothers like my own "changing with the times," choosing to halt imports on shame and judgment. My mother did not seem to have considered this option. Or, perhaps I never convinced her of the appeal of my ways. Because it was undeniable that my forays into what she called "loose culture" did not advertise its advantages. For instance, in college, I lost my virginity to an aspiring animator named David Cho, who turned our sexual encounter into a Claymation short that depicted me crying and bleeding a lot more than I actually had. When, a month later, he traded me in for a sage-scented white folk singer classmate, I had a breakdown, stopped attending classes, and turned in a plagiarized paper on Bluebeard to a course called Fairy Tales and Folklore. (I cried to the dean, a white man, who kept the incident off my record. "I see this kind of thing a lot with Asian

Americans," he said. "It's like they breed you to succeed and then things go wrong and—" He snapped his fingers as if to say, *You disappear.*) When I confessed the incident to my mother, admitting that my spiral had begun because of a *boy*, she told me if I went on like this, giving myself away to anyone and everyone, I'd wind up fragmented, less of a person, like these oversexed Americans. She was not entirely wrong.

The years of bad blood were why, when Killian and I decided to get married after two years of dating and one of cohabitation—for health insurance purposes, we claimed—I did not invite my family. Killian and I tromped over to the New Haven County courthouse. Lia and Killian's friend Corey were our only guests. Killian was thirty-five, I was twenty-eight, and it all seemed, to me, not like the real encroachment of adulthood, but like a game, a way of playing at adulthood. The lack of ceremony—no red sari, no white horse, not a catered samosa in sight—made things feel especially unreal.

I did mean to tell my parents. But I just kept putting it off. Whenever I called home, language failed me. How could I translate myself? My mother had always deemed people who married outside the fold *very strange*. This was one of her most vicious, damning categorizations—*strange*. Her whole face would wrinkle in disgust whenever she said the word. Did I need to repulse her yet again? And so, I said nothing for two months. Then three.

They found out, of course; Lia told her sister, who was Maneesha's old classmate, and Maneesha ran straight to Mommy. My parents called and said if Killian and I went to the temple with them, took their blessing, they would welcome him. It was a solid plea deal that I should have taken, but that word—*blessing*—pissed me off. It was close to *permission*. I told them as much. They said I had hurt them. I barely spoke to the other Satyanandas for the three years of my marriage, half of which we spent in India, anyway; distance made estrangement easier. Plus, Killian did not like my family—or, he did not like *me* around my family, as he often said. "You change. You shrink, like you're hiding from your actual self. It's hard to watch you become invisible."

When I left Killian, Maneesha said it was good "all that" was ending. "Ajay and I want Naina to know her chikkamma," she said firmly. Harmony for the next generation justified mending ties.

My mother, however, does not forget, let alone forgive. She has a deathbed list of people to curse in her final moments that includes the florist who brought zinnias instead of marigolds to Maneesha's wedding. You can imagine where I stood.

These days, I spoke to my parents by phone once a month for ten or so minutes, or when they came to town to see the Good Daughter and the Sweet Grandchild, who had not yet disappointed them. It was a tenuous, frigid truce.

Dharma didn't blink when I told her about the rift: "Sometimes, the apple falls from the tree and rolls all the way down the hill and that's fine." Dr. Kim, however, seized on the matter like a rottweiler catching a squirrel in its maw. I'd read a blog post she'd written for Asian American Pacific Islander Mental Health Awareness Day in which she discussed the communitarianism supposedly endemic to the entire Asian continent and its surrounding isles. The way we aren't individual, sovereign selves; the way we, unlike Westerners, are products of collectivist societies, forever filially burdened. I could feel her faith in this totalizing notion burning into me.

"Help me understand something," she was saying now. "You feel that you are turning your back on your family's ways. Right? That's why you didn't get married in a temple, with a priest, to a groom they selected?"

The frond flopped on my forehead again. I wondered if the plants were a test. A truly self-empowered client would get up and move them.

"Sure. Though Maneesha's marriage wasn't arranged. It was just *approved* of." I bit the cuticle on my right thumb, too hard. It went a hot, irritated red.

"And yet you *did* get married. Did any part of you think being married would make them approve of *you*?"

"They didn't like Killian."

"You told me they were unhappy that you were living with him before marriage, so wouldn't being married resolve that?"

I *had*, in moments of private fantasy, imagined declaring the news to my parents with triumph rather than trepidation, announcing that they *had* to accept my life, and Killian. That by their own standards, I was no longer a slut but a wife, which made me good. But that meant accepting their terms and judgments.

"Yeah, maybe. But only if I did things their way. I guess in theory, I'd like to get along with them, but in practice, I don't want to have to make concessions to be the kind of person who they *would* get along with."

"You don't want to compromise."

"Not on my selfhood."

"So, Sanjana … what *do* you want?"

I frowned. "Do people really know the answer to that?"

"Do *you* think they do?"

I massaged my temples. "I think some of my friends do."

I'd once had more compatriots. Then I left the country, and everyone became parents. When I returned, they were transformed. I tried to maintain the connections—with Jameela, for instance, my best college friend. I took the train to see her in Philadelphia twice. But she and her wife were public defenders with no childcare. Jameela fell asleep, her face plonking straight into a bowl of ice cream, and asked after Killian, forgetting that I'd just left him. She'd admitted, apologetically, that yes, she had lost touch with a lot of her non-mom friends. Not out of malice or exclusion; she just needed people who *got* it. This was a natural changing of the seasons. She was surrounded by new women who recommended tear-free shampoos and toxin-free cribs to her, who passed on hand-me-down maternity sweaters and onesies. *They got it.* I had chosen not to get it. Thereafter, we both stopped trying.

"The ones with real lives know what they want," I said.

"I didn't know one life could be *realer* than another."

"I mean," I said, "people with careers and money and credit cards and houses and partners and *kids.*" I paused for a breath but knew, an instant later, that ending on kids was a mistake.

Dr. Kim leaned forward, her tongue darting out like a lizard's. "It sounds like you feel angry with these women," she said. "For having children."

Behind her, in the aquarium, a fat brown fish floated horizontally. I wondered if it had expired in the middle of our session.

"That would make me an asshole," I said.

"That's certainly not what I intended to imply."

"I dunno," I said. "Maybe I'm angry. Hey, I think your fish might have died."

Dr. Kim angled her head to see and emitted a sad squeak. It was the first time I'd seen her emote. Then she turned to face me again as though nothing had happened. Her features were more determined now, vengeful, haloed by the blue, fatal waters. "Anger," she said, "is a secondary emotion. It conceals something else."

"Such as?"

"Such as—jealousy."

I stiffened. "You're not supposed to ask if women want kids. It's considered rude."

When I was younger, children seemed as inevitable as death and taxes. I assumed I'd have them, someday, but I never felt that essential, deep-flesh craving for offspring that Jameela, for instance, described. I also had a serious aversion to my own physical involvement in motherhood: when I imagined having to bear, birth, breastfeed, and nurture, a dizzying fear set in. Ambivalence was my official stance for many years. When the matter arose, I said, *maybe later, not now, not yet*. Some people left that alone. But a certain kind of woman saw herself in me. They'd say, *I didn't want them when I was your age either, and then* ... Others came on stronger, telling me that baby fever could strike without warning, and if you hadn't prepared for it, it would kill you. Maneesha was the most aggressive. She called me once while I was still in India with Killian, in our Chilly War, and ordered me, through tears, to freeze my eggs. She was dealing with secondary infertility, she said, and was currently at an offshore medical facility in Barbados—*Barbados!* she cried, as though the geography were the great imposition—trying to conceive baby number two. She did not want me to suffer as she was. "You can't trust *anyone* about your fertility. You can't trust doctors. You can't trust boyfriends, or, sorry, your *husband*. I know you'll get angry at me for saying this, but I am your sister, so I can say it: you can't trust yourself right now, because you might change your mind. Then it will be too late! Ask Mommy for the money if you have to. Forget about the fight. You know what adulthood is? It's making choices. And if you make the wrong one—there's no going back." It was violating, being told that one day I would wake up, transformed overnight like Gregor Samsa into a Sanjana who wanted something the Sanjana of today could not imagine wanting. A mother was in me, just waiting to burst out.

"I did not ask if you are jealous of your friends who are *mothers*," Dr. Kim said. "Maybe you are jealous of the *babies*, in the way that an older sibling is sometimes jealous of a newborn. Your friends neglect you, just as the parents of a newborn may neglect their older child."

This was the point at which I could have Shouted My Abortion at Dr. Kim. It would have been a kind of trauma trump card. But also, my choice not to mother would, in Dr. Kim's hands, become about *my* mother.

Instead, I said, "That's a little infantilizing."

"How so?"

"I mean that you just compared me to an actual child."

"I don't mean to agitate you, Sanjana," she went on. "I am merely trying to tighten the connections between parts of you that I am still coming to understand—and which, I hope you'll accept me saying, you are still coming to understand."

Dr. Kim's eyes darted to the clock above my head.

As I gathered my bag, she turned to examine the dead fish. I imagined her crying as the door shut behind me, the surviving fish swimming in her tears.

At home, I packed my bags to move to Maneesha's. I would be subletting my studio to a poet who was spending her summer writing a chapbook of sestinas about nipples (inverted ones, third ones, chafed ones). I was drinking—Smirnoff and soda—and scowling down at my India things. The day I left Killian's and my place in Bombay, I took just one suitcase with me, abandoning piles of clothing, books, jewelry, and diaries. I'd taken pleasure in ditching not only him, but all the crap of that life. The stuff I had taken—hotweather clothes, mostly linen or cotton, natural dyed—had somehow spoiled in storage. Everything smelled damp and rotted. When I tried it on, all the clothing looked like it belonged to someone else. Over the past year, I'd shed too much weight.

Annoyed, I plonked my drink on the nightstand and slunk into bed. I reached for my vibrator and opened Pornhub on my phone. Uninspired by the pulsing, seething oiled bodies, I switched over to Zillow instead. I set a minimum total price of $750,000 and scrolled as I masturbated desultorily to a listing that boasted French doors and built-in bookshelves with ladders and window nooks. Twelve-foot ceilings and gleaming hardwood and a vast kitchen island. The blankness of an as-yet unlived, luxurious life. *Jealous*, Dr. Kim had said. *Jealous* didn't seem to cover it. I wanted to shatter and be reborn as a two-dimensional, pixelated figure, wandering through these vast homes, careless, my brain shut off, my needs all met. Just as I switched the vibrator all the way up, my thumb slipped, and I slid out of Zillow and into my iMessages, where an unread text awaited me, from a second unknown number. It had arrived within the past half hour.

I seeeeeee you!

I bolted upright and scanned the vicinity. My blinds were lowered. My room was dark but for a single floor lamp in the corner, next to a tattered armchair. I edged to the window, tugging my underwear up, and cracked a slat open. The street outside was still and dim—a summer stupor. One block away, one of my neighbors, a divinity student, slumped up her stoop, hauling groceries, her figure just visible in the yellow light of the nearby laundromat. No other signs of life.

I wrote:

what
where

I swigged more of my drink, willing a response. And then, in real time, came a photograph. I recognized the location immediately. The gray turmoil of the Arabian Sea to the left; the hazy, polluted sky above. The wide palm-tree-lined boulevard, dotted with auto-rickshaws and blue cool cabs and kaali-peeli taxis. Carter Road: the seaside promenade not far from where Killian and I had lived, in Bombay.

The shot was backlit, washing out a cluster of faceless figures. But even with the imperfect angle, I recognized him. His shoulders hunched up to his ears. His neck craned down. Six foot four and pale as a vampire, Killian was always conspicuous in India.

A few inches to his right stood a woman. I couldn't make out her face. She had short black hair and wore a long blue dress. They didn't seem to be in conversation. His entire body was angled away from her. But her chin was cocked slightly in his direction, as though she were addressing him, while he remained absorbed in the ocean.

A burst of messages was now pinging in from this stranger—who, I registered, had a +91 country code. An Indian number.

> I waved but you didn't see me and I had to run to the airport!!! Going to bali!
>
> You look GORRRRGEOUS nice haircut!!! So chic and short
>
> Coffee or a drink when I get back???
>
> Omg I'm so stupid, not coffee, no drink!
>
> Eep!
>
> Beans spilled!
>
> DW bb I can keep a secret 🙊🤰
>
> ok on plane theyre yelling at me to turn phone off but soooo excited for you guys

I replied:

1) who is this
2) who told you

But my correspondent had gone silent.

I scrolled back to the picture of Killian and the woman. I supposed I could understand why someone would assume she was me—she was next to Killian. But she did not *look* like me. Her hair hung in a coiffed bob, for one; mine, curly and untamable, drooped to my breasts. She was perhaps five foot four and curvy; I am five foot seven, tall for an Indian, buttless and surfboard-breasted. The texter was probably a white expat who couldn't differentiate between brown girls. A white expat so peripheral to me that I hadn't even bothered to save their number. Just as I began to feel annoyed about the quotidian racism, I squinted and pinched the photo to zoom in. Closer up, I saw that the woman's dress was indigo, ikat-printed, with a long slit up its side.

My neck went cold—a trickle of melting ice. Goose pimples rose on my skin. I stood, and as the blood rushed to my head, I became acutely aware of how drunk I was. I drifted to my duffel to riffle through the mildewy palazzo pants and maxi skirts and crop tops. My fists closed around what I was looking for but, in my sodden state, had briefly believed would not be there—my ikat-printed, side-slitted indigo dress. I brought it to my nose. It reeked, but it was real, in my hands.

4
Impostor Syndrome

The first time I saw Killian, he was nude. Pale, toned, illumined by an unflattering cone of yellow lighting, like Michelangelo's *David* on display in a Walmart. I was in my first year of graduate school, attending something called a Naked Supper Club at the home of a forestry school student named Elsa, who hosted monthly dinners consisting entirely of foraged vegetables, roots, and fungi. Elsa had several housemates, most of them PhD candidates whose favorite hobby was threatening to drop out of their respective programs for a more stable life. There was a dreamy man named Ronald who studied the physics of music; his primary partner, Wendy, a public health student who hoped to force the city into legally recognizing throuples one day; a heroin-chic comp lit fuckboi named Rhys who was rumored to be a Kennedy cousin; and Killian Bane—not a graduate student but an actor.

I was there on my fourth date with an art historian named Viktor, who'd known Elsa since prep school.

"You have *really* great conversations at these," Viktor had said, after recounting the housemates' names and school affiliations, as we traipsed up the hill to East Rock. "Nudity levels the playing field, you know. And don't worry, *no one* looks good naked."

Viktor and I had fucked twice already, which made these ostensibly reassuring words seem cruel rather than comforting.

I spotted Killian as soon as Viktor and I arrived and shed our clothes in the foyer. I wish I could say that I noticed Killian's eyes first, which were green, keen, and feline, or his shock of black hair. But obviously I noticed his dick, which was very small. The smallest I'd ever seen, actually. In coloring and features it was commonplace—pinkish, circumcised, mercifully flaccid. From there I registered his torso, shoulders, etc., which were muscled but not bulky, and hairless, like a Ken doll, or a swimmer.

Viktor smacked his head on the coat rack as he stood up from untying his sneakers. "Ow!"

Killian glanced over at Viktor's *Ow!*, and right then I was reminded that I was naked, and he was naked, and everyone was naked, and all these people—these hipster white people who would normally have terrified me with their cultural confidence and manner of taking up space unthinkingly—were, beneath it, also just undignified hunks of flesh. The room seemed very cold and very bright and I was sure everyone would see lust starting to prickle on my skin. And not for Viktor.

Suddenly Killian was in front of us, smiling. At first I assumed he knew Viktor, but my date had already slunk off to kiss Elsa on both cheeks. I looked his way long enough to notice how his eyes swept her pixie, porcelain figure, and how he dropped his hands to his crotch. I was only too happy to turn to this new man, whose gaze was fixed on me. The green eyes were especially vivid up close.

A single gray stripe shot through his black hair, near his left temple. Like Indira Gandhi. Despotic. I noticed then that he seemed older than me, and older than the other grad students; later, I learned that he was thirty-three—a distant age.

"Great to see you," Killian said, enthusiastically.

I had never been noticed so plainly before. The guys I liked, lanky Art Boys, were dark haired with hooded eyes and slouchy postures and opinions on the French New Wave, and all of them—white, Black, brown, Asian, mixed—went for cream-skinned wraiths. Plathy types. Elsas. It embarrassed me, later, to think that it all came down to my desire to be recognized, even if the recognition was a lie. I am basically plain. I have shiny hair and unblemished skin, though aunties are bitchy about its darkness. But I have one of those forgettable faces, particularly for people unaccustomed to distinguishing between the nuances of brown features. So when someone looks—really looks—something happens to me. An admixture of surprise and gratitude is stirred up, indistinguishable from desire.

It took me a moment to realize what he'd said. "Have we, er, met?" I asked.

"*Just say we have*," he whispered. "The Future Senator cornered me." He jutted his elbow at someone I'd met at the grad school bar—another naked white man, a 2L at the law school who was being mentored by a confirmed war criminal in the Global Studies department, with whom he was co-writing a tome called *Great Man Theory*.

I didn't blame Killian for fleeing the guy, but I was still befuddled by the way he'd made for *me*. "Sure, yeah. Great to see you. How, um, how have you been?" I pinched the skin at my wrist, unsure. I had never been a performer of any kind. I am actually a terrible liar; it was why I so unsuccessfully concealed my double life from my parents.

"A biologist!" Killian said loudly, hamming it up for the Future Senator, who was scowling at Killian's taut ass as though he'd been robbed of an immensely edifying conversation. "Thank god, I've been wanting to talk to one."

"Anthropologist." I sniffed. "You just said I'm a biologist because I'm Indian."

"Oh, no, not at all. You know, I have some Indian in me," he said, at a more normal decibel. I squinted. He was very pale. It sounded like he meant that he'd eaten naan for lunch. "I mean. My mom's Irish, but the other half is Indian. I know, I came out white."

My eyes flitted to his penis. Was there some tinge of brown amid the pink? I had only seen one Indian man's penis, during freshman orientation week; the guy had dumped me the next morning, saying he could never Be With a girl who gave out hand jobs to practical strangers as I had.

"Oh," I said. "Are you from … the north?"

"No idea." He shrugged. "My mother was a hippie. Got pregnant by some Indian man when she was traveling, and never saw him again. Anyway, I was not *assuming* you're a biologist. I'm just doing research. I'm playing one in *Who's Afraid of Virginia Woolf?* at the Rep. I need to interview some jaded academics. Are you jaded?"

"Not yet," I said. "I don't think I've actually seen the play. Or the movie."

"Hm. I mean, it might depress you. But you should come see it. For me, at least." He pulled his face into an impish grin that affected me instantly. He lacked symmetrical, leadingman features. There was something off-center about his nose, and his chin was too wide. But all together they added up to someone particular. Memorable.

We drifted into the kitchen, where Killian poured me some earthy natural wine, and I learned that he had moved to New

Haven for the year. He could have commuted from Brooklyn, but he wanted to live with a bunch of "almostbitter" academics. "I had to properly immerse. To study your kind."

"That seems vampiric," I said. "What are you offering in return?"

"I could give you some acting tips. You struggled back there."

"I don't need to act."

"Everyone has to act, all the time," Killian said. "Every time you lecture or post up at a seminar table—that's all a performance. But you academic types, you don't like to think that way, do you? You people lack an improvisational spirit. You know what I mean?"

I was not sure I did, but I was also not paying much attention to his monologue. I was trying to memorize his physicality—the sharp dip of his collarbone, the ripples of his biceps, the golden ratio proportions. I kept thinking I might not be in close proximity to a body like this very often in my life. As we talked, I had to periodically press my legs together.

"Hey," I said. "I just thought of this one. What happens if someone gets horny at a naked dinner party?"

He frowned. "What?"

"Exit, pursued by boner," I said. "Ha. Ha."

He laughed suspiciously hard at that, so hard I began to suspect that there had been some mistake, that in the darkness he'd confused me with someone sexy enough to elicit this kind of try-hard masculine desire to impress. Later, he would brag that he was not like other men. "You're not *classically* beautiful," he said once, as though congratulating himself for having interesting taste. "But classical beauty is Eurocentric."

At some point, Elsa clanged a gong and announced that it was time to dine. We were shepherded to a long table made from scavenged wood and seated, still bare-assed, on mismatched vintage chairs and love seats with peeling upholstery, beneath a rusty chandelier. The house was vaguely sinister in the manner of those old northeastern homes, and the wind battered the structure and the place creaked and moaned, soundtracking the night.

We picked at chanterelles and morels and drank the sedimenty wine and popped edibles afterward, and I found myself bordering on something like ebullience. I had been lonely and afraid all year. It had seemed like a giant stroke of luck that I had been admitted to such a fancy graduate program after flailing through undergrad, after the David Cho affair. Lia said I was merely suffering that classic female affliction, impostor syndrome, which she had learned about recently from a Women in Law conference she'd attended. *Impostor syndrome*: it made me sound like I had been body-snatched. I wasn't so sure. I had come to suspect that I was one of those people whose identity was just very thin.

Before the evening wound down, Killian touched my elbow and asked to exchange numbers. Behind him, Viktor was lying on a Moroccan rug, tripping out on twenty milligrams of sativa, his head on Elsa's concave stomach. Rhys was suggesting they have something called a *kale orgy*, in which they all ate leafy greens off each other's naked bodies and "went from there," and the Future Senator was saying he'd have to excuse himself for career purposes if things progressed to full-on group sex. I felt no guilt in trading in Viktor for this better model.

I asked Killian how to spell his name as I entered his information into my phone. He told me, and added that he'd changed the spelling when he was twenty and did a stint in Los Angeles. His name used to be C-I-L-L-I-A-N. But there was already Cillian Murphy. He needed to be himself, not a knockoff.

"Plus, people were always calling me Silly-en, rather than Killy-en."

"It's a major difference," I said. "Silly versus kill-y."

"Well, maybe you *should* call me Silly-en," he said. "*Kill* sounds dangerous. I wouldn't want you to think I'm dangerous. Really, I assure you, I am a fool."

5

Home Safe

For the first week of my house-sitting gig, I barely slept. Maneesha had told me I was not to use her bedroom, because I would corrupt her and Ajay's Tempur-Pedic, which was contoured to their bodies. I was allowed the guest cum mandir room, where the double bed had been shoved against the wall and surrounded by a phalanx of gods and goddesses, three-foot-tall bronze idols from the import store. There was Krishna, the impish baby; Lakshmi, the goddess of wealth; and Parvati, who oversees fertility. When I did manage to drift off, my dreams were of those divinities taking on vulgar forms—fanged wildcats, cackling monkeys, gargoyles. I remembered how my parents had explained nightmares to me when I was small: a dream, they said, is a scrambling of your daytime reality. Your dream brain could take the same images and feelings that were scattered disparately throughout a given week and turn them into a monstrous anagram, a nonreality that is frightening *because* it rings familiar. I remembered campfire tales from my youth, of cleaver-wielding dolls and murderers masquerading as clowns, and I soothed myself with a recurrent thought as I tried to suppress the nightmares, a thought that would have infuriated my mother: that the gods and goddesses in Maneesha's house were nothing more than scary stories, invented to give shape to the epistemic darkness.

Put off by the eerie sacredness—and in search of the profane—I retreated into Naina's room, where the deities were stuffed animals, endangered or extinct creatures manufactured with recycled materials: a tarantula, a bonnethead shark, a fennec fox.

Every morning and evening, I took Jerky on a walk to East Rock, but other than that, I confined myself to the house, with its central air and fundamental distance from the world. I got my sunlight when I let Jerky into the garden every few hours and stood there, watching him huff around, avoiding posting to his social media feed. Apparently, Naina, our parents, Maneesha's in-laws, and a coterie of her and Ajay's friends depended on @beefjerkypup for their daily endorphins. All I'd contributed so far was a shot of Jerky peeing on Maneesha's tomatoes, noting in the caption the benefits of urine for tomato cultivation, a tip I'd learned from Elsa. That needled my sister.

It was curious to inhabit Maneesha's life, which seemed so comfortable from afar. I saw now the extreme machinations required to maintain that comfort. I was to polish the stainless-steel pans after each use with a solution called Bar Keepers Friend, lest they appear, well, used. The wineglasses were to be treated with a microfiber cloth and a mixture of vinegar and water to keep them from growing cloudy. I should throw lemons but nothing else into the Insinkerator, and use the Roomba once a day because I shed strands of my thick curly hair everywhere I went, and Maneesha did not want to come back to find a "rat king" formed from my locks. I didn't do any of that. I just lurked, mourning the person I might have become had I chosen a different job, a different partner, a different pattern of behaviors over the past thirtytwo years. I might own a house like this, or like the ones I jerked off to on Zillow. I might have been happy. I might not have been myself, but that would have been no real loss, as I did not particularly like being myself.

Days passed. I spoke to no one. The only sounds were of Jerky's weak, heaving lungs and paws skittering over the hardwood, as well as the vague jangles of Maneesha's security system, something called a HomeSafe. It consisted of menacing black circles mounted to the garage door and to the exterior rear of the house. There was probably a beady eye in each circle, witnessing and recording. I would not have put it past Maneesha to be nanny-camming me on her iPad from her Athens sabbatical. The HomeSafe sensors lit blue and chimed every time there was "irregular" activity nearby, making no distinction between chipmunks and burglars. The constant jangling startled me at first; I could not shake the sense of another being stalking the house, the house itself trying to warn me that I was endangered. I felt sad for Maneesha: she lived in a state of constant poised anxiety that an outside beastliness might intrude on her immaculate life—violent crime in the streets, squirrels in her tomatoes.

Through it all, I kept vigil over my phone. I texted and called my second mystery correspondent, the one who'd spotted "me" on Carter Road, via a WhatsApp call that rang and rang and was never answered. They'd said they were headed to Bali—perhaps they'd switched off their Indian number. What bothered me was why they thought I was pregnant. The only way to account for that information was Killian, which meant this correspondent had to have spoken to Killian recently. So I tried to reach Killian again, emailing, texting, and calling, just in case his phone was active again. But he maintained his silence, a silence that was beginning to feel less like stubborn anger and more like torture.

I also texted my first correspondent, the one who'd sent me the throbbing pink heart and the angel baby emoji, the one I'd dismissed as a wrong number. I couldn't help but wonder now if I'd been incorrect. I asked them who they were, who they were trying to reach, and if *K* meant *Killian*. I got no reply for several days, until they wrote back: wrong number.

This should have been a relief. The angel baby *wasn't* meant for me. And yet I couldn't shake some lingering fright, some sense that its arrival in my life was not an accident.

I had been almost happy, for a while, in Bombay—in that magnetic city, performing the job I thought I wanted to do for the rest of my life. I spent nearly two years conducting fieldwork in the slum at the heart of the city, Dharavi, which was a metropolis unto itself, thronging with potters and leather tanners and plastic scavengers; homegrown doctors and homegrown gurus and homegrown mephedrone cooks. I was hardly the first anthropologist to descend on Dharavi with notepad in hand. We outsiders were constantly carpetbagging, clumsily trying to frame it with phrases like *public health pyramid* and *informal economy*. I myself came there because of a septuagenarian healer, Nakusha. *Nakusha* meant "unwanted," and it was a common name given to girls whose families cursed them for not being born male. Today, people flocked to be cured of a variety of ailments by Nakusha, and I, too, came to behold the healing, a pilgrim in my own right. Every day for months, I squatted on the floor of a fourhundred-square-foot temple and witnessed Nakusha shut her eyes and quake and quiver and place two leathery hands on the heads of her postulants and rid them of their qualms. Infidelity. Infertility. Sexual inadequacy.

After my days with Nakusha, I'd feel my borders pleasantly erased as I subsumed myself in the anonymity of my commute home—the streets Jenga-packed and jigsawed with auto-rickshaws, rich people's buffed black Audis en route to the financial district or film studios, salwar-kameezed career women urging their mopeds through traffic. Sometimes I took a cab home from Dharavi, but more often I rode the train, cramming myself into the women's car, which was always raucous with color. Lemon-lime bandhani dupattas and the pastel ridas of the Bohra Muslims and red saris slashed with gold zari.

From the station, I'd hop in an auto, crossing Linking Road and catching a glimpse of Colonel Sanders, blinking down from a gigantic KFC sign, his fluorescent white face surveying the masses, reigning over the shopwaalas selling polyester clothing to the aspiring middle classes and the child beggars supplicating at idling autos.

Past the KFC sign bloomed our neighborhood: Bandra, a historically Catholic area that was also home to the film industry. My auto would edge through the streets brimming with glassy high-rises abutting fisher villages, then down the leafy alleys where longtime residents lived—cobblestones littered with copper pods in the spring, Goan aunties in floral dresses sipping feni on balconies, and white plaster Virgins peeking out from cornices. I'd come to a stop at the foot of Mount Mary, the southern edge of Bandra, where Killian's and my building was situated. One of our many neighbors was a beloved cricketer, who lived in the penthouse ten floors above us. To reach my stairwell I often had to push through a crowd of tourists gathered to gawk up at the athlete's balcony. Once a day he emerged to wave magnanimously down at them. I would make my way into my building, passing the guard, and the neighbors' drivers, who lounged in the shade of the car park and polished their charges' European imports endlessly. I'd trudge to our 2-BHK, brushing by maids hauling trash or groceries up and down the stairs, and stand on our jute mat, eager to escape the pungent scent wafting down from the Chimbai Road fish market.

And then I'd open the door and be alarmed to find Killian there, shirtless, pacing the house with a script in hand, running lines. I'd be startled by the fact of the palatial, ocean-view flat itself. The place had come semi-furnished, like many expats' apartments, and the furnishings included several enormous wooden crucifixes, the subtle touches of our ancient addled landlady, Miranda. We had traded on Killian's Catholic roots—and Miranda's assumption that I had converted to marry him—to get into one of the nicer buildings in the area. (Many Bandra residences were only open to Catholics.) There was particular moral scrutiny toward young couples like Killian and me; posh housing societies regarded childless young people with suspicion, assuming that they were faking a marriage to live in sin. We'd had to show our marriage certificate to Miranda and her middleaged son John-Matthew and the president of the housing society Isabel and her husband Simon and so on; each one had made photocopies of the certificate and distributed it through the building. To put a fine point on it, Killian decided to frame the document. He nailed it up right next to one of the crucifixes in the living room. It was the way that certificate hung, next to the agonized Jesus, whose divinity was not real to me, that made the marriage feel even more like an invention. It seemed—I seemed—like a counterfeit. A forgery of someone else's idea of what a wife was supposed to be.

My problem, during those days at Maneesha's, was that I could not write about Bombay. Things went horribly wrong near the end of my time in India. My fellowship money was nearly all spent when I got an email from a grad student at Brown, Inés, with whom I was friendly. She was writing to let me know that she was defecting from the app. She linked to an email newsletter she was starting on post-academic life, in which she hoped to counsel other grad students on alternative options to increasingly unstable university careers. Her central recommendation seemed to be that all of us start advice dispatches of our own. She also mentioned, in the note, the latest jobs report from the American Anthropological Association, which said that there were three teaching positions available, on average, every year; usually one was tenure-track, and two were uninsured adjunct gigs that paid around nineteen thousand dollars a year. This was not the first time I'd seen comrades defect from academic life. Elsa had become the social chair of a private club in New York. Rhys now did something called *content agnostic management* for a hedge fund. Wendy took a position as a public policy liaison for a sharing economy start-up; Ronald composed music for a boutique ad agency. Inés, though, had been one of my last fellow travelers.

I panicked. For the next three weeks, I did not go to Dharavi but instead tried to put together a paper to submit to one of a handful of journals. Anything to bolster my weak CV. I wrote, turning Nakusha into not a person but a *unit of analysis*. I flipped through my notebooks, trying to find structure, numbers, things that resembled data, which even humanists demanded these days. I wrote and rewrote. Buckets of rain drenched the Bombay streets, rising ankle-high. When you stepped outside you might find a dead rat floating face up, being carried to the sea. I was happy not to leave Killian and my air-conditioned, dry home, our little glass box in the sky.

When I emerged from my bunker, I returned to Dharavi to find that Nakusha was not in her temple. But her elderly, stooped brother-in-law was, and he told me what had happened: Nakusha had been coughing. Too much. Even a few weeks ago, I had noticed it. I had promised to get her an inhaler from the local chemist's. I forgot. She began hacking up blood, grew feverish. She went to another healer—my mother would have said *a quack*—but not a hospital. Hospitals were expensive. And she had the gods on her side. Except the gods weren't strong enough. Pneumonia could act rapidly on older people. She had been dead for two days.

The brother-in-law said he had called me, more than once. But it had been an unknown number flashing up on my screen, and I ignored those, especially in India, where spam was plentiful. The brother-in-law did not read or write, so he could not have texted or WhatsApped. He didn't have to tell me why he'd tried to reach me. Even my dwindling fellowship money, meager in America, could have easily covered Nakusha's hospital bills. But I had retreated into my career, making Nakusha an idea, not a person. Losing her reminded me of the eternal problem of the position of anthropological observer. You are never, yourself, converted, never a part of the world that you purport to understand. It was a terrible way to live; it was like not having a body at all, like being a concept instead of flesh.

So, I wasn't writing at Maneesha's. I wasn't even editing college application essays—the "job" that had sustained me during my medical leave—as I'd been fired from that gig in May when I told an ambitious Asian teen that being an ambitious Asian teen didn't count as a personality. My boss, Hardik, had said that I'd failed to empathize with Asian Americans who were "rightfully" sensitive about being treated as one indistinguishable blob in the admissions process. I was living off my sublet money and counting down the days until the semester started and my meager grad student salary returned to my bank account.

In the evenings, I occasionally wrote Killian more emails, to no avail. You've made your point ghosting me, and I'm sorry I disappeared on you. But you must want a divorce as much as I do at this point, I wrote. Come out come out wherever you are, I wrote. I tried the two texters a few more times, even calling one night while very high. I spent the rest of my time selfabusing like a teenage boy and bingeing classic horror—*Rosemary's Baby*, *The Wicker Man*, *When a Stranger Calls*. The films did not help my nightmares, but I sought them out nonetheless—the jump scares, the stranger's breath on the hero's neck. Fear in scary movies manifested in satanic rituals and axes slammed through doors. It had a form. It was not so abstract as it was in life.

I went back to Dr. Kim a few times out of a sense of obligation, a need to prove to some invisible audience that I was in fact *working on myself*. Exasperatingly, Dr. Kim had decided to fixate on my "jealousy" problem—my ostensibly repressed desire to be like other women.

One day, squinting dubiously at me, she said, "You told me you often got caught, as a teenager, when you broke your parents' rules. Did some part of you *want* to be caught?" She tented her fingertips below her chin. "To be seen as you were, instead of as they wished you to be?"

Dr. Kim's aquarium had been restocked with plump, bright goldfish. They zipped through sprigs of coral and dove toward pebbles at the bottom of the tank. The creatures looked like toys designed to trick my inner child into confessing trauma.

I blanched. "Maybe." I was stung by the idea that I might have motivations that were secret even to me, that I had missed for fifteen years. "But I don't regret being myself." I crossed my arms, defensive.

Her fake plants were drooping worse than ever, perhaps because the air-conditioning was cranked up so high.

"*Don't* you?" she asked breathily, panting with the epiphany of it all.

A fake fern tickled my neck. I stood. I tried to move it but knocked it over. Soil and sod—real clods of white-speckled dirt—spilled over the carpet.

"Why do you have a fake plant in real soil?"

"That's not a fake plant," Dr. Kim said, untroubled by the mess. "Sanjana, as we've been discussing, anger can often conceal jealousy, which itself conceals regret, and regret can be—"

"*Really?*" I fingered the flappy green leaves tinged with yellow, which I'd thought were waxy, but no, they were soft, organic. "I *totally* thought this was fake."

"You know," Dr. Kim barreled on, "I wonder what it says that you thought this plant life, which I've picked out and repotted and watered to foster a nurturing space, was a *false* life. As though nurture is something you feel you must reject. Was your mother very nurturing?"

Once, at Nakusha's temple, I met a woman named Kamda who might have been diagnosable, in DSM terms, as a schizophrenic. Kamda presented before Nakusha in the midst of an episode that was warping her reality; she kept trying to kill a demon she believed had taken up residence in her head. Her brother had brought her in, and he seemed to find her condition more comic than dangerous. "She gone mad," he kept telling me matter-of-factly, in English, sibilant on the *s*. Nakusha dropped low to meet Kamda, who was squatting on the ground, thrusting her head into the wall, first softly and then with increasing violence. Down there, Nakusha whispered something I could not hear to Kamda, who halted. Then Nakusha drew Kamda to her sweaty white blouse, placed one hand on Kamda's left ear and the other over her eyes.

The scent of Nakusha—sweat and sandalwood—seemed to fill the whole room as Kamda took great heaving, suckling breaths. The goddess descended in a silent, violent whoosh, and Kamda crumpled to the floor, sapped. The demon had spilled out of her. The incident left an impression on me, and sometimes in my lowest moments, I pictured myself ramming my own head into the wall so hard that whatever was possessing me would leave me behind. What I wanted was to be held in Nakusha's hefty, firm arms, to be cleansed of that devil that both was and was not me.

Day ten at Maneesha's, and I was staring bleakly at a part of my dissertation draft subtitled "The Literature of Possession in Postcolonial Nations." Beneath the header I had written zero words. My phone buzzed. I answered rapidly, on instinct, thinking immediately of Killian, and of the faceless texters I'd been harassing over the past few days.

"Didi, Didi!" a woman was shouting, through static. A roar of traffic surrounded her, the honking and skidding of vehicles. "Sanjana Didi!" A few other voices rose, a supporting chorus. One was nasal, screechy, shouting, "Pyaaz, pyaaz, pyaaz!" I shut my eyes and was transported back to the cobblestoned streets of Bandra: the onion seller clattering down the alleys, waking me every morning as he hawked his wares.

I removed the phone from my ear and saw this was a WhatsApp call. And for a change, I actually had the contact saved. *Shazia Maid Bombay.*

I was embarrassed to admit that I hadn't thought of Shazia in at least a year. She'd only been in our lives for two months or so, between March and May of the year prior. Killian had hired her without telling me. It happened when I went away to Delhi for a conference. Upon my return, I was greeted by a willowy woman with a long, thick braid slung over her shoulder. She stood in my doorway, cocked her head to the right, and stared coldly, as though *I* were the intruder.

"Who the fuck are you?" I'd asked the woman.

"Didi," she said—sister. Deferentially. And then I saw the jhadu in her hand, and the slight stoop of her shoulders that maids get from leaning over constantly to clean up after their charges.

Apparently, over the weekend, Killian had gotten sick of the constant dust coating the apartment. He'd called up an expat friend and found Shazia, to whom he'd offered twelve thousand rupees a month, above market rate, for daily cooking and cleaning. We had fought about it. A *maid*! I'd cried. I couldn't be one of those foreigners who got used to such comforts. He'd said we were a grown-up, married couple. This was what people *like us* did. "But we aren't married *like that*," I'd insisted, and he'd asked what I meant, and I'd said, "Like, husband-wife, married—we're, like, *health insurance* married," and he'd balked.

"Shazia Didi? Kya sab theekh hai?" I hadn't thought in or spoken Hindi for ages. The language came out shaky and childish, each word overpronounced. "All okay?"

"Hanh-ji, Didi." She had to raise her voice to be heard. "Kya aapko kuch khaana ya cleaning ki zaroorat hai?"

She wanted to come cook or clean for me. Befuddled, I explained that I had left Bombay and was living in the US again.

"Nahi, nahi, Didi, good news? Maine good news sunna hai! Aapko madad chahiye hogi. Bahut zaroori hoga."

Good news: I recognized that phrase of hers. One of her favorite refrains. On weekend mornings, if I slept late, Shazia would run into my bedroom, shouting at me to awaken. She seemed to be employed by some other Sanjana who instructed her to boss me around. If I motioned that she should leave me alone, I was tired, she'd crouch on the bed and begin stroking my belly, whispering,

Good news? For a while I was confused about why a Muslim woman was proselytizing the gospel, until I realized she was asking: Was I exhausted because I was pregnant? Why wasn't I pregnant yet?

And now she was saying that she had at last heard the good news. I would need help. It was necessary. She wanted her job back. She had spied an opportunity—but how?

I asked her if she had seen Killian. The last time they would have spoken to each other was the day, last May, when he'd fired her. He'd done it while I was out of the house, the same way he'd hired her. He'd said she had become overfamiliar. He had found her, more than once, wearing my clothes while I was out. "She seemed to think that she was the lady of the house," he'd said, and I'd refrained from saying that, in a way, she was.

I pressed: "Killian Bhaiya, Didi."

"Didi, Didi, aapki awaaz nahi aa rahi hai!" She couldn't hear me. The line cut.

I called back once, twice, three times, to no avail. She was probably out of data. There was no use sending a message; Shazia could read, but she panicked at the sight of chunks of text on her phone and never replied.

My heart was thumping quickly. I scrolled over to the message I'd received from my second texter—the one with the photo. I zoomed in on the person standing next to Killian, the one in the indigo dress. She was still backlit, still washed out, still faceless. My eyes dropped to her stomach. Was some other explanation possible? Could it be that Killian had, in the past year, found a new partner and knocked her up already?

The woman's belly looked completely flat. But one of her arms was bent, just slightly, pressed against her midsection. It might be nothing, that gesture, that stomach-cradling. It might also be something. It was a matter of interpretation.

6

Self-Help

The spring Killian and I first started dating, he was playing God. Understudying God, technically, in a two-hander off-Broadway called *Waiting for G.* For sixty-nine minutes, no intermission, two unnamed characters, M and G, sophomorically debated the existence, power, and justice of a loving god until, in the final moments, G revealed himself to be God, deciding whether to leave the world to its fate, which the playwright helpfully enumerated in Seussian rhymes ("cruelties and rising seas and police brutalities!"). At the end of the show, God—occasionally Killian—disappeared in a puff of red smoke. That the actor playing G contracted the Zika virus and Killian went on most nights, and that *Waiting for G* earned rave reviews, told me I did not understand the theater, or at least other people's consumption of it. "*You* were great," I always told Killian when I took the train down to New York to see him, which wasn't entirely a lie. In those early days, Killian was an undeniable talent, even when saddled with inane material. As one reviewer put it in the *Who's Afraid of Virginia Woolf?* write-up, it was easy to miss Killian Bane if you did not keep your eyes trained on him for an entire show. But if you let your gaze fall squarely on him, you saw how the whole story seemed to unfurl from his sphinxlike, smoldering expression.

He purported to be, in his heart, a stage actor, but when an agent from CAA began courting him, promising television and film opportunities, Killian promptly abandoned his theatrical dreams for the screen. He landed a recurring guest star role as an immortal warlock on a teen paranormal romance show that filmed in New Mexico for tax purposes. He shot a prestige pilot in which he played a traumatized Iraq war veteran who had gone in search of his father, having forgotten, due to traumatic brain injury, that his father had been killed in the *first* Gulf War—ostensibly, the showrunner claimed, a comment on the way history "rhymes." The whole thing was to be filmed in gray-blue, with long, uncut shots reminiscent of *Children of Men*.

I kept expecting Killian to break up with me as his star rose, and perhaps I mistook the novelty of those early years together for love. We had always seemed mismatched; I assumed I was one of his many forays into the ruck of human experience, that he was trying me on temporarily as a way to better understand others—some kind of artistic research. But the dumping never came; instead, I moved into Elsa's group house when he finished with *Woolf*, and he began splitting his time between New Haven and wherever he was filming. "No one expects this," he'd say, before swinging me out to a party with him, as if to say he knew people pictured him dating some bird of a blonde, or an Elsa, whereas I was so random as to be hip. I often felt like his accessory—his anthropologist girlfriend!—and adopted a uniform of big gold-rimmed glasses and black cowl-necked sweaters, to be sure I was delivering on whatever promise my epithet implied.

But I don't think Killian would have stuck with me if things hadn't begun to sour for him professionally. Execs passed on the war vet pilot, calling it too close to *Memento* and the Bourne trilogy. And what was supposed to be Killian's next break—a historical drama about nineteenth-century Irish American railroad workers called *Poor Paddy*—got what he claimed was a bad edit. The night we attended the premiere, which the only real "name" in the movie skipped in order to shoot a fantasy epic in Macedonia, Killian drowned his sorrows in five whiskeys, turned his green eyes on me, and said, "We should be married. Why aren't we married?" I was not sure exactly when, but I had, at some point, stopped picturing life without him. That phrase—*can't see myself without you*—was both romantic and strangulating. Now there he was, plaintive, proposing, so certain about me, which made it seem simple enough to be certain about him in return. "You keep me in touch with what really matters," he went on. "Also, I need to not work for a while, so I'm gonna lose SAG-AFTRA health insurance."

We took no honeymoon; instead, Killian melted down. He had long planned to survive on the creative vim that went into being an artist, but art had begun to sap him of his selfhood. Go on playing other people, he began musing on his bleakest days, and you eventually become a husk of yourself. He lost confidence, stopped getting callbacks, quit bothering with self-tapes. His agent dropped him. Killian took a side job running after-school drama in New Haven public schools, but found himself too depressed to "recruit these young people into the pyramid scheme that is the failing arts in America," as he put it, and also the kids didn't respond to Harold Pinter.

He claimed to be writing a play, which morphed into a feature, which morphed into a pilot; once, I stumbled upon him writing and he shut his laptop so quickly I imagined the words on the screen as Jack Nicholson's typewriter in *The Shining*, just the words All work and no play makes killian a dull boy, forever and ever. Though I knew it was a violation, I opened the computer later and examined the work in progress: a clumsy attempt to dramatize the death of his younger half brother, Cormac, who had, at sixteen, fallen or jumped off the roof of his high school, where a few kids had been passed out, cross-faded on alcohol, crystal, and acid. Killian told me that he always wondered if Cormac had meant to die or if he'd thought he could fly. If his death had been caused by his imagination constricting—the diminishment of options that came from growing up working class and fatherless—or ballooning, engorging grotesquely to make him believe that if he took a step off the roof, the air would carry him somewhere better.

I did not find these incarnations of my new husband *attractive*, but they did provoke my empathy. I felt that we were in the same boat, he stuck on the bottom floor of the pyramid scheme of the arts, and I at the base of the pyramid scheme of academia. I wanted to help him regain his faith—that "improvisational spirit" that he had once believed in as fervently as his lapsed-Catholic mother believed in the Holy Spirit. I was waiting for the promise of our early courtship to be fulfilled. I had come to depend on his buoyancy.

Killian and I had been married for about a year when I won my fellowship to go to Bombay. I was surprised when he greeted the news as though it were the greatest joy of his life. Like the veteran he'd played, he was interested in his paternal roots; as he'd told me on the night of the Naked Supper Club, his mother, Mary, had gotten pregnant while backpacking around India. Plus, Killian said, he'd heard of half-Indian actors making it in Bollywood. See: Katrina Kaif. There was even one entirely white woman, Kalki Koechlin, who had somehow been allowed to slide through the whole industry getting cast as brown. If they could do it, he could, too. All he'd have to do was learn some Hindi and learn to dance. Then, when we came back to America, he'd have a bolstered résumé. Or if things took off, maybe we would even stay there. I could write books free of the university system and he could be a bona fide superstar. He seemed to imagine that the nation was waiting for him to arrive. I didn't want to prick his new confidence. My life had become a game of waiting out his depleted selfhood. Waiting for K. I was willing to let him think or say anything en route to regaining his swagger.

In Bombay, while I spent my days with Nakusha, Killian studied Hindi, worked with a vocal and diction coach, attended dance workshops. He got a job as a personal trainer at the gym where all the Bollywood stars worked out. He paid "coordinators" (lecherous quasi-agents who demanded upfront payment for a foot in the door) and booked some auditions. But his Hindi was miserable; he couldn't wrap his mouth around the aspired consonants or the retroflex *t*'s. And he couldn't dance. His only roles were those of British baddies. He beat revolutionaries within inches of their lives, threatened good Hindu girls' honor, was bested in games of cricket by plucky anti-colonial upstarts. He was always killed off in vicious ways: stabbed with bayonets, decapitated by whirling chakras, trampled to death by elephants. "I'm *Irish* and *Indian*," he told everyone for whom he auditioned, hoping, I think, that his roots would disqualify him from playing a colonizer. But no one gave a shit. Perhaps they could tell that he had a conqueror's mindset himself: he had come to the Global South thinking it would bend to his will and was frustrated to find otherwise. He was always having to grow out a handlebar mustache to twirl villainously.

So, he began to follow the route well worn by many a failed actor before him: he went woo-woo. While taking still more undignified gigs—performing as a Disney prince for rich little girls' birthday parties in South Bombay; running improv workshops for corporate team-building retreats—he also went cult shopping. During his fallow LA years, he'd had his more spiritual phases. Never full-blown Scientology, but always a yen for self-improvement. Now he hired a Vastu Shastra consultant to rejigger the layout of our house so the energies would flow better. He worked with an Ayurvedicist to revamp his diet, discovering that his frequent dreams of "water bodies" meant he needed to quit all salt, alcohol, and carrots. He poured a whole lakh into homeopathic skincare products designed to make him ageless; they were all infused with whitening agents that stippled his skin with angry red bumps (and, ironically, made him paler and more colonial-looking than ever). He was hypnotized weekly by an artist-life-coach named Shiv, who made house calls and drew his brother Cormac out of him again.

(Once, as Shiv was departing our flat, leaving a trail of incense and a shuddering Killian clutching a ratty coconut in his lap, he whispered to me that I'd made a grievous mistake with my nose piercing. My silver stud is on the right side, but, Shiv chided, Ayurveda makes clear that left-nostril piercings release juices for reproductive well-being. "You must menstruate more than average," he said knowingly.)

Killian began spending time at the Hare Krishna temple in Juhu. I spotted a tambourine and a saffron robe in the closet once. He attended a series of workshops led by an internet "poet" who had published an illustrated book of "poems" called *Touch My Trauma*. Killian paid ten thousand rupees for her to teach him to not just touch but manhandle his trauma into submission. "You need selective amnesia to act," he told me. "But I've been weighed down recently. That's why things aren't working. I need to forget everything I was so I can be anyone again."

"How are your dance classes going?" I asked. "How about the Hindi?"

"I can *not* learn a new language right now, Sanjana," he said. "I'm still not fluent in myself."

Again, I kept waiting for him to become the person I'd fallen in love with, though much of me now suspected that he had only been briefly playing the part of that man. Still, I told myself I would not leave. I dreaded explaining myself to my family, to Lia, to myself—barely thirty, and a divorcée? Which is why, when Killian returned from the *Touch My Trauma* workshop in Powai and told me he'd had a borderline religious experience, and that he now saw what he needed to do to access not only his "creative selfhood" but also "get in touch with the wider shimmering life force that imbues all of humanity," I was relieved.

"It's been all about me, me, me," he said, dropping to his knees and burying his face in my thighs in what I assumed was apology. "All about who *I* am, rather than who I ought to be in relation to *others*."

"Well, I didn't want to say anything," I replied, running my fingers through his hair. I *did* understand. Both of us had chosen what we thought of as monastic higher callings, *vocations* rather than jobs. Art! Thought! What could be more fulfilling than these pursuits? And yet as we aged, we were discovering that these vocations were vulgar, not transcendent, riddled with immaturity and instability.

"I figured it out, though," he said, speaking into the sweaty crease where my thigh met my crotch. His breath came steamy on my vulva. "It's you," he whispered. A kiss. "I love you so much that I want more of you. I always have."

"What do you mean *more*?" I asked, tilting my neck back, feeling hot and flattered.

"I want to serve something beyond myself. I want to make art that's about the most important human experiences. I want to be a vessel, Sanjana. For Meaning."

"Sure," I said.

And then he turned his face up to me, his chin pressing too hard on my clitoris.

"We need to have a child," he said.

"What?"

"I *saw* it," he said, dreamily. "I wish you'd been there, Sanj. It was total clarity. Everything went white for a second, my whole brain, and my past just seeped out of me—Cormac and my mother and my selfishness—and I realized that the *something higher* I've been needing to serve, it's not Krishna or Buddha. It's another, vulnerable being, who you and I make together, and tend. I realized that's the meaning of life, Sanj. It's *always* been the meaning of life. In order to make universal and moving art, I have to belong to human history.

To do the most ancient thing. Then I'll understand. I was *made* to be a father first, and an artist second."

The intensity of his gaze on my stomach in that moment made me think of the husband in *Rosemary's Baby*—the actor who sells out his wife to the satanists, swapping her womb for his success.

"I'm sorry," I said, my hands going clammy. "I'm not sure *I* am ready. Now, or … ever."

"Take your time," he said, bravely. "You waited for me."

But as his eyes flashed to my midsection, I detected dread. His sanity, our future, the very purpose of life, apparently, now depended on me. On my body. I split in two, right then. Half of me found this, his latest avatar—Daddy Killian—absurd. The other began wishing, fervently, that I could be converted, as he had been. I wanted his new clarity for myself. I knew that purposelessness was dangerous. I feared the self-annihilation that comes from not knowing why you are alive, from seeing your life add up to nothing. And so, we agreed to wait for each other, neither of us knowing when, or whether, the other would arrive at the appointed meeting place.

7

Where's the Beef?

Over the next week at Maneesha's, the strange messages did not cease. The day after Shazia's call, I got a WhatsApp from an Indian number. It arrived when I was at the liquor store. I had just cashed my subletter's check and wanted to reward myself with some Tito's. The fortysomething desi owner demanded two forms of ID. As I handed over my debit card, I checked my phone to see an image: two doves perched on a thin branch, superimposed atop a pink sunset. Above the birds was some cursive text:

> *Congratulations. A child is the greatest blessing from Our Lord. May God forever look after your new family.*

"You okay?" the cashier asked. I must have gasped. He was craning his neck to peer at my phone screen. "My uncle, he sends me and my sisters a WhatsApp every morning. Picture of a rose or a tulip or some bullshit, with cursive, you know? *Good morning may all your best wishes come true.* We desis, we once broke the internet with all the WhatsApp good mornings."

"I'm not Indian," I said, reaching for the Tito's.

The guy frowned, still gripping my debit card, my school ID, and my driver's license. His eyes dropped to the plastic and focused on my name. "Really?"

"Yeah, fucking really," I said, and snatched them all back from him, violently.

"Well, solidarity, man!" he yelled after me. "You totally could be!"

Outside, I called the number. The air was rich with the smell of collegiate drunk food: buffalo meatball subs, Singapore noodles. My stomach roiled.

"Who is this?" I snapped.

"Hallo, Mrs. Bane?" The voice trembled. An elderly person.

I rolled my eyes. I had never been Mrs. Bane. The only people who had ever called me that were the nosy aunties in our housing society and my old landlady, Miranda.

"Miranda?" I asked. "Miranda, did you get a new phone number?" In India, people were always acquiring different (or additional) phone numbers. Miranda's son John-Matthew was a real estate broker whose chest pocket perpetually bulged with three phones—two smart, one flip; each of the Androids had two separate SIM cards. Killian thought John Matthew was a drug dealer. I had to explain to him that this was just the way of my people. I once heard someone call it Multiple Phone Personality.

"Hallo, Mrs. Bane, very best wishes to you and your husband!" She was yelling, not because of an inordinate amount of traffic around her, or even a staticky connection, but because she was an Indian of a certain age who remembered the days of bad international phone lines.

I was stepping into the crosswalk and nearly knocked into a cyclist. "Miranda, have you spoken to my—my husband, recently?"

"No, Mrs. Bane, not recently? Is there some problem?"

"So, uh. Is he not … back? At the apartment?"

Miranda breathed hard. "Mrs. Bane, I do not want to get in the middle of some marital issue."

"Yes, well," I snapped. "We're getting a divorce. And I'm trying to reach him."

"Mrs. Bane. Please do one thing. Please think. With a child—"

"Who told you I was pregnant?" I shouted, matching her register, though a rational part of me knew that she wasn't really angry—just confused. Someone stopped on the street next to me—a woman, concerned.

There was some scuffling and the phone was being moved, and then a deeper voice boomed through the line. "Who is this?" "Is this John-Matthew?" I asked. "John-Matthew, it's Sanjana, your mother's former tenant, I—"

"Mrs. Bane, congratulations, I am sure you are excited, but you are upsetting my mother—"

"Stop fucking congratulating me! I am not fucking pregnant!"

"Mrs. Bane, you cannot speak this way!" John-Matthew was yelling now, too. "This is just unacceptable NRI arrogance, you people, you come from America and—"

"I haven't lived there in a year! I haven't been pregnant for a year!" I shouted. "Because you know what I've been doing? I've been fucking my way through Connecticut Tinder! Do you know what Tinder is? Miranda? It's for people to fuck strangers!"

Mid-tirade, I realized they'd hung up. I stood holding my phone limply in one hand. I felt the eyes of a few sidewalk spectators on me, including the woman who'd stopped when I first yelled that I wasn't pregnant. She looked to be in her early forties, with shiny chestnut hair, and she wore flowing oatmeal-colored linen and Birkenstocks. Her lips puckered, not in disdain but in sympathy.

"Are you okay?" she asked, approaching me gingerly, with a little shuffle in her step.

I was staring at my stomach.

"I think my ex told people I'm pregnant," I said. "And …

I'm not. Not anymore. I was. And then I wasn't."

"May I give you a hug?" she asked.

I found myself nodding.

She drew me to her. "I'm so sorry," she whispered in my ear. I almost pulled away, afraid that she had misunderstood me—that she thought I had miscarried, or lost a wanted child; that this was not my *sorry* to take. But there was something about this woman's arms around my neck, her moist forearms pressed to my shoulders, that made me not want to move. I stayed still, sweating on her, and it wasn't until she said, "There, there, let it out," that I realized I was wetting her shirt with tears.

The next night, afraid to be alone with myself, I called Max. Not so much to talk as to fuck the weirdness out of me.

He arrived at Maneesha's bearing Thai takeout and a slightly befuddled expression at the urgency of my booty call. We smoked, drank too much, watched the original *Stepford Wives*. I was losing the edges of things. A half hour in, when Max said he had to pee, I shouted, "Pee on the tomatoes!" Obligingly, he slid open the screen door and walked out to the yard, bringing Jerky with him. I followed after what I thought was a respectful amount of time. Max was done, fly zipped, staring at the slivered moon and the black tented sky. Jerky sprawled at his feet, content. Jerky liked Max. All living creatures could sense his gentleness.

"Hi." I stepped behind Max, wrapping my arms around his waist, not caring that the gesture was dangerously intimate. He pulled my palms to his belt buckle. I had been trying to teach him to be mean during sex, but alas, the Harm Reducer had no talent for even consensual cruelty. Everything was clunky, performative. I could feel him straining against his natural tendencies when he said I was going to do exactly what he told me to for a little while.

Hesitating, he attempted to clarify: "Is, uh. Is that the kind of thing you want?"

I didn't answer. Behind us, the blue motion sensor of the HomeSafe jangled and lit up, but I had forgotten what that sound meant. I left myself and dropped to my knees on the grass.

After, we sat on the patio furniture. With urgency surely hastened by our mix of substances, he gripped me by the shoulders. His soil-hued eyes met mine, ferociously.

"That bossy stuff," he said. "I don't want to do it if ... something happened to you."

I snorted at the juvenility of the word *bossy*. Vocabulary befitting Naina's report card.

"What do you mean *happened*?" I reached for the vape on the patio table. I took a long drag, then forced it into his hand. He held it slackly. "Like, the abortion ... was it after assault?"

I fingered his hair, which hung to his shoulders. He frowned a shaming frown, like I was emotionally blue-balling him. "I was married," I said, as though that sufficed. I waited for his expression to shift, or for him to recalculate my senescence.

A minor twitch around his eyebrows. "Did your husband hurt you? Because it would affect how I treat you. During sex."

I threw myself back on the patio pillows, which were damp from the previous night's showers. I was supposed to bring them indoors after each use.

"He didn't rape me. He didn't hit me. He just got me pregnant."

Then I leaned over and barfed in the tomatoes.

In the morning, I awoke in Naina's room to several discoveries. Some sweet ones: Max, asleep on the floor in a *Jungle Book* sleeping bag, his hand stretched toward me. A lined wastebasket by my head, a glass of water on the nightstand.

And then, the disasters: My phone, alit.

A storm of messages in all caps, from Maneesha.

The worst: NAINA SAW YOU. ON THE HOMESAFE.

In sum: Naina missed Jerky. Wanted to see him.

I wasn't posting to the doggy-gram. Naina kept asking for the pup.

Naina had recently learned "Where's the beef?," kept shouting it.

Maneesha's response to her crying daughter: sedate her with a screen. She gave her the iPad.

Naina scrolled through the HomeSafe recordings. Watched for Jerky in the backyard. Saw her first blow job instead.

Maneesha's worst nightmare.

I had, yet again, breached the barrier of the Satyananda moral fortress that was supposed to keep American immorality at bay, its encircling moat a chastity belt.

Then there was one more text, from Maneesha: ALSO YOU HAD SOME RANDOM DUDE IN MY HOUSE *AND* LET HIM PEE ON MY TOMATOES???

I called. If Maneesha heard my voice, I would be a person, not just a grainy porny figure. But instead of clicking the voice-call button, I hit video, which meant that when I popped up on Maneesha's screen, she saw that I was in her daughter's bed.

She'd tugged her hair into a tight ponytail, which was contracting her features horribly.

On the floor, Max stirred. My eyes flashed toward him, involuntarily. Maneesha saw, sensed the presence of an additional person in the room.

"Oh my god. You're in Naina's room. You didn't. Not in my kid's bed."

"Nothing happened in here," I said, panic creeping into my voice. I spoke through my teeth, praying Max would understand the urgency of the situation.

"I am so done with you, Sanjana," she said. "I don't want you around my dog, let alone my daughter."

"You don't even like Naina," I said. "She's too much like me."

"You are a narcissist!" Maneesha shouted. "You think you're some kind of feminist pioneer, like there haven't been a million lonely, selfish bitches before you." I'd never heard Maneesha use the b-word. "You're just a … I was going to say *woman-child*, but you're not even that. You're a *man-child*. You think you're better than other people who want their lives to be about someone else. Get *out* of my house. Mommy will come get Jerky."

She hung up.

"I got you in trouble," Max said, his face falling. There was something so total in the way he said it, with the inflection of a little boy. *In trouble*, as though there really were some kind of omniscient authority floating above us, judging. In our case, the eyes watching us had just been a seven-year-old's. "Where are you going to go?" he asked. "You sublet your place, right?"

Before he felt obligated to offer his own apartment, I said, "Brooklyn."

Lia didn't ask what had happened. She just registered the snotty sounds of my crying and told me to shut the fuck up and get on the first train to Grand Central. I could stay in the guest room. But just for a bit. They were converting it into a nursery.

8

Give Me the Epidural!

Killian and I went to Goa a few weeks after Nakusha died, a few days after I sent Alisandra an email informing her that I would be dropping out of the program. Killian handled the arrangements: he'd learned of a cooperative farming community called Moksha Living from an actress who'd gone there to recuperate after a demanding role, and he believed the place might do us good, too. We were to be guests of an Israeli woman named Rivka and her husband, an Indian man named Stalin. Stalin was the son of Bengali Communists. When I asked why he'd never changed his name, he cited the other Stalin, M. K. Stalin, chief minister of Tamil Nadu, and then added, "Anyway, did you change *your* name just because it's difficult for some people?" and I said no, but wasn't Stalin a bit more evil than any Sanjana he'd ever met, and he said that could change anytime, not to get too holy about it. "You're very in your head, aren't you?" Rivka, observing the exchange, said.

Stalin had made money in e-commerce in Bangalore, then bought the land in Goa and started a family with the much younger Rivka, whom he'd met straight off the hummus trail that transported her ilk from the IDF to the Indian seeking industry. India was dotted with twentysomething Israelis, all smoking hash and replaying kibbutz fantasies inherited from their parents' generation in a new landscape that, to them, seemed deliciously, appealingly blank.

Moksha was home to fourteen adults—thirteen Europeans and one Aussie—and three children. All except Stalin were white. The residents shared the labor of planting, harvesting, cooking, cleaning, and chicken tending. About half of them had digital-nomad jobs and tithed portions of their income to support the commune, while the other half worked on community tasks full-time. Many residents kept vows of "noble silence"—no speaking, gestures, or even eye contact—for large portions of the day, especially in the morning and evening.

On our "welcome tour," Rivka provided stern instruction. The bathrooms especially had many rules. The composting toilet yielded "humanure" for crop-raising, an extension of Elsa's pee-on-tomatoes principle. "Poop," Rivka said, sagely, "is also food." Sawdust served as flushes, water as toilet paper. Babies used no diapers; rather, their parents observed their faces closely to determine when they were going to urinate or shit before racing to the toilets to hold their children above the holes in the ground. This form of potty training required total connection between parent and offspring.

The last directive on our tour was a reminder that Moksha was an alcohol and drug-free zone. There had been some Russians recently, and, well …

At dinner that first night, we sat in a circle under a thatched hut adjoining the house, and one Australian Indian woman asked, in a chanty way, "Tell us your names, please, guests, so we can pronounce them correctly." We told them, and in chorus they responded, "San-ja-na! Kill-i-an!" several times. Then large pots of vegan stew were passed around, though it was too humid for stew. Over dinner, Stalin and Rivka gabbed about their family, a brood of "unschooled" autodidacts. Their daughters were fluent in English, Hindi, Bangla, and Hebrew. One was now pursuing a yoga course in Rishikesh; another had chosen the "urban gluttony" of Tel Aviv. Their third child, a miracle baby born of the elongated fertility produced by the Moksha-mindful life, was "twentynine months old."

As I attempted to swallow the stew, the Aussie, Olga, cozied up to me in a female-secrecy fashion. She told me about how, back home in Sydney, she had run a community group that attended the Sunday seafood market each week, where they bought up all the lobsters and shellfish—the only still-living creatures—and released them into the ocean. She asked if I had children. When I squealed, *No!*, she looked offended. That was when I saw her son curled into her side, paging blankly through an illustrated book called *I Was Born in a Hut!*

"Do you like the book?" I asked the boy.

"Like the pictures," he said, and jammed his thumb in his mouth.

"How old is he?" I asked, cautiously.

"Lennon's a very wise eight," she said.

She seemed disappointed when I told her I was an anthropologist.

"*How strange the customs of the natives*," she said, in a gobliny voice.

"She's retired," Killian said, and Olga smiled approvingly.

In our room that night, I told Killian I'd found the chanting creepy. "Like, 'We accept her, we accept her, one of us! One of us!'"

"They just wanted to say our names correctly. You're always complaining that people get yours wrong."

Hearing our names chanted that way had not felt welcoming to me. In their mouths, our names changed from our names into discrete sounds and syllables, mere noises. It was menacing.

I raised my suspicions about Lennon's illiteracy and likely unvaccinated status. "He shouldn't be sucking his thumb at that age!" I insisted, but all Killian said was that I seemed to be jumping to a lot of conclusions.

"Also," I said, "I'm not retired."

"You dropped out," he said, to which I did not have a good response. "Don't feel bad. I'm thinking of retiring, too. Or taking a long hiatus until I've reset my inner life to make real art."

"This place is so fucking white," I said on day seven. We were on the beach, arguing. Rivka had recently asked me to hold an infant over the toilet, since its mother was nowhere to be found. I'd said no, in front of other residents, and Rivka told me I was a Western individualist. In the morning I woke up to a pile of Ayn Rand books on my doorstep. It was a passive-aggressive bit of ideological terrorism. It also meant someone at the co-op owned a pile of Ayn Rand books.

Killian said he didn't disagree that Moksha had a "race problem," but that what mattered more was that these people had located *Meaning*. Weren't we both proof, he said, that art and thought did not fill you up but rather made you less of yourself? How had *he* spent the past fifteen years of his life? Staring at himself in a mirror. Trying not to settle too hard into being himself so he could be anyone else. He was nearly forty and had nothing to show for his life. Had he helped anyone? Touched anyone? Foamy water lapped at my toes; the tide was coming in. Another wave rose and whacked me in the calves. I stumbled.

"I see that happening to you," he said softly. "To us. What will we add up to?"

Irritated, I stormed away, then hitched a ride on the back of a motorbike to a party beach in Calangute dotted with neon glow lights. A German offered me Molly and I accepted. I made out with a woman from Auckland with bright pink hair. Eventually someone dropped me back at Moksha. Still rolling, I kissed Killian and told him I was full of love for him and his strange ways, and I was sorry to have been so stingy with my affection for all the people at Moksha, who were only doing their best to spread more love in the world, and, and … and …

We had sex. For the first time in weeks. I had stopped taking my birth control pills, in part because he was on a Tantric kick, which entailed him not emitting sexual fluids. It had seemed torturous to me, a monthslong blue-balling, and I assumed he was jerking off in the shower, so I didn't ask questions. Plus, Tantra meant more focus on me. I came constantly and never had to deal with semen. But that night, Killian plunged deeper than usual as he was finishing, and whispered: "I want to put a baby in you."

I tried to push him out, but I realized later that I had tried only in my mind. My body did nothing. It remained wet and pliable and available and gave him no indication of the way in which my reality was not overlapping with his.

I spent the next day white-knuckling through the post-MDMA crash, and that night when Killian reached for me, I didn't have the energy to stop him. It kept happening for a week, then two. We fucked more than we had in years. Multiple times a day. He had started to sob lightly during sex; he was perpetually damp, soggy with new purpose. I didn't crave a child. But I had no job now, and no plan for a new career. I didn't have an answer to his question—*What will we add up to?* What would *I* add up to? There was a reason so many people had children. Wasn't there? Killian once argued that it was a bit like Pascal's wager, the case for belief under uncertainty: the possible spiritual gains from having children were infinite; the possible losses material, but comparatively smaller. Of course it took trust, faith, a measure of irrationality. But you did it because it was an act of vibrant hope, because you trusted something beyond you. So, did it matter that I couldn't see *it*—the blinding, bright clarity that Killian had witnessed—just yet? Wouldn't it come, as I swelled, as I birthed, as I finally held new life in my hands?

I consented to all that followed. For two months. Hours of silence every morning and evening, dish-scrubbing and toddler-potty-holding, and constant sex. At Moksha, there was no risk of failure. The only task was what was right in front of you. Peel the potato. Sit on the sand. Open your legs. Stalin and Rivka had been right: I was too in my head. As I thought less, anger and anxiety bled out of me.

I knew that Killian had started finishing inside me. I knew I hadn't restarted the pill. I had left my body and was hovering above myself, watching me—her—get fucked better than ever by a man who had started to whisper, whenever he finished, some iteration of his intention to impregnate her. *I want to put a baby in you.*

I never said yes. I never said no.

I thought of how I'd felt on Molly, kissing the Kiwi girl, then coming back home to mount Killian, and I thought, perhaps motherhood is like that, only to a better end—all that oxytocin roiling up in you, but instead of slutting around, you give the excess love to a helpless, wailing creature? I thought I could understand the desire to fundamentally expand yourself with something that grew, when everything around you was shades of decay.

And then, one day, I woke up and tried to remember the date of my last period. I'd never been regular, even with the pill.

"Where's my birth control?" I rummaged through my duffel. "Fuck. They took them. They hate drugs—they said that. On the first day."

Killian nodded seriously, an adult hearing out a distraught toddler. It had started to rain, and monsoon was coming down in a vicious sheaf on the tin roof of the main house.

"Or *you* took them," I hissed. "Did you get all Catholic?"

He shook his head woefully, but there was little surprise. It was as though he knew I'd been under some kind of spell. "Sanjana." Cool dishonesty draped him. "I thought we were finally in agreement."

"If I wanted an abortion. Would you support that?"

"*She blew up, and then she went down*," he said viciously. For a minute, I did not recognize the line. And then it came to me: Nick, the biology professor he'd been playing when I met him, speaking to George in *Woolf*. Nick, explaining that he'd married his wife, Honey, because she was pregnant, but it was a hysterical pregnancy. Nick, bitter by the second act: so young, and his marriage, too, already a farce. I understood what Killian was saying: that he had married me erroneously. I had not known that children had been there, lying in wait for us, in his imagination, the whole time; I had thought his desire for them was a whim, but now he addressed me as though our unborn children were the invisible dark matter holding his universe together. "I was going to be a father," he said. "I was always supposed to be a father." He took a step forward. He grabbed my wrists. Then he seemed shocked at the ferocity of his own movements. His mouth dropped open. "No, no, no, no, no," he said, folding into himself. Then he ran from the room, teary again, like a little boy who wasn't getting what he wanted.

That night, Killian and most of the Moksha kibbutzniks sat in evening meditation on the sand, ascetic even as the honks of motorbikes and yelps of coked-up Russians intermingled with the waves. I, too, had been propped crosslegged, but unlike the others, I was fidgeting, unable to locate equanimity. I was trying to commune with my womb. I didn't feel scared or sacred. I just felt divorced from my body. I tried to understand what might be in me. A monster that would rip me in two? Or a private, secret purpose?

I opened my eyes. Up the hill from the beach, near the garden, the illiterate Australian boy Lennon, naked from the waist down, was running around aimlessly, ignored.

I got up and went to the main house. I found my bag under the hammock, pulled out my bug spray, and started squirting it on my legs. Rivka approached. She was breast-feeding the toddler. I shuddered. My hands went to my own tits, which I could not imagine secreting milk.

Rivka asked me, syrup in her voice, if I was using a product with DEET in it?

I examined the bottle and admitted I was.

Her tanned face hardened. DEET, she said, was bad for children. "You are spoiled," she said, speaking rapidly and softly; she did not want to be overheard. "Me, I sat in silence twenty days before giving birth, each time. I ate nothing after eleven. I needed no silly drugs. I had reached an understanding about pain. It is an understanding our ancestors had. My people had it. You are Indian. Your mother has it. I caught my babies in my own hands; I planted their placentas in the earth. Now mango trees grow over each one. You? You complain about mosquitoes."

She paused. "You are pregnant." I froze. "When you give birth," she went on, "you will say, 'Give me the epidural!' When your child enters this world, you will say, 'My teeties hurt, do not make me feed my child this way!' and you will poison them with formula.

"You look down on motherhood."

"I don't," I said, feebly.

"You do," she said, irritably. "You are like a man. A capitalist pig-man. You think it would be better if women did not get pregnant, want babies. You find us weak. This attitude, this is why there is no protection for mothers. This attitude, this is why we must create places like Moksha. You understand nothing."

I lingered beneath the banyan tree, wishing she would reveal to me the thing I couldn't understand, to show me the bright white light that had blinded and remade Killian at the *Touch My Trauma* workshop. I willed her to change me or save me. I stared blankly until Rivka, confirmed in her suspicions, walked away.

Hysteria in the literal sense—an illness of the uterus— blacked out the rest of my night. I have no memory of leaving Moksha. I only recall arriving back at our flat in Bombay, packing, buying a same-day flight to JFK on my rarely used credit card, racking up a debt that I took months to pay off.

I waited two months to call Planned Parenthood. I was willing to feel something for whatever was in me. Willing to change my life if love stirred. But I felt only violation. By the time I went in, at fifteen weeks along, it was too late for the pills, too late to bleed it out at home. They sucked it from me and I was not different then, either. I was as empty as I had been before.

9

Bloody Mary Bloody Mary Bloody Mary

At Lia's, on the door of my new, temporary bedroom, hung a twenty-week sonogram in a personalized yellow frame. It read, *Welcome, Tadpole*. The photo was a Rorschach test. I knew I was supposed to see the gray-white that signified *child*, but my eyes first went to the duskiness surrounding the pale, grainy uterus: the deep black of Lia's body.

Lia and Gor had painted the room a gender-neutral soft olive, one accent wall covered in orange-jungle-print wallpaper. There was a problem with the fabric chandelier, Lia warned. The bulb kept flickering. A loose wire. After sundown, if you left the faulty light on, tigers and giraffes and orangutans sprang out at you from the shadows.

I was invited to make myself at home, but it was difficult to do so amid Lia and Gor's nonstop preparations for "Tadpole" (no pronouns yet). Lia was finally showing, delicately, like an actress in *People* magazine so skinny she might be accused of faking her pregnancy. The Grigoryans were eager, babyproofing ages in advance, readying for when Tadpole would crawl and stand and walk. They covered sharp furniture edges and outlets and replaced a square table with a round one. They latched drawers, the freezer, the garbage bin; examined labels for toxins. The cat, a tabby named Sandra Day O'Connor, sensed transformation and hid under beds and boycotted the litter box. The pioneering justice's skittishness was especially concerning to Lia given the dangers of cat poop for fetuses. I found myself constantly cleaning up after Sandy.

Meanwhile, Lia wandered the apartment in a daze. Pregnancy, she reported from the front lines, was a horror show; she'd known her body would technically no longer be just hers, but she had not planned for all the ways it would revolt. Her nose ran constantly. She had hemorrhoids and back pain and night sweats and Gor wouldn't fuck her, ostensibly for fear of jostling Tadpole, but she suspected the real reason was that her vulva had puffed up "like a purple ski jacket." Prenatal yoga was bullshit, but she was too tired for anything more arduous. Sometimes, when I opened my bedroom door, I'd find Lia standing on the other side, zombielike, shadows ringing her eyes, staring at the blurry sonogram.

"Does it feel … *miraculous*?" I asked once.

She bumped her belly against my waist. "Want to commune?"

I backed away with more disgust than I intended, and from the way she winced, it was clear that the belly thrust hadn't really been a joke. I was confused, because she'd been complaining about strangers and coworkers trying to stroke her stomach. *I* felt no right to her body. Wasn't that respectful of me? But no, she wanted *me* to touch her. She wanted me close.

Another time, Lia crept out of her bed in the middle of the night and slithered into mine, hissing in my ear: "This baby is not the most important thing about me. Promise me you won't treat me like it is." I promised, and she fell asleep, her breath hot on my shoulder, her blond locks spilling onto my neck, like when we were kids at a sleepover. We used to bully each other into going into the bathroom, switching the lights off, and shouting *Bloody Mary Bloody Mary Bloody Mary*, then waiting for Mary to appear in all her gory murdered glory. Lia could always fall asleep after, but I always stayed awake, as I was doing now, lingering in the witching hour. I let my hand drift onto Lia's stomach as she snored lightly. Her shirt had ridden up and her skin was exposed and dusted with a thin coat of fuzz, and her belly button protruded like a swollen pinky toe. I waited for something to change as I touched her. Waited for her conviction—her ability to name and love what was within her—to emanate, warm, through her skin. For a kick, the quickening. Tadpole did not stir for me. I had waited like this for my own insides to tighten and contract and bloom with new love, and there was nothing then, either.

I drifted off, in the dark solitude, where Lia and I were the only real things. All else was a story of a future as yet unseen.

Upon my arrival at Lia and Gor's, I'd apologized for being a bitch about Tadpole, and Lia had adopted that sympathetic affect again, lowering her voice. "This must be hard for you," she said. For a moment I wondered if she'd guessed about the abortion, and relief cooled me, but then she said, "You still have time." "For?"

We were making up the double bed in the future nursery. Lia tossed me a pillow and a pillowcase. "All this stuff." She jerked her head as if to say, *A house, a home*. I remembered, suddenly, helping her move into her first New York home: a closet-size bedroom in a Greenpoint apartment shared with two Craigslisters. We had scrubbed the place for hours to rid it of an ominous chemical scent, and when it still reeked ages later, Lia had collapsed on the floor, half laughing, half crying, and rubbed her snotty face on my shirt and admitted that she was terrified—what if she did not figure out how to be a real person, out here?—and I had touched her hair and promised that I, too, felt like a cipher to myself.

"Kids, if you want them," she said now. "A partner, if you want one. You're just in a shitty life season."

I nodded, shoving the pillow into the silk fabric and zipping it shut.

"Any word? From Killian?"

"No. I've been trying to track him down. Well, sort of."

She frowned, her attorney brain switching on. "Let us know when you need a lawyer."

"I don't have any money, Lia," I said, which was true. My income from editing college application essays was dwindling, and when my grad school stipend restarted in August, it would barely cover daily expenses.

Lia flushed. She had become one of those rich people who found it gauche to discuss finances.

"He can't ghost you forever," she said. "Are you seeing anyone new?"

"Not really." Max was gone for good. He'd texted once to make sure I'd gotten to Brooklyn, and then when I replied saying I didn't want to see him anymore, he sent a too-quick response, agreeing with my *decision*.

"*Do* you want any of this?" Lia asked, kneeling to tuck in the fitted sheet. I dropped to meet her and pulled my side. It stretched like one of those life nets used to catch suicidal jumpers. "Do you want to be married again? Have a family?"

I almost replied with my old line: I don't know, or Not *yet*.

"I don't think so," I said. "But not wanting it is its own kind of … hard."

"I guess I can see that," she said, pulling a strained expression that suggested she could not. "You know, Gor and I are, sociologically speaking, the exception. Our generation is having fewer babies than ever. It was in the *Times* this week. People can't afford to buy homes, so there's nowhere to *put* their families. Statistically, *you're* the majority."

"Lia, *you* bought a house."

"We bought a *condo*," she said, with a dignified sniff.

She beckoned me to follow her to the kitchen. Sandra Day O'Connor appeared out of nowhere and bit me on the toe. "Oh, she's just love-nipping," Lia said. "Anyway, you're a grad student. Don't you know a whole bunch of child-free types? Gays and stuff?"

We'd had this conversation before. *Find your people*, Lia loved to say, which always stung, as I'd sort of thought she was my people. In college, she'd once asked if I was sure I wasn't a little bit gay, because the LGBT groups might take me, and if not them, then maybe the South Asian Student Association?

Now Lia continued, "Or is this, like, an Indian identity thing?" Her voice lowered to a respectful hush on the word *Indian*.

"I think it's an *identity* thing," I said, thinking of Dharma and her desire to believe that my shit was all attributable to immigrants. That what I was feeling had nothing to do with her.

Lia's head was buried in the fridge. There were at least ten more sonograms of Tadpole on the stainless steel. "I'm fucking starving. It's like my body's trying to make up for the first couple of months. I couldn't eat anything salty. I never knew salt had been, like, the great joy of my life. It's all so weird."

Sandra Day O'Connor leapt onto the countertop. Lia chided her.

I took a deep breath. "I've been meaning to tell you ... I've been getting some weird shit from *strangers* these days." I had waffled on how much to tell Lia about the texts, initially figuring I'd say nothing because explaining the roots of the mix-up would require me to tell her about my abortion, and I assumed it was in bad taste to discuss abortion with a pregnant woman.

But matters had grown more bizarre by the day. Everyone who'd contacted me—the unknown texters, Shazia, Miranda—had since vanished into the ether. There was a record of the messages and calls, which was the only thing that led me to believe I was not insane. At night I opened the photo taken in Bombay and stared at it furiously, as though the woman in the picture would suddenly move, turn over her shoulder, wink at me, finally, revealing some secret.

Then, the night I arrived at Lia's, I checked my phone to find that I'd been added to a WhatsApp group without my consent called Bandra Expat Moms. I scrolled the list of members—hundreds. It was not the first time I'd been dropped into a WhatsApp group that then flooded my notifications all day; that was daily life in Bombay. I wrote to the whole group: how did you people get my number?? and someone said I was free to leave whenever I wanted, but please see the group's guidelines for conduct: rudeness was not tolerated. Then someone else replied suggesting they institute a zero tolerance policy for meanness because otherwise what example were they setting for their children? and someone else said to be kind above all! because the whole point was that they were all going through something together and hadn't they been snapping at partners and electricians and maids on occasion, due to stress? and someone else said to please call maids *domestic workers* and asked by the way what the charge was for a night nurse in Bombay because her friends in London swore by them but she found the idea a little old-fashioned but also it was India and wasn't it *good* to provide employment opportunities? I'd planned to lurk on in the group, to see what happened next, but after twenty-four hours I *was* kicked out. The last message I could see was an opinion poll on the zero tolerance policy. The future moms had elected in favor, voting me off the island.

It was all so strange that I had actually booked an appointment at a free clinic during my first week at Lia's to have the position of my new IUD checked. When they'd told me it was fine, I had whispered to the physician's assistant: *You're* sure *I'm not pregnant?* It was as though the past were overlaying the present. All these texts seemed to be emerging from some other realm, a parallel universe in which I had not left Killian on that beach in Goa, in which I had not had the thing sucked out of me, and when I was very high I had the thought that perhaps the other timeline had grown hungry, hungry like an evolving fetus, and decided it was time to devour the life I'd tried to make on my own terms. I did not say any of this to the PA, but she must have spotted the glimmer of crazy in my pupils, because her tone changed, and she spoke to me as though I were extremely stupid and perhaps unstable. I was not pregnant, she explained. Hardly anyone got pregnant with an IUD. I begged for proof. I could feel it in me, I said. I hadn't noticed fast enough last time, but I knew now. Don't they say *a mother knows*? The PA showed me, clearly, the arms of the implant, extended into a superhero T, then asked if I needed a referral for a therapist.

I was still deciding whether, and how, to share some of this with Lia when I heard the sound of Gor's keys in the lock.

"Babe," he called. "Did you order dinner?"

It occurred to me that Killian might have been in touch with some of his old friends in New York, so I tried reaching a few of them.

No one had heard from him in years, but one did offer me heavily discounted tickets to an off-Broadway show. I accepted, as I owed Gor and Lia a thank-you gift. So, off we went to see a highly acclaimed reinterpretation of *Macbeth*, which attempted both a contemporary setting and a gender reversal, such that Macbeth was now Marissa Macbeth, a corporate VP with designs on the CEO gig who needed to lean in a bit further, and Lady Macbeth was now Lionel Macbeth, a laid-off white guy who drank beer in his wifebeater and feared becoming a cuck. Lionel Macbeth delivered some of Lady Macbeth's original lines, accusing Marissa of being *too full of the milk of human kindness* when she wanted a breast-pumping room in the office. And instead of shouting, *Are you a man?* when goading her to oust her corporate nemesis, he shouted, *Think like a man, bitch!* As we spilled into the street, Lia said, "Super thought-provoking," and Gor said, "I thought Macbeth was a guy in the original?" and I said I wished they hadn't cut the bit where Lady Macbeth says she'd *dash the brains out* of her own child if her husband demanded it, and Gor said, "I don't think showing an ambitious woman killing her baby is really the right picture to offer the world in this day and age, given the future of the court," and Lia said, "I mean, the whole point is to show how men are the real villains behind females perceived as villains!" and that's how I ran out of money.

The anxiety of being financially useless sent me back to my old college-essay-editing job, but my ex-boss once more declined to offer me work; the ambitious Asians I'd slighted had left him several furious reviews calling him and me racist. I emailed Alisandra asking about the mysterious departmental "hardship funds" I'd heard of some people receiving. I got an auto-reply; she was still in the field.

Given all this, I was particularly distressed when, ten days into my stay in Brooklyn, Gor pulled me aside and asked me to leave.

"Don't tell Lia, but we're hosting a surprise early baby shower next week." They would need the room for Tadpole's new bounty. A diaper pyramid. A Moses basket. A DockATot.

"What is a DockATot?" I asked.

"A place for the baby to moor, or something," Gor said, looking hassled. "A *dock*. But, uh. When do you get your apartment back? Like … August?" It was mid-June.

"I'm going to India soon," I heard myself say. It just came out.

"Great. It's great you have that going on." His shoulders, which had been creeping up to his ears in awkward anxiety, relaxed. "For fieldwork?"

"Uh, yeah," I said. "And to divorce Killian."

The phrase arrived smoothly, naturally, like playing a part.

That night, more frantic than usual, I performed what had become my routine, systematically contacting everyone who'd contacted *me*. (Everyone except Shazia, whose number had been disconnected, for, I assumed, financial reasons; and, obviously, Miranda.) No one answered. I swapped windows to Beef Jerky's social media pages, which I'd been using to stalk the expat crowd and all of Killian's friends whose names I could remember. Some of the profiles were private and did not accept a strange dog's follow request. There was no sign of Killian anywhere—no more pictures of him with, or near, that short-haired woman; no selfie against the hot orange sunset. It was as if he'd never existed at all.

I began scrolling through my contacts to see if there was anyone I hadn't already tried, which was when I saw the obvious answer.

I was probably always going to have to look in the mirror, turn off the lights, and call Mother Mary: Mary O'Malley Bane, my mother-in-law.

At first, I had tried to like Mary. She'd suffered in a specifically female way that elicited my sympathy. After Cormac's death, Mary shed her already mystical strand of Catholicism for Wiccanism and animism, taking comfort in a syncretic mélange of eldritch beliefs. She prayed to Cormac, who now dwelt, she believed, in the trees. A few years later, she found further salvation in the American Dream of multilevel marketing. There was a makeup company, a leggings company, a health drink company. Mary was always trying to recruit you into her downline. ("You don't have to do a thing except *precisely duplicate* a tried-and-true system for success!") She frustrated Killian. There was no dealing with a person so warped by disappointment and delusion. I decided I wanted nothing to do with Mary after she cracked a joke, when Killian announced he was moving to India with me, about Indians eating monkey brains. Killian understood my anger, and I hadn't spoken to Mary since.

But now it was time. The morning before the baby shower, I took a walk to Brooklyn Bridge Park to call Mary. In daylight, not darkness.

Right before I dialed, I remembered Killian's advice about how to handle his mother—and mine, for that matter. Young people saw the world as an infinite road forking off to endless possible smaller alleys, he'd said, but people like our mothers were on the other side of those many branching paths, having already chosen the routes down which to proceed. Their greatest fear was the possibility that they had made a mistake. I should not flaunt how much of my life was yet to be lived, he said. I had always thought this explanation was wrong: my mother did not make *choices*; life happened to her, and she lived it, and I suspected Mary felt the same way.

Mary picked up on the first ring and chirped, "Who's this?"

I said, "Uh, hi, Mary, it's Sanjana."

She said, "Oh, love, did you get a new number? I wondered when you'd call back."

"Back?"

"Honey, I'm just in the car going to that conference, the NutriBoost Community Elevation I told you about? Isn't it the middle of the night there? Are you getting woken up at all hours? Cormac used to kick and fuss but Kill was calm—"

"Mary, wait—"

"Is everything okay?" I could hear her pulling over, the quieting engine, the scrabble of gravel. "Honey, is it Kill?" She sounded panicked, and her voice was closer, like she was speaking on her actual phone rather than the car Bluetooth. "Is he safe?"

The terror in Mary's voice made me wonder about the moment she heard of Cormac's death. I reminded myself that at some point, she had gotten the call a parent is never supposed to get, and it had ruptured her reality. I should be kind now—part of a world that apologized to her for all it had taken away.

"I was calling to ask *you* that," I said. "When was the last time you heard from him?"

"Honey, has he come out of the silence?"

Something possessed me to ask, "Mary, when was the last time you and I spoke?"

"I don't know, honey, a month ago? I've been calling—"

"Mary," I said, attempting steadiness. "That wasn't me."

It took a while to calm her down, and longer to glean everything she knew. From what I could gather as she hyperventilated through tears, someone—she kept saying *you*—had called her around this time last year, asking to make amends. They were *family*, after all, and anyway, it was important that Mary be in touch with *her*, rather than Killian. He was entering a period of prolonged silence. At this point, Mary stopped and asked me, "But how can I trust you?" and began accusing me of not being me, which was tricky because technically I was not the person she thought I was, but I *was* me. I had to prove myself in a number of ways, first by switching to video chat, showing my ID, then copping to personal details: what was our last conversation, the eating-brains thing, and so on.

"But you are frigging with me," Mary said, not for the first time. "You could be anyone just trying to frig with me and my son and daughter-in-law, I mean—"

"I'm not anyone," I said. "*I'm* me. *She* could be anyone— why would you trust someone who told you that you couldn't talk to your son for a whole year?"

"No, well, you're making me sound like ... he's sent *postcards*! Jesus, Mary, and Joseph, I mean, she looked just like you, only with this lovely shorter, straighter haircut, and ..."

"White people often can't tell brown people apart," I said. "Now, that's not fair, all this white people this and white people that, I'm just *Mary*. I'm Irish, I'm not *white*. We were the Blacks of Europe, you know."

"You are white," I said. "It isn't an insult to call you white."

"Honey, my point is, Killian was just in one of his phases this year, you know how it is, he goes ages without talking to me, and it was so nice that this time *you* were, well, *she* was San-jay-nah, I thought you'd changed." She spoke the last bit in a whisper. "I truly wanted that for us, sweetheart."

"So she's nice to you," I said.

The night of our nuptials came back to me. Killian and I went to an Irish pub with our tiny wedding party, and I got trashed, and he was suddenly struck with guilt that we'd had no parents in attendance, so he slipped off to call his mother. He brought her tear-stained face back to me on video chat, whispering that I should say sorry for going to the courthouse. I took the phone, shakily, and Mary told me that she'd always wanted a daughter. She and Cormac's dad, Pat, they'd tried. It was lonely, all those boys, no company of women. The totality of her desire for me was frightening. It made me think of an Indian village bride sent from her parents' home to her in-laws. I couldn't remember what I'd said in response. I imagine it was unkind.

"Like a daughter," I added. "She's like a daughter to you?"

"So it is," Mary said, sadly.

"Well," I said. "If that's his new partner, she *can* be your daughter-in-law. I just need to divorce your son. Did she say where they were? This woman?"

"Not Moombay, it was someplace, gosh. Not Goa. I know Goa, they have Catholics there. It was somewhere I can't pronounce... and oh, dear. Oh, sweetheart! Does this mean—?"

This was when Mary told me the worst part.

The first day this Other Me called Mary, she offered an explanation for why Killian was entering his silence. They were mourning, she said. A traditional form of mourning. She must have run with Mary's ignorance of Eastern religions.

"What were they mourning, Mary?" My voice grew grave, thin.

"Oh, honey, well." A sob. "She said you'd—she'd—they'd—you'd—lost the baby."

Mary was crying huge, chest-wracking sobs. I tried to make a soothing shushing noise.

"I told her," she finally managed to say. "I told her, just keep trying, you know. I told her—they can save your life, children. When you can't remember why you're here, even if the unthinkable happens and you lose them, they're your gravity. They keep you on earth. Because you know. You know you mean something, meant something, to someone. You know why whatever Creator we've got put you here, and knowing that … it's worth something, honey. It is. Sweet-heart, I saw myself in you. And when I heard you were going to be a mother, I thought, yes, yes, that's what that girl needs, a good *reason*. A reason to keep going."

A Buddhist man once told me not all ghosts come from dead people. Some are a sliver of a living person's soul, karmic manifestations of dissatisfaction or regret. The fragment of the living person falls away and torments the person from whom it came. Only when Mary and I had hung up did I settle into the realization of the thing that had been encroaching for some time: the fragment of me that had split from me when my marriage went to pieces, when I went to pieces. An actual Other. An impostor. Someone who had seamlessly taken over the shell of my relationship with my still-husband and my so-called mother-in-law. This creature had spied my life, seized it, thinking, *Well, she's not using that.*

10

Devil Eggs

Walking back to Lia and Gor's, I pulled out my vape and took a few too many hits. It was hard to assess my baseline state of mind when I already felt high. Ever since that first bizarre text about *K*, I had been losing myself. The past was rising up again, reborn.

Maybe it was my fault for keeping secrets; maybe failing to speak about my marriage over the past year had deepened its inexplicability. But it was a lie, this era of Shout Your Abortion and *Touch My Trauma*. It was all the emotional equivalent of that auto-rickshaw dick I'd seen in Bombay: no one really wanted to look at it. And there were so few ways to hold one's history, to make it make sense without letting it overtake the present and future.

When I opened the door to the condo, I found Lia perched on the couch, wearing a floaty pale yellow cotton dress that made her look like a cake, her blond hair the soft wavy icing. The room was packed with balloons the same yellow as Lia's dress.

I'd messed up the date of the shower. It was today, not tomorrow. Lia was surrounded by a gaggle of women, and her gay male friend Ryan, who looked like he wanted to die.

"Shit," I said, as everyone's heads turned my way. "Uh.

Surprise! You're pregnant!"

Lia appeared untroubled. She rolled her large blue eyes. "I had no idea," she said.

The other women, also trussed up in Easter egg hues, raised cold Emily Post eyebrows. Lia's mother Anna, whom I'd always known to be glacial and stern, was stroking her daughter's shoulders with a novel tenderness. Lia's sister Martina and Gor's sister Carine were in the mix, too, and everyone seemed comfortable touching Lia's arms, feet, and belly. Lia herself had her jaw set stoically in a fashion I recognized, as though someone had unleashed a jar of poisonous spiders and set them crawling all over her and she knew she had to remain very still, or they would kill her. I had seen this expression on her face a few years before, at her bachelorette party. I was nominally maid of honor, but her college friend Raphaella had done much of the planning, which meant it was Raphaella who hired the starved-looking male stripper at whom Lia grimaced for three minutes as he shook his sinewy G-stringed ass in her face. That night, she'd shouted at me, saying she thought I knew better, I was supposed to be her friend who *got it*, and I'd said I thought she liked *mainstream things*, and she'd said that was a very insulting thing for me to say.

Ryan zoomed over. Poor Ryan, so often treated as an accessory of the straight-girl gang.

"It was supposed to be *all genders*," he whispered.

"Uh, the *hubby's* here," I said.

"Yeah, that *totally* counts."

I tried to make myself obscure, taking a seat on an ottoman between Ryan and Raphaella.

"So, we're voting on names!" Raphaella clapped her hands at Lia's colleague Lucie.

Lucie, teetering on high summer wedges, hauled out a poster board from behind the couch, on which a number of index cards were stuck, each bearing possible baby names, all written in a bubbly sorority font.

"Wait," someone asked. "Are these boy names or girl names?"

Everyone squinted, reading: *Carter. Cameron. Rory. Alex.*

"They're white names," I said to Ryan, who'd stood to assemble a plate of deviled eggs, which were labeled *Angel Eggs*: marshmallow angels with toothpick spines had been stuck into the whipped yolks. There were also pigs-in-a-blanket designed to look like swaddled infants. The centerpiece, a giant hollowed-out watermelon filled with fruits, had been arranged to look like a huge-eyed baby staring up from a bassinet. The baby's face was a hunk of pale honeydew, its eyes genetically modified blueberries, its tuft of hair on an otherwise bald head a plump strawberry. For dessert there were cake pops trussed up as rattles.

I took two. Munchies.

"We're going to choose the name in advance and then give it to whatever comes out!" Gor said. "Gender aside! Right, babe?"

Lia gave a resigned sigh. "We did say that would be fun, in the abstract," she said.

This was the compromise: Lia had refused a gender reveal party, but those around her decided an early baby shower was essential. People expect to be included in the experience, Lia's mother and sister and sister-in-law and mother-in-law had all told her.

Someone snickered: a racially ambiguous, possibly South Asian woman next to me. She turned around, and her eyes fell on me. I smiled, relieved to have a partner in scorn. The woman did a double take and slopped orange juice on her wrist.

"Is that a mimosa?" I spoke slowly. My tongue felt like molasses.

Her jaw dropped.

"Oh my gosh," she said. "Are you—Sanjana? Satyan?"

Sanjana Satyan—at least, that's how I heard it.

She pronounced Sanjana correctly. I decided she was desi.

"Uh, yes—Satyananda. Have we met?"

I tried to remember if she'd been a bridesmaid. I was still eycing her drink.

People were cheering for *Emerson*. Lucie marked tallies. There was less love for *Brooklyn*, which the room decided was too on the nose.

"No alcohol," Ryan whispered, handing me a flute and sniffing his own.

I stuffed my face with two Angel Eggs and realized that I was really very high and possibly even getting higher. They felt like Play-Doh in my mouth but I wanted, like, ten more. "Oh, wow, no," the eager brown woman said. "I'm Tara, I work with Lia at White and Feldman? I had no idea she was friends with you!"

"What's next, Sis?" Gor asked Carine.

"Since middle school," I said to Tara. "Wait, why do you, uh." Trying to keep pace was like trying to wade upstream against a heavy current. "Wait." It was obvious now, though I struggled to speak through the denseness of my high. "Tara—who—"

"Well, we could open gifts," Carine said. "Tara, would you?" Tara stood to attend to the present table, piled high with offerings, before I could finish my sentence: *Who do you think I am?*

Lia hastened a quick hand, waving. "No, no, I can do that alone, it's a little … tacky. In front of everyone." Her eyes fell on me, then Ryan, in a silent plea for help. We were, apparently, the ones she believed could stop this, but I was not in control of my faculties, and now I had a mouthful of Angel Eggs.

Anna said, "Honey, that *is* what's done."

"No problem," Gor said in a hearty voice. "How about the crafts?"

I stood, realized I had been trying to stand for a whole minute, then felt proud of myself for standing. The others were being instructed in onesie decoration by Carine. I elbowed past Raphaella and some lawyerly types and found my way to Tara, who was fluffing gift bows.

"Tah-rah," I said, deliberately. "Are you ... South Asian?"

"What?" She looked offended.

"This thing. This weird thing has been happening. With brown women. Are you brown?"

She stiffened. "My biological father was Indian."

"Why, how come, how come did you know my name?"

She frowned. "I—I think I made a mistake," she said.

"My hair," I said. "Is it my hair? It's longer? Curlier?"

"*Yes*," she said. "Your hair!"

I seized her by the shoulders. It was not intentional, but I had been moving so dazedly that I honestly didn't know I could perform such a violent gesture. Yet there I was, gripping Tara and shaking her and saying, "Who is she? Who—?"

"Tara!" Carine called. "Can you—the stencil set? It's under the gift table."

Tara backed away, looking terrified. She ducked under the table, extracted a Tupperware of fabric stencils and pens, then went to help Carine.

I made to follow Tara, but then Ryan was by my side. "*Please* drink with me," he said, linking his arm through mine. He was really leaning into the brief camaraderie we'd established at Lia and Gor's wedding, when we were the only ones willing to indulge in giggles as Gor delivered his vows in an acrostic poem (*L is for love, I is for infinite, A is for always*). I threw one more glance at Tara and allowed myself to be tugged into the kitchen.

"Gor wants me to have a drink," Ryan hissed. "He was like, 'Leave the ladies to it.' I'm afraid he's going to make me smoke a cigar."

Gor looked annoyed to find me attached to Ryan. I was watching Tara intently, and she seemed to feel my eyes on her back. Someone was calling out that Ilana was here and couldn't get in, the buzzer wasn't working, would anyone go down for her? Tara shot to the door before I could meet her eyes again.

"So, you forgot," Gor said to me.

"Yeah, sorry. Can I have a drink, too? Or is this … boy club?"

"'Course," Gor said gruffly. "It's just beer." He said this as though it would dissuade me. "My friends all bailed," he added to Ryan, apologetically. "We were trying to make it nontraditional and stuff, but they thought the invite was just for, like, wives and girlfriends." He looked genuinely sad. "Men don't always know how to be involved in this stuff."

"In fatherhood?" Ryan asked, icily.

"You mean, like … good models. For being good dads." I kept one eye on the door in case Tara came back.

Gor looked alarmed that I was offering a lifeline. "Yeah," he said warily.

Watching Gor have an intense emotion was like watching a rooster try to shit an egg. The other day Lia had told me she was pissed at him, because he claimed there was nothing to prepare anyone for becoming a parent, and she'd bumped him with her belly and shouted, *Maybe for you, dude!* For Lia, Tadpole was already here, altering her, weighing on their lives and plans; for him, the baby remained an idea. I had surprised myself by understanding him rather than Lia.

My expression must have gone loopy as I considered my solidarity with Gor, because Ryan hovered his face in front of mine as if to check whether I was still inside my skull.

"So," he said. "How's your thesis?"

"It is fucked," I said, slapping my palms down on the counter in an attempt to snap to. I thought, *Don't be high.* "Totally fucked." It was the first time I'd said that aloud to anyone, but as I said it, I knew it was true. "My main informant died. I dropped out. Of my PhD. Then I dropped back in. On, like, probation. But I think—I think I have to drop out. Again."

"I didn't know that," Gor said. He uncapped and distributed three IPAs.

I almost said, *How could you know?* Gor had never asked me a question as long as he'd been with Lia. His love language was beers and barbecues and brunches; golf and frisbee golf and something called Topgolf. Conversation bored him. Being with him had changed Lia, too. There had been a kind of urgency about her, once. She'd approached people with a hunger to comprehend. When Gor arrived, it was as though he quelled everything about her. At first I'd thought he was intellectually euthanizing her, but then I realized she was happier this way. To her, all the frenzy of before was not an inner life spewing out, but angst. She *liked* feeling less.

"How come *they* don't get drinks?" I asked, pointing to the women in the other room. "Is ... is everybody here pregnant?"

"I think they are," Ryan whispered. "Like, in their souls."

"Those are mimosas," Gor said, pointing at the jug of what I'd thought was orange juice. "Do you think I'm some kind of pig who doesn't think women should drink?"

"Um," I said.

"My mistake!" Ryan said. "They were just not super strong, I guess!"

"I offered Ryan beer, specifically."

"Me and beer," Ryan said, slapping his stomach.

Gor leaned over toward me. "You know, this is what she's afraid of. That you'll judge her, treat her as backward."

"I promise," I said with intense effort, "I will like *your* kid." I almost said, *Ask Maneesha*. I might not be who you'd entrust with diaper changes, but I loved Naina in my own awkward, distant way—a way men have always been allowed to love. I couldn't say my sister's name, though, nor could I cite her or Naina as successful examples of my maturity and grace.

Ryan said, helpfully, "Kids are just people. They can be assholes. My baby is an asshole."

"You have a baby?" I asked.

"Oh, well, he's not entirely mine. I gave my friend some sperm, so he's, like, biologically mine? I'm kind of an uncle. It's a good level of involvement for me. Anyway, he's an asshole, but I love him anyway? I think that's the coolest thing about the whole experience."

I placed both hands on my stomach. It seemed possible that I was getting higher. From the corner of my eye, I thought I saw Tara reenter with a brunette at her side. "Whoa," I said. "That does sound cool."

Gor glanced between Ryan and me, suspiciously, then turned back to the living room, where everyone was bent over their onesies. Carine was saying, "Okay, if you're not going to open all the gifts, we have to do mine, because—" and she opened a bag and withdrew a bunch of giant blown-up masks of Lia's face, like the ones Raphaella had brought to the bachelorette party. The faces were attached to Popsicle sticks with holes for eyes, on which were superimposed the word *Mommy-Boss*. Twelve MommyBoss Lia masks were being distributed around the room, and everyone was waving them in front of their faces, giggling and preening, and the real Lia was staring at me with an expression of revulsion, mouthing, *Help!*, which was when I decided it was time to shout my abortion.

I yelled, "ABORTION!"

I was still super high, so I thought I had said the whole thing—"I had an abortion!" But I just got out "Abortion!"

Half of the women's heads snapped violently in my direction. The others were turning more gradually, processing. Lip-glossed mouths fell open in stupefaction; tweezed eye-brows shot toward hairlines. But before anyone could come up with an adequate response, Lia gave a horrible little jump and her hands landed on her hips and she wailed in pain.

My stomach rose into my throat. *I cursed her!* I thought. A spinster demon had swept into the house and infected Lia! My toes clenched. I was doing the firmest Kegel of my whole life, as though trying to keep an imaginary head from crowning out of my own vaginal canal. Lia yelled that it felt *pointy*, her belly was *sharp*! Raphaella, an ER doctor and new mom, jumped into gear, grilling Lia. Someone whispered—*twenty-four weeks?* People froze, terrified. Moments earlier, everyone had been so pleased with themselves, certain of what was to come. That was the whole point of this ritual, I thought, to trick ourselves into believing that we could shape an experience that was, fundamentally, out of anyone's control. The games and gifts were all a way of enforcing form and structure when what awaited Lia, and all of us, was formlessness, the raw material of a life as yet unlived. Enraptured by my own stoned mental eloquence, I felt a great tenderness toward the entire room.

"It's Braxton-Hicks," Raphaella was saying. "It's gone now?"

Lia nodded. "I'm okay. It happened the other day, too."

Everyone exhaled.

"Braxton whatsit?" I whispered to Ryan.

"False labor," said Lucie, nearby.

"It still feels *spiky*," Lia said, poking her stomach and speaking through gritted teeth. "But it's fine." She stood, shaking off her sister's tending. Her face relaxed. She arrived next to me and leaned her head on my shoulder. "Freaky shit," she said, to me and me alone.

I wrapped an arm around her waist. My molasses high had been replaced by paranoia. "That looked … very real. Should we go to the hospital? What if you, like, die? Or *it* dies?"

Into my hair, Lia whispered: "Take me to the hospital if it gets me out of here. *No one* asked me what I wanted."

She tugged me to the food table. People turned away, perhaps assuming she was chastising me for my outburst. Leaning over, she said, "Maybe we need to get *you* out of here. Why the fuck would you shout *abortion* at a baby shower? Is that some kind of new protest move? Most of these women"—she lowered her voice—"they're pro-choice, but still."

"I apologize," I said, scanning her face for genuine anger and locating none. "I am extremely high on marijuana."

"Fuck you," Lia said. "I'm jealous."

Tara sidled up to me. Her eyes narrowed distrustfully. "What *is* your name?" she asked.

"Sanjana," I said.

"Sanjana Satyananda," Lia said, at the same time.

Comprehension dawned on Tara's face, followed by horror. "No way," she said. "Uh. This is weird? I'm sorry, you just look *exactly* like this person I follow? This influencer? And I mean, she almost has your name" She pulled out her phone, tapped away, then lifted it to display a social media profile.

The banner above a grid of photos showed her name in clean black font: Sanjena Sathian. She had a quarter million followers.

"I mean, I know other Tara Patels, but your name is rarer? And—"

I ignored her. I kept staring at the grid of images on Tara's phone. My eyes fell on the most recent photograph. My first thought was: *I don't remember taking that picture.* It showed a brown woman, standing in profile, wearing a cream tunic and gripping her stomach. The caption read, Still waiting on dat bump.

I hadn't taken that picture, of course. It was not me.

But there was, yes, a likeness, something that had been imperceptible in that image I'd received weeks ago, where she'd had her back to the camera and been washed out. Here, though, I saw it. Something to do with the cock of her head, her dark complexion, her insectoid, protuberant eyes not quite in proportion to her face. There were differences. Her hair was shorter and straighter than mine. She had a better nose: more delicate, round. Her breasts were large, blooming out of her bra.

Dr. Kim would have been proud of how quickly I was able to name my feelings: I was *jealous*. She looked like a more sensuous version of me. She probably had what my yoga teacher in India had often told me I lacked while adjusting me in happy baby: open, childbearing hips.

I examined Sanjena Sathian's hair. I liked it. It framed her face. Our faces. Our face.

Lia, her eyes on Tara's phone, screamed—an actual howl. Everyone's heads whipped our way.

Someone yelled, "Is it real this time, or is it fake again?"

II

Women, Being Softhearted

My childhood home, just outside Boston, was a petite blue colonial. Plain, old, unpretentious, faded by years of difficult winters. The roof was newly tiled in gray, not black, but other than that, it looked almost exactly as I'd left it four or five years ago. My mother was mowing the lawn when I stepped out of the taxi I'd taken from the Alewife T station.

"Hi, Mommy," I said, when she'd turned off the machine.

She turned, and the first thought I had was: *That is not my mother.*

When I was fourteen months old, my mother went away for two months to take care of her own sick mother, our ajji. She left Maneesha and me in the care of our other grandmother, Appamma, who had still-black hair and all her teeth and was only fifty. When my actual mother returned, I refused (I am told) to be held by her for a week. *Only Mommy!* I cried, and reached for Appamma. Seeing my mother in the yard now was not that mental glitch, not a failure of recognition. I did not believe that I was encountering an impostor in my mother's skin. Rather, I experienced a sharpening of perception. She was not *mine*. She was just a person, in her own right, who did not owe me her body or her shelter.

"You look good," I said.

My mother has always been what one might call *handsome*—tall and dark, with a thick, black Frida Kahlo unibrow. Her hands, death-gripping the mower, looked arthritic. She has always been too proud of her slenderness, in a way that surely must have harmed Maneesha, who was a rotund child. (Ajji said *healthy*.) The truth was that I resembled my mother very closely. The truth was, as Maneesha often said, "You are exactly the same person." Same temperament, same phenotype, opposing worldviews. "What's worse," Maneesha added once, "is that you two can't live and let live. You could get along if you both didn't act like you're in the middle of some clash of civilizations all the time."

"Aiyyo," my mother said. "Why have you mangled your hair?"

I'd done it at Lia's, the night of the shower. After we'd all been assured that she and Tadpole were safe, I'd hidden in the guest room piled with still-wrapped presents while Lia and Gor argued. Lia, Gor was saying, had been rude by not opening gifts and thanking people individually. She was retorting that she hadn't asked for any of the baby shower stuff, especially not this early, especially not as a surprise. Gor said wasn't that what people did and Lia yelled, fuck the etiquette, she was sick of etiquette, all she wanted was to be left alone with a pregnancy pillow and her vibrator, and Gor replied, in a too-loud voice, "Well, go hang out with Sanjana, then, because she has *no* etiquette." They went to bed angry. While they slept, I crept into the kitchen, stole their shears, and pulled up Sanjena Sathian's profile. I zoomed in on her photo and got to work. I was setting out on a journey. I had this feeling that I needed to depart incognito. After, I tucked myself into bed and masturbated, one hand on my new hair. I had not thought of Killian sexually in a long time; I had stopped desiring him well before we went to Moksha, but the old pleasure came back now, as though this new Sanjena had swooped into me. I pictured myself pushing him against the wall, as her, guiding him in, in charge of the encounter. I pictured the surprise in his green eyes at the switch, and then the release, vaster than ever before.

I left for Boston in the morning with all my shit, after writing Lia a note saying I was sorry I'd been difficult lately, that I was sure I'd love Tadpole, that she could talk to me about all the baby stuff and all the *personal* stuff if she wanted because I was still her friend who *got it*; I folded over the note, wrote *LIA*, not *LIA AND GOR*, and stuck it to the fridge, beneath the sonogram. I planned to head straight to Logan airport with the money I hoped my mother would give me, and from there to Bombay—and to Killian.

I knew he'd be wherever *she* was, because I'd stalked her cursorily on the Megabus. I saw what I needed to see: a picture of three hands—two white, one brown—tenderly cupping a belly so mildly curved you'd assume it was post-burrito bloat, not pregnancy. It was captioned We can't wait to meet you!, followed by a slew of emoji. There was also a selfie she'd posted a few weeks earlier, in which she flashed a thumbs-up next to a sleeping, shirtless Killian. Caption: Me being an insomniac while my partner is conked out. #gendergap #pregnancy #futuremommas #futuredads.

The picture that unsettled me most had been posted about a month earlier. In it, she appeared to be spinning, caught mid-twirl, her short-haired head thrown back, chin to the ceiling. What bothered me was not her face, but her surroundings. Behind her was my landlady Miranda's favorite crucifix. Next to Miranda's agonized Lord and Savior hung a black wooden frame, and in it: a copy of my marriage certificate. They hadn't even bothered to take it down. A story appeared to me, about Killian's new life. If he and Sanjena were living in our old flat, she might be passing herself off as me. You didn't draw attention to things like divorce or new partners in conservative Catholic Bandra's housing societies. I could imagine Sanjena slipping in and out of the large building covertly so none of the hundreds of neighbors or the rotating cast of security guards realized Killian's life had been interrupted at all. She was me, now, living under the assumed alias of *wife*. I wondered if that was why Killian didn't want to divorce me—if remaining married was somehow important to his doings there. Or if he was in denial: I hadn't left him at all. He was still with me. Me 2.0. I pinched the image with two fingers to zoom in on the certificate. The text was barely visible but I knew what it said from memory, because I had often stared at it in horror as I wandered through our flat, realizing how deeply I had sunk into this mistake of a marriage.

To certify that
Killian Bane *and* Sanjana Satyananda
were united in marriage on this day
the 13th of June *in the year of* 2014.

I could discern the black hulking shape of Killian's John Hancock flourish above *Groom*. Above *Bride* there was nothing perceptible. It looked as though I hadn't signed at all.

"You look like a Muppet," my mother said, now circling me. "I will fix it. Come."

She steered me inside, into her and my father's bathroom. "Appa is at a conference in Chicago," she said, noticing me glancing around. My father and I were not close, and spoke even less frequently than my mother and I did, but she and I were often better behaved in his company; he served, if not a peacemaking function, at least a civilizing one.

"Where's Jerky?" I asked. Maneesha had said the dog would pass to my mother's care.

"Pah, that dog?" my mother said. "Ajay's sister has it."

"Him," I corrected her.

"I come from a place where dogs belong in the streets," my mother said menacingly. "I will not call it a him."

I sat on a chair in front of my mother's vanity. My reflection resembled her, Sanjena. My face was exposed, my bone structure now sleeker and sharper. I had a new air of confidence.

Then my mother lifted a handheld mirror and showed me the back of my head. I had to admit that it didn't look good.

"What possessed you, hm?"

"I don't know," I said, truthfully.

She ran a hand through my curls. Flakes of dandruff landed like powdered sugar on my black tank top.

"You're the one who told me never to get a professional cut," I hedged, which was true; for years, I'd performed my own trims. "You said people would steal our hair to make wigs." This had indeed been her mantra when Maneesha and I were young, and the image stuck: someone else *wearing* me.

"When did I say that? Maneesha's hair, maybe. It is soft. Yours is too rough for any wig and all. Mine, too. I do not remember the things you are always claiming I said." She snorted as if to add, *My word against yours.*

She opened her drawer, pulled out some hair scissors, and began to even things in the back. Neither of us said a word as she worked. A vast, overwhelming silence sat at the heart of my relationship with my mother. We were afraid to speak to each other.

The silence often made me think of my grandfather's funeral in Mysore. I was twelve, and I had just gotten my first period. My mother told me to keep my Kotex hidden for the duration of our stay in India. If one of her more orthodox relatives saw pads, they might challenge my right to participate in the funeral. "Nonsense," she said of the old practice, but it was not a battle she wanted to fight.

When it was time to transport my grandfather to the crematorium, I stepped near him to take one final look at his ashen face, but as I did so, some auntie grabbed me and thrust me into Ajja's study. At first I feared I had leaked blood and was being quarantined. Moments later, the other women followed. Someone shut the door. An auntie explained that we women now had to lock ourselves up, in silence, while the men went to the crematorium. We could emerge once they had returned to chow down on the vegetarian buffet. Seeing my huff, the auntie in charge clarified: "It is because, you know, women, being softhearted and all, become very agitated. Wailing and weeping and whatnot." The silence, apparently, left space for a more dignified grief. It tamed us.

We sat in Ajja's study for an hour. Not everyone took the rule seriously—some women gossiped in Kannada and Tamil. But my mother didn't speak, instead paging somberly through my grandfather's copy of the Gita, and Maneesha and I followed her example, sitting stiff and tearless as rigor-mortised bodies.

Then, when the men clomped back to the flat, everyone except the three of us stood to enter the kitchen. My mother, her eyes on the Gita, heaved a great sob, a wrenched sound I had never heard from her before, and her tears splattered the page. I was petrified to see her reduced this way and shielded my face. She howled that she'd ruined her father's copy. An auntie manifested to sedate her. The sob was swallowed. Other aunties dried the book, and my mother was restored to her unflappability, within which she'd dwelt for twenty years hence. Every time I tried to speak to my mother, I had the sense that I was pressing up against that silence, which concealed something savage and dangerous. It was a kind of compassion, this silence, my distance.

"See, now," my mother said, lifting the handheld mirror again. She had fixed the back of the cut. The ragged edges were more rounded, appearing more intentional. "You look a bit mannish, but that is the best I can do."

"Thanks, Mother," I said.

She made a little spitting noise. "You are here, so, what? Chai?"

In the kitchen she said, "No one has heard from you," as she pulled two mugs from the cabinet above the sink. She didn't have to stretch to reach the highest shelf. She is taller than I am, five foot nine, pipe-cleaner legs and limber torso. She has done yoga every morning at six since 1970-something. She refuses breakfast, as a practice; for lunch, she eats a single ghee-less roti with sprouted moong and achar, and for dinner, brown rice khichdi followed by fat-free cottage cheese for dessert. She does not sing or dance, even at weddings; does not read novels or watch movies. She takes pleasure in competence and order, in the accomplishment of tasks and the neat arrangement of her calendar, her family, her life.

"I know what your generation calls your behavior," she went on. "You are ghouling me."

"Ghosting, Mother. And I'm not ghosting you. I've been … busy. Writing my dissertation."

She opened the cabinet and pulled out tea leaves, whole cardamom, and her spice mix. My mother's afternoon chai is one of her only indulgences. From the fridge she grabbed a nub of ginger root that resembled a crooked big toe. For a few minutes, she pounded the cardamom and ginger in her mortar and pestle with such ferocity that I wondered if she was picturing herself pounding my face.

Once the pot was on the boil, she turned her back to it, standing worryingly near the waggling blue flame. "I received your letter," she said, crossing her arms.

"What letter?"

"A letter is very nice for you, isn't it? You get to tell your story, talk in your terms. You go on and on, saying how everything is my fault. A letter is not a conversation; a letter is some angry manifesto-shmanifesto."

"What *letter*?" I said again.

She frowned. "Are you forgetting things? Is it your psychiatric issues? Or are you blacking out drunk and all?"

"*Mother.* Jesus Christ."

"Who is Mother, what is Jesus this Jesus that? We have nothing to do with Jesus."

"I didn't send you any letter," I said. "I don't even own stamps." I tried to recall the last time I'd been to the post office. I certainly didn't make a habit of epistolary correspondence.

She scowled, charily, and left the room, returning a minute later holding a piece of lined, ripped paper and an envelope covered in ink and postage stamps bearing the Indian flag. She handed both to me. I examined the envelope. The address—my parents' home, here in Massachusetts—was not in my handwriting. I thought I recognized it from somewhere, though. It was slanted, printed in all caps.

"This was mailed from India," I said. "I don't live in India anymore."

She shrugged, bending over the pot to examine the progress of the chai. "How do I know you haven't gone back there? You don't tell me things."

"I would tell you if I was *leaving the country*," I said.

"Yes, daughters usually tell their mothers when they are leaving the country. Or getting married."

I snatched up the letter and began to read. My stomach plummeted. I *had* written it—a year earlier, to expel an inner demon. Not to send. I knew I had drafted many versions, scratched them out, over and over. I knew I'd left every incarnation of the note in a spiral notebook that remained stowed in Killian's and my flat, in Bombay.

> *M—I don't know how to say this. I am afraid to tell you the way I've always been afraid to tell you things, ever since I was little. You think I am too private, that I lie and am two-faced, but I only keep things to myself because there's nowhere to put them in this family. I might have to be honest now, though. I ~~am~~ might be pregnant. I can't decide what that would mean to you. I am married. But I'm married to someone you don't approve of. I ~~might be~~ I could be a mother. And I wonder if that would make me understand you and if it would make you understand me. I keep picturing you showing up to help. You're different, with Naina. Would you be different with my baby? Would you see me more like you see Maneesha? Maybe that's what you want. Maybe if my life looked more like yours*

It ended there. I knew what I'd been thinking of when I wrote it—the way, when I was a teenager and we fought, my mother used to shout: *You'll understand me one day, when you have a daughter, when* she *gives you hell.* Perhaps I was doomed, now, to never understand her. Perhaps I had chosen not to understand.

At some point while I was reading, the tea had finished brewing. When I looked up, my mother was holding the pot over each mug in turn. Tea ribboned out in a thick, dark helix. It would be bitter.

"When did you get this?" I said softly.

"Few months back." She clanked a wooden coaster and the mug in front of me. "Drink. You can have sugar if you want. I do not take it."

"I know you don't take sugar, Mother. I'm not pregnant, by the way. *I* didn't send this. There's someone messing with me," I said. "It's been happening all summer. They've been in my apartment. My old apartment, I mean. They've gone through my things, and they decided to ..." I trailed off, hearing how insane I sounded.

"So you did write it." My mother's unibrow raised in amusement. "You had an imaginary twin when you were very small," she said. "You remember? Her name was Sahana. Sahana killed Maneesha's doll. Sahana wet the bed. Sahana ate all the Girl Scout cookies. Then, no more Sahana, and just your ... lies."

"I do not have an imaginary friend anymore, Mother. I wasn't—I mean, I was never ... I was never going to have a baby." Fumbling, I took a rapid swig of the chai and nearly burned my tongue. "I'm trying to get a *divorce*."

She yanked the letter from me. It tore slightly at its left corner. The paper had weakened over the past year. She flicked it, evidently untroubled that it might rip further. "Is this what you think of me? That I am one of these women who needs cute-sweet-cutie-sweetie messes of grandchildren? That you could have some baby and come to me and everything would be all perfectly fine, so-so simple because I am so-so simple?"

"Well, not exactly," I said. But my mother *was* different with Naina, though. The child softened her roughest parts; when I pointed this out to her once, she said, *That is the point of grandchildren*. They offered a second chance to raise a child, gently, forgivingly, redemptively. "But ... I thought you *wanted* me to have kids?"

"You will not have children," my mother said. "This I knew a very long time ago."

"So, you weren't … happy? When you thought I was pregnant?"

"I never thought anything. I thought only that this was a very *strange* letter. I know you. I know you do not think about *duty*. It is not one of your interests. If it were, you would be …" She trailed off, lifting her mug, appearing to nibble on its rim, chipmunk-like.

"So raising us was … a duty," I said.

"Pah, do not try to trap me and all," she said. "Children *are* duties, that is a fact. If you had children, my duty to you would be different. *I* did not *want* children, you know. I am not so nurturing. But I understand. I understand my role. What is to be done?"

I didn't point out that my mother had accidentally quoted Lenin. I took another sip of the chai, which was quickly cooling.

My mother blinked. "My only point is that I do not take my whole identity from you two. I did my duty then with you, I do my duty now with Maneesha and Naina and Appa. Life is life. I do not go hunting-shunting for some big mysterious purpose in being Missus Mommy or Missus Wife or Missus Doctor or now Missus Ajji. It would have been very bad if you and Maneesha were the center of my world. *You* have gone off, now. What would I be left with, half of myself only? That is how these stupid women lose themselves."

"Actually," I said. My mother scowled, so I spoke quickly. "I think that's what made you a good mom." I didn't qualify. "You kept your whole self."

The great contradiction: I meant what I'd said, but sometimes I wished she *could* have given in. Her self-protectiveness was the most visible heritable trait she'd passed on to me. My mother abhors feminism, which she calls an excuse for Western women to do *this-that-and-all* with their bodies, but there was something unintentionally political about her coldness. It was like a strike, a refusal of the thankless labor with which she'd been tasked.

She glanced aside, embarrassed, even as her mouth twitched upward in a rare smile.

"So," I said, my head hurting from all I could never know about my mother. "You aren't upset with me for not wanting children. But you also think not having a child means I'll never understand *duty*. Or family."

"Pah," my mother said. "No need to do so much talking and talking. You don't have to go *on and on* talking about things."

Dharma once suggested that my mother might be jealous of me. She had wanted to come to America to work for herself, but her father had decreed that she could only leave the house as a married woman. I had been allowed to individuate, to be a self apart from the family unit, to obtain education without having to marry. How unjust. Dr. Kim might have proposed an alternate theory, though: that *I* was jealous of my mother, of her disinterest in purpose. Her straightforward way of living in action and gesture, not thought. Perhaps it ran both ways; perhaps mothers and daughters were doomed to look at each other this way, not as people but as foreclosed selves.

I finished my drink uneasily. The chai was sour and cold and I felt tremendously sad. I had failed to translate myself, failed in turn to hear her, and now it was all over, and the silence of that locked room at my grandfather's funeral would descend once more, possibly forever.

"Did Maneesha tell you?" I asked. "Why I … left?"

My mother kept her back to me. She stared out the window above the sink, at a neighbor power-walking. "I do not want to discuss these things," she said. "These things about the way you choose to live. Let it be. Do not send me *strange* letters like this. Do not do *strange* things in your sister's house. Just … do not be so *strange*."

And then I knew that everything she had said to me she'd said with great effort, speaking through a curtain of shame and disgust, in spite of her moral fury. This was her attempt at a gift.

"Fine," my mother said, still not looking at me, as I clanked my mug onto the counter with finality. "You want some money?"

I felt nauseated. "It's—it's for the divorce," I said, in the tiniest voice possible.

"Because of this new boyfriend," she said.

"He's not—he wasn't—"

"Ah," she said, calculating. "You do such things without even being boyfriend-girlfriend. With anyone, everyone."

She had been right to keep us from discussing the Home-Safe incident. Sometimes, silence was useful. Sometimes, it was the only thing that kept two people together, however tenuously.

I stood. "I take it back," I said. "I don't want money."

"You need it. I'll give it," she said. "You are my daughter."

I have no idea what it is like to create a new person, to hope you know them, only to find them filled with mysterious or even repugnant desires, to lose them to forces you disdain or fail to comprehend. I imagine it must be awful, like turning over a stone in your pretty garden to find maggots writhing beneath. I imagine that I have caused my mother tremendous pain. As I shut the door to my childhood home, I thought: *If I could be another person, I would.*

Part Two

Mr. Golyadkin looked as though he wanted to hide from himself, as though he were trying to run away from himself! Yes! It was really so. One may say more: Mr. Golyadkin did not want only to run away from himself, but to be obliterated, to cease to be, to return to dust.

—Fyodor Dostoyevsky,
The Double
(translaten by Constance Garnett)

1.

Motherland

I counted, on the first leg of the flight to India, five squalling infants. In their every cry I heard frustration. What a hassle, the babies seemed to be saying, that we must journey across oceans mere months after our fontanels have closed, because our families insist there is something eternal and essential to which we belong on the other side of the planet.

I am not a monster: I felt for the five brown women on the plane who paced the aisles and hushed and cooed and rocked complimentary bassinets, lifting thin blankets to offer up breasts, multitasking like so many multi-armed Hindu goddesses. One mother cast apologetic glances at all who glared; the other four studiously avoided eye contact with the enraged, sleepless passengers.

Perhaps these women had not so much as dozed in months. Or perhaps their oxytocin levels had been raised so high that they were, before my eyes, being healed by their own babes. I read once about a woman whose depression was wiped out by way of orgasmic childbirth and mothering, that pink new baby smell better than Zoloft. I would never know. This lack of knowledge now struck me as tragic, not because I wanted to have birthed but because I wanted access to the Self on the other side of birth.

But I could not deny what Dr. Kim had said to me a few weeks earlier: I was more like the babies than their mothers. I had, after all, once been one such infant; growing up, Maneesha and I were toted to India every two years, where we spent winter break being whisked between relatives' homes. The routine was mechanical: We'd sit in a living room in awkward silence, unable to remember how exactly we were connected to these people. I'd scan their faces, checking for resemblance, and find nothing. Our parents and the aunties and uncles would ask, "Health is good?" and everyone would give that zigzag nod of half assent, half dismissal. An adult would turn to Maneesha and me and ask, "Studies are good?" and we'd murmur yeses. Twenty days of this and then we'd be on the plane back, having ostensibly paid tribute to our ancestry.

It may have been my dissatisfaction with these trips that sent me to India on my own. I knew there was *more* pulsing beyond our relatives' doors, and I noticed the way my mother seemed afraid of the country she'd left behind. Though in America she invoked India as a source of her conservative morals, she seemed almost allergic to her actual birthplace: the smog made her cough, the food made her sick, and the water made her break out in a hot red rash. The anal-retentive control our family exerted over these archetypical diasporic returns to India was, I decided as I got older, about safety. If the first generation could export a stable picture of India, they could draw clean lines around our lives.

Perhaps the wailing babies on my flight to India already sensed this happening to them, the calcification of their personhoods.

One of the babies commanded my attention more than the others, because she seemed to be named Anjana or Ranjana, I couldn't tell; either way, her name was close enough to mine that I kept sitting up as her parents begged her to sleep. Somewhere over the Atlantic, Anjana/Ranjana's father misapprehended my interest in my own name for an interest in his baby. He was holding Anjana/Ranjana for the first time all journey, only because his wife had gone to the bathroom. His daughter, dressed in so many frills she might have been a doily, had spat up on him violently and was now wailing with the passion of a diva delivering her climactic aria. The father kept looking to the lavatory, then the baby, and then he caught my eyes with a pathetic gaze. Though I could not understand what possessed me, I asked, "Do you need help?"

I had not offered any of the women help. But this man seemed so useless, and I presumed myself less useless than he. Before I knew it, Uncle-ji had wordlessly placed his baby in my hands and opened the overhead compartment, out of which spilled a jute bag of Harvard printed T-shirts, a mug, and a poncho. He began sorting through his treasures.

Anjana/Ranjana was glowering at me in this way I remembered baby Naina looking at me, with alien obstinacy, a gaze not of pure discovery but of fury that the world was so befuddling. I was relieved to find myself moved. I was a woman who could hold a baby, halt a baby's tears.

Then, I looked up to find the child's mother in the aisle, saying her baby's name, which was not Anjana or Ranjana but, actually, Anjali.

The mother yanked Anjali from me and began spewing a string of abuses at her husband (now wearing a muscle tee reading

Harvard Extension School), among them, What do you know about anything, you worthless broom dog of a man.

Like the children, I had a mission related to history, only mine was more recent. I was finally going to get my divorce, which meant finding Killian, and this Other—Sanjena, my impostor, my replacement. Before getting on my plane, I had sent Killian another email, expecting nothing in return. The habit had become something like a recently agnostic person kneeling in prayer. This time I told my still-husband that I was en route to India, and I'd be landing the following afternoon. I added something new to my routine, too. On the second leg of my journey, from Dubai to Bombay, I purchased in-flight wi-fi (flush as I now was with Mommy money) and, still logged in as Beef Jerky, reopened Sanjena Sathian's profile to scroll through her perfectly lit, precisely gridded life. She shared her food—a wooden table laid out with glass jars of herbs and jams and honeys, captioned with musings on holistic nutrition before, during, and after pregnancy. Moms say they become a whole new person when they get pregnant, but we can begin becoming that new person long before we get pregnant!, she wrote. We have to begin caring for ourselves early and often. Our bodies can't produce love and shelter for another being on demand if they haven't been producing that love and shelter for *us* all along. She shared her reading material: *Motherhood, Disrupted: Ten Big Ideas for Transforming Parenting* and *Your Job Can't Love You Back (But Care Work Can): A Parent's Manifesto* and *Lean Out: A Feminist Mom's Guide to Really Having It All.* Caption: #amreading. She shared her insights into conception: the trick, apparently, was balancing holistic treatments with Western medical interventions. She shared summaries of her "deep dives" into studies on the value of acupuncture, Traditional

Chinese Medicine, Ayurveda, and Islamic wet cupping, all of which could be used in concert with IVF or IUI.

She also shared about how all this sharing could be scary, writing of the terrors of inviting others into her life before carrying to term: a lot of people don't tell these stories until they've had "success," but I think we need a siblinghood of people going through it together! In one post, she mentioned an ongoing project about community for pregnant people and intended parents currently in beta—more soon! Her captions referenced a seemingly endless fertility journey, and at least one miscarriage. She wrote of a "Rainbow Baby"; I discerned this to mean a baby born after miscarriages or stillbirths. She invoked an entire lexicon of suffering and magical thinking. I could see how her followers might dive headlong into her world and feel less alone. People bonded by shared distress born of desire. A pregnancy influencer: a twenty-first-century fertility goddess.

Lia had recently told me about this phenomenon of becoming obsessed with the internet avatars of women who were your inverse. She and Raphaella were besotted with *tradwives*, coiffed white females who chronicled their lives in hobbit-hole cottages in the countryside, knitting baby booties, baking gluten-free muffins, and gently interrogating the value of vitamin K shots for newborns. Raphaella had a cousin who'd converted to complementarian Christianity after meeting a corn-fed evangelical at the University of Iowa. The cousin had dropped out of her MFA program in book arts, then taken up homesteading. Raphaella was convinced that this cousin was fundamentally happier than she, a boss-bitch ER doctor married to a finance dude. When Lia first told me about their shared tradwife kink, I scoffed at their voyeurism, thinking it regressive. Now I understood: Sanjena Sathian was a resident of the Other Side. I couldn't *not* look.

As I sank deeper into the Sanjenaverse, I also hunted for a sight or mention of Killian in the bright, cheery squares and peppy posts. But oddly, Killian wasn't a mainstay on Sanjena Sathian's profile. There was that photo of him on Carter Road, and the one of him sleeping while she cheesed. There was one of him from the side, posted five months earlier, in which he was meditating in full lotus, the soles of his feet beaming up from the crevices of his knee joints. There was one two months before that, of him doing a headstand on a beach. But Sanjena's brand seemed focused on *her*.

I kept scrolling until I reached … the end. Sanjena's very first post was on July 1 of the year prior—just weeks after I'd left Goa. It was a selfie of her and Killian. They were on a beach. Sanjena had laid her small head on Killian's shoulder; his chin rested in her hair. Her expression was all unruly joy—protuberant eyes, beaky mouth; tongue lolled, teeth bared. She seemed oblivious to history. His eyes looked askance, toward the ocean. There, captured in a single frame: the end of him and me, the start of him and her. As though she had sprung from me the day I turned my back on that old life.

I wavered, hovering over the screen, my neck cramping. I opened the direct message tab of @beefjerkypup and typed a note, moving too furiously to think about punctuation or sense.

> Hello I am not a dog I am the original Sanjana
> Call off these goons contacting me I am not pregnant you are
> haha congrats
> also fuck you
> I am coming
> I am coming for you
> You both
> And then you can have him

Killian I mean
I don't want him
But get out of my life

Then I stowed my phone.

I slept, tumbled into a jigsawed dream: Lia held up a mewling infant. The child had Killian's shocking green eyes, and Lia said, like the satanists in *Rosemary's Baby*, "He has his father's eyes." Lia then morphed into a woman in an airport who, in profile, was my twin, but a twin who walked away too quickly for me to see whether she resembled me straight-on. Then the airport faces vanished, replaced by many round geometries. I kept bouncing between them, a bump here, a bump there, before I woke up and realized that the bumps were the runway. We had landed and people were standing in the aisles before the plane came to a complete stop, and children were bursting into fresh tears. I was back.

I cleared customs, watching an auntie scurry through the *Nothing to Declare* lane, bearing a tote packed high with Cabot cheddar cheese and Honeycrisp apples. While withdrawing rupees from the ATM, I eavesdropped on some Indian women my age giggling about whether they were going to be hassled for bringing in a "neck massager" purchased in Amsterdam. An immigration official stamped my passport with so much gusto that the red ink bled onto the pale blue pages. I rolled my suitcase through the automatic doors and into the smoggy Bombay air, making for the prepaid taxi stand, where I forked over five hundred rupees for a car to Bandra.

I did have a plan. But it is a truth universally acknowledged among immigrants and expats alike that as a stranger in a strange land, you begin to act in ways that render you foreign to yourself.

I was headed to the parking lot to meet my driver, gripping my prepaid ticket, when I glimpsed a woman standing in the arrivals area wearing a starched white uniform and holding a sign bearing the pink logo of a company called Maharashtra Women-Driven Car Service. The woman leaned on the barrier amid a throng of male drivers, who had been sent by hotels and corporations to collect their charges. Each waved a placard with a name and a destination: *Mr. Syed Mirza—JW Marriott Juhu*, and *Dr. Takeishi Yamamoto— Taj Hotel Land's End.*

The Woman Driver's sign read *Mrs. Sanjana Sathian— Pune.*

I felt a tingling, chilled awareness: the creature intuition that warns you you are being watched. Could we really both be arriving on the same day, Sanjana and Sanjena, converging here? I had to know. I skulked to a food court near the drivers' waiting area and lingered there for five minutes, then ten, then fifteen. After twenty minutes, I ordered a creamy cold coffee at Starbucks, not tearing my eyes from the Woman Driver. The problem was, in India, I never give a false name at cafés, as I do in America, where I say my name is Sunny. So when the barista began calling: "Cold coffee for Sanjana?" the Woman Driver's ears perked up.

Guilt was written all over my face. In that instant, I made a fateful decision. I walked right over to her, said, "That's me," and followed her to her car.

2

Women-Driven

The driver's name was Irene. She was from Mizoram, in the northeast. "Basically, I am also from foreign, like you," she said in English, wrenching my suitcase from me. "By the by, they have spelled your name wrong. On the order. S-a-n-j-E-n-a, they told me. I had fixed it."

"Some people spell it that way, with an *e*," I said. "Or, at least one person does."

"Is it? In America?" Irene gave a snort of amusement, as though at the very notion of America.

I hesitated as we approached the car, a silver Maruti Suzuki. "Who ordered the cab?"

Irene came to a wary halt. "It says on the slip that you only ordered it, madam."

"Ah." I thought fast. "Can I see the bill? You have it there?"

Scowling, she dug in her pocket and handed over two pieces of paper stapled together, one white, one pink. There, pencil-scrawled and already fading: *Mrs. Sanjena Sathian— airport pickup—BOM to (near) Pune—cash on arrival.* I calculated. Killian must have gotten the email I'd sent from the plane. So, he was back online and had been selectively ignoring me. But when had he moved to Pune? Maybe it was the air—Killian was always concerned about Bombay pollution; Pune was a slightly smaller city, and not so far from Bombay that he couldn't commute to auditions or shows. Or maybe—*near* Pune, the bill said—he had decided to settle in one of the hill stations to raise a baby in more peaceful environs. Possibly he had quit acting for good to embrace the higher purpose of fatherhood.

I had been holding the papers too long.

"Ah," I said. "It was my husband, I think. Gora man. He gives my name because his is hard for Indians."

It came too quickly, that word, *husband*. I remembered now how often I had needed to use it here. *Husband* covered a lot. It explained your status to electricians and aunties and flirtatious men; it was a protection, a slotting-in to expected realities.

"Yes, madam," Irene agreed, satisfied.

She struggled to toss my suitcase onto the roof luggage rack. It would have been inspiring if she'd done so with ease, like a man. I helped push it up, where it sat, unsecured, relying on centripetal force alone.

"Do a lot of people want women-driven cabs?" I asked, as politely as possible.

"Foreigners, like you. Sometimes, they think I am just a boy." Irene took her seat. "I put my hair up and they do not notice. They may be unfamiliar with our faces, you know, cannot tell the difference between boys and girls. Other times, they have read the news and think they will be raped in India and all."

We set out. I felt a twinge of guilt that Sanjena might arrive at the airport to find herself without transport. But it was poetic justice. I could take her car. She had taken my life. As we inched through Bombay traffic and toward the highway, Irene asked, "Madam, you are some kind of celebrity, is it?"

"What?"

"They told me," she said, sheepishly. "They're telling me to be very cautious with you. Your privacy. That there is some necessity for tinted windows. I am discreet, madam. I have driven for two famous playback singers, and one Bollywood actress. I will not tell you who. I will say only that one was in *Dhoom 5: Make More Noise*. That is all I will say." She made a self-satisfied *hmph*. "But, madam, forgive me. I had not heard of you."

"I'm ..." I considered issuing the correction, but decided it would only cause confusion. "I'm an influencer."

"And you influence about what?"

"Uh," I hedged. "Pregnancy. And ... motherhood."

"Oho." Her eyes flitted to me in the rearview mirror. "Miss Sanjana, you are expecting?"

I thought of Lia at that word, *expecting*, and missed her immensely. "Erm, yes."

"God bless," she said. "Myself, I do not have any. My husband, he is useless."

"I'm sorry to hear that," I said.

We were zipping down the highway at reckless speed. My stomach turned.

"What do I tell him?" she asked, flooring it past a shabbylooking tollbooth, where a man waved angrily at us to slow down.

"Didn't you have to pay something there, at that toll?"

"Scammers," she said. "They try to trick you. Stand there and look so important and you think, it must be real, but it is not. My husband, Sanjana Madam. You have some ideas? We have tried everything. Our minister, he says it is me, but I know, it is not me. Because, before, I have—well. I stopped it, once. So you see, I know *I* can."

"Oh," I said.

"So, what is your suggestion?" Urgency emanated from her.

"Oh, I really don't know," I said. "I guess ... just ... just keep trying." I scanned my memory for something on Sanjena's profile, or something Nakusha might have told one of her visitors. "Maybe, like, give him some Ayurvedic stuff to eat. I think urad dal helps men's, you know. *Seed?*" I gripped the door handle. My impersonation of Sanjena was going poorly. I cleared my throat and spoke as myself: "Or, maybe think about whether it would be so bad. If you didn't. Would it be the end of the world? To be childless?"

Irene harrumphed, jerking the steering wheel especially vigorously to avoid a cow loitering in the right lane. The driver of an orange-garlanded Ashok Leyland truck bearing the sign *Don't Be Horny, Horn Not Okay Please* slammed his horn down as we passed.

I was sad to know that I'd let her down. I wondered if that was what it felt like to be Sanjena. To hold influence. To matter.

Irene zoomed on. I tried to doze, but after about an hour of sleeplessness, I gave up. Just as we approached Pune— according to highway signs—I reactivated my old Indian SIM card to see if Lia had contacted me. I'd left her that long handwritten note, after all, and figured a compassionate reply must be in the works. I had no WhatsApps or texts, but there, in my inbox, was her name.

At least, I thought it was from Lia. But it was not from her. It came from an email address I hadn't seen used since her wedding—liagetsthegriGLORYan. Their hashtag, apparently required for contemporary nuptials. I'd been BCCed on what appeared to be a mass blast. It read:

Dearest Beloveds,

Greetings! As some of you already know, we are PREPARING TO SPAWN! Huh? We mean we are getting ready to welcome Tadpole, our beautiful baby-to-be!!!!!!!

Things are about to get weird. Yes, we will sniff our baby's butt in front of you. Yes, you will all see Lia's boobs and Gor will not be allowed to complain. Yes, you might meet the pet behavioral coach who's coming to help Sandra Day O'Connor adjust to her new "colleague on the bench." (Apparently kitties do not love babies?) Yes, we know we're crazy. Love makes you crazy!

But seriously: as problem-solvers by nature, we've been reflecting on the biggest challenge with contemporary parenthood, which is: it truly takes a village to raise a child. Unfortunately, that's not the reality of everyday life in Good Old New York City these days. Therefore, parents become isolated.

So, we wanted to issue an invitation to you guys to join our village! Be here for the big things, from first words to first steps to first day of school to first date (someone has to help Tadpole have ~game~ and it won't be us). Be here for bedtime! For story time! Bathtime! Diaper time! If you don't have kids yet, try on Tadpole as a trial run! We want you in our lives, and in Tadpole's. TL;DR: Come babysit! (Haha! But actually …)

All our love,
Gor, Lia, Sandy Dee, and Tadpole

There was a picture beneath the note. Gor held a squirmy Sandra Day O'Connor over Lia's belly. They stood on their balcony, with Brooklyn splayed out behind them. The cat looked likely to bolt, committing kitty suicide.

A hot knot of rage rose up in me. In my note to Lia, I had exposed as much of the past year as I could—the abortion, Maneesha, Killian, the strange calls, my sense of isolation as everyone else carried out their fuller, richer lives. In response, I'd gotten not the sort of sensitive reply Lia would have offered in the past but a mass email wheedling me to, what … watch Gor diaper a squirmy purple newborn? Everyone— even Lia and Gor—knew there was something wrong with the way the world was set up. But they were so *inside* it that the only reinvention they could perform was to ask *me* to join *their* "village," a village conveniently located on the ninth floor of a doormanned condo building.

We'd finally reached Pune. Outside was a clothing boutique and two cafés, one with a patio on which a mix of hipster Indians and foreigners mingled.

"Do you know how to go from here?" Irene asked.

I said I didn't. My mouth tasted rotten.

Irene, her face visible in the rearview mirror, frowned reprovingly, as though this did not add up.

"I'll get directions from someone, Sanjana Madam," she said. "You sit."

After a few minutes, she returned. "Madam," she said. "This place is very high up in the hills, did you know?"

"Oh," I said, swallowing the lump in my throat. "Yeah, sure."

"It will be one more thousand rupees to go so far," she said firmly.

I shook my head in a desi side bobble. She drove on. As the car climbed a winding, bumpy road into lush green hills, I became aware that I did not have a plan for where to stay. I decided I would ask Irene to wait while I located Killian. Then she could take me back to a hotel in town.

Suddenly, the sky cracked open. It was the beginning of monsoon season. Irene flipped on her lights, drove a distance more, and jolted to a stop. The rain plummeted down, striking the hood and roof like bullets.

"Here, madam," she said.

Through the rain, I could make out gigantic iron gates, their wings spanning two stone pillars. Behind them was more foliage, wilder and thicker even than that lining the mountain roads. The trees swayed, casting a pattern of alien shadows on the drive. For years after, I would wake to discover that I had been dreaming of this image, my first sight of the compound. The moment on the precipice of change, when the world I'd come from was still more real than whatever lay beyond those gates; the moment when I could have turned away from what followed.

"Madam," Irene said, warily. "This place looks quite dark."

We stepped out. My luggage was soaked. We had forgotten it when the rain hit. Irene was distraught.

"It's fine," I called through the downpour. "I'll go to a hotel tonight and dry everything there. Leave the bag. And can you wait here, while I run in to find someone?"

"No, no," said a raspy voice. "You have to stay."

A figure stood just beyond the gates, beneath a giant black umbrella. Through the downpour I could make out a woman, her curvy silhouette framed by a billowy kurti, which might have concealed a protruding belly.

3

Baby Moon

I stood immobile in the driveway, certain of who was under the umbrella. I was about to see the other me. I wanted to see her more than I could remember ever wanting anything. My whole body was a single, throbbing pulse. Perhaps I had been dishonest with myself prior to pulling up outside those iron gates, believing that all I felt was annoyance at Killian or mild curiosity about Sanjena or disorientation from the summer's strange letters and calls. What I felt was, in truth, more intoxicating.

But then the person standing beneath the umbrella shuffled out of the gate and revealed herself, beneath the glare of Irene's headlights, to be white.

She was lanky, about my height, with a mane of sandy hair and eyes as gray as the Atlantic Ocean. Her name, she said, proffering a hand, was Mireille. She had plump, careless pink lips. She worked for Sanjena, she went on. I was being greeted by a surrogate.

Irene's eyes widened when she heard Mireille say she worked *for* Sanjena. "Wait," she said to me. "You are not Mrs. Sanjana?" Mireille lunged at Irene and me. I teetered on my back foot before realizing she was only extending her umbrella so it covered me more than her. She laid a warm, dry hand on my shoulder, rooting me to the earth. To Irene, she said, "You should go. The roads take time when it's pouring like this."

I was fighting to maintain calm in my voice. "Where's Killian?"

"Everyone's asleep," Mireille said.

"Then I'll come back tomorrow."

I inched nearer to Irene, but she was looking at me with renewed confusion, even fear. She gathered that I had lied to her, and she couldn't understand why.

"Do you have a hotel reservation?" Mireille asked sweetly.

"Yes."

"No, I don't think you do," she said. "You weren't even sure where you were going. Everything is booked. There's a big EDM festival on. And this"—she pointed to the gate—"is a four-star resort."

I hesitated. Mireille seized the chance to hand Irene three thousand-rupee notes. That was all the incentive Irene needed to unload my suitcase, duck back into her car, and floor it down the mountain. I was alone. There was no choice but to follow this stranger to the gate. I struggled to stay under the umbrella; behind me, my suitcase rattled awkwardly over the sodden path, its wheels sticking occasionally.

"I'm glad you found the car," Mireille said, tapping a key-pad to reopen the gate. She had to tilt her head into the onslaught of rain to do so, and when she pulled back, her hair was soaked; she resembled a soggy golden retriever, and she shook herself like one. "We worried you might miss it."

The gates swung open, revealing a path, and a plastic sign attached to a wooden stake, on which was printed—I squinted—*Welcome to the Shakti Center.*

"May I help you with your bag?" Before I could object, Mireille tugged it away, handing me the umbrella. "I don't mind getting wet."

"What *is* this place?"

"As I said," she replied, "it's a resort. Sanjena can tell you everything herself. She's the eloquent one. Be careful—it's very slippery. You wouldn't want to fall." She said the last bit mockingly.

Mireille's accent was almost Indian, all rolled *r*'s and per-cussive *t*'s, with an additional throaty francophone edge.

"Where are you from?" I asked.

"Here and there," she said into the rain. "Come, come, *Sanjana.*" She sounded disdainful when she said *Sanjana*, almost reluctant to admit it was my name.

"Wait," I said, remembering. "Why did he put *her* name on the car?"

Mireille turned coquettishly over her right shoulder, her chin cocked, as though she'd been waiting for me to inquire about this.

"I imagine it was a joke. Don't worry, she's found it all very amusing."

"And where is *she*? He? I mean, where are *they*?"

"She sleeps early these days," Mireille said. "She's exhausted, of course. She would have liked to come greet you, but—"

"No need," I said sharply. "I'm here for Killian."

Mireille, a few paces ahead of me, kept rolling the bag up an incline. The wheels left a trail of mud that was almost instantly washed away by the rain. My once-white sneakers, soaked and squelching, were fast turning bronze.

"That's none of my business," she called. "Here, we re-spect the privacy of the past."

The pompous phrase came out of her mouth in swift, strident percussion—*the privacy of the past.*

"What does *that* mean?"

I caught up to her and tilted the umbrella so it was covering both of us.

"It means," she said, at a more normal decibel, "that we don't care who anyone was before this particular moment."

We had reached a roofed hallway. A line of doors ran along the right side; to the left, the rain slanted in. The umbrella shielded us slightly, but staying dry was a fool's errand at this point.

Mireille stopped at the end of the corridor.

"This is you." She pushed open a door with a bow, like a bellhop, then flipped on the lights to reveal an opulent suite: pastel blue walls that looked freshly painted, not a scuff in sight. The bed was king-size, enclosed in a mosquito net that looked like a gauzy, regal curtain. A kantha quilt, olive green. In the window: two cane-backed reading chairs with deep mustard-and-cream upholstered cushions. A secretary roll-top desk, mahogany wood.

"I'll have your things washed and dried and ironed tomorrow." She paused, as if waiting for me to object. I didn't. The thought of freshly pressed clothes was inviting. "And someone will come by with Bournvita and pj's in a few minutes. That's the bathroom. I've switched on the hot water geyser for you. Hit the red button when you're done. Breakfast is between seven and eight thirty. Mealtimes are fixed." She said the last bit sternly before stomping out.

I took her suggestion and stood a long while in the steaming hot shower, feeling time and the journey slither down my back. A four-star resort, she'd said. Killian and Sanjena were posted up in luxury. Perhaps this was what Lia referred to as a *baby-moon*. Perhaps they were just enjoying the considerable disposable income that was the province of many American expats in India. But this didn't account for why Mireille had seemed to be Sanjena's assistant, nor did the average resort have catch-phrases like *the privacy of the past*. Too tired to question further, I settled for scrubbing myself vigorously, watching muck accumulate on the immaculate white, then slip down the drain.

When I got out of the shower, I found, as promised, a folded white nightgown and a mug of Bournvita with a plate over it, both placed carefully on a side table in the entryway. Someone had been in the room, feet away from me, while I stood naked in the steam.

I tried to sleep, but jet lag kept me awake. I hadn't enjoyed a full night's rest since before Lia's baby shower, which felt like eons ago. But my mind was alight. I tossed and turned, shuddering into a shallow, dreamless sleep for ten minutes at a time, then zapping into wakefulness at the sound of a persistent mosquito in my ear—it had busted through the netting. I could feel it surveilling me, predatory and bloodthirsty.

It was after three a.m. when I gave up, stood, found my phone, and tried to get online. I would have liked to google this place, the Shakti Center, but there was neither service nor data, not even a password-protected wi-fi network in the vicinity.

Using my phone as a flashlight, I padded outside, thinking I might get a signal somewhere else within the resort.

The building where I'd been put up was single-story, stretching long like a ranch house. Above, the sky was a wild dome of stars, the moon gibbous. The rain had stopped, but the air was sticky with the bated breath of the next storm. This was the deathliest quiet I had experienced in a long time.

Then I saw it: a pinprick of yellow light emerging from a round building some yards away. Ahead of me, up a slanting path, was a tiled pathway leading to what looked like the lobby.

I'd strode a few feet in the direction of that light when I felt my right ankle roll. I yowled and flashed my phone down to see an uneven section along the path. I lifted my ankle, gingerly; it was tender. Then, as I hoisted my leg up, the phone slipped from my hands, landed in the mud, and proceeded to slide, down into black thrush. As it fell, its flashlight illuminated the steepness of the drop-off—the whole hotel appeared to be built into the flank of the mountain, and below, a great crevasse gaped. I heard a thud as my phone settled somewhere. Its light went out.

I stood in shock a moment, then decided to keep heading toward the lobby in search of help, wincing each time I put weight on my ankle. When I got there, I jiggled the handle to open the door and found it locked.

I rapped on the window.

"Hello?" I pressed my ear to the glass. No noise; only the sound of my own breathing. "Hello?" I said, more loudly.

The light inside flicked off.

"Killian?" I knocked so hard on the glass that I could feel it start to shake. "Killian!"

I stood, keeping all my weight on my good ankle, and tried the door more insistently. It gave. It had not been locked at all.

I edged into the building. The foyer was vacant: no luggage carts or sofas for guests waiting to check in, no coffee tables, no wall of pamphlets advertising tourist attractions— local temples, nineteenth-century forts, zip lines through the jungle. Not even a rug to soften the coldness. The ceiling, latticed with mahogany rafters, threw a weird waffled pattern on the bare marble floor. There was a front desk, unstaffed.

I hobbled on down the long hallway beyond the lobby, suppressing the pain swelling in my leg. The overhead lights flickered automatically, illuminating a worn crimson carpet. I tried the first door on my right—locked. The first on my left—locked. I went on like this. Around one corner was a set of swinging doors. I gave them a shove, revealing a laundry room with a huge, industrial-size white washing machine. I kept going down the main hallway, trying doors until one opened.

There, before me, in an antiseptically bright room, was a wheeled cart covered in paper. Enclosed in plastic atop it were several sharp silver instruments. Scissors; a can openeresque object. Next to the cart: a tan bed, lined with paper. Two steel legs sticking out—stirrups.

The rest of the room came into focus. A metal Godrej cabinet, a sink, a glove dispenser. The silver instruments were forceps and surgical scissors and specula. All arranged as though someone had been here in the middle of the night, telling a patient: *Spread your legs. You' ll feel some tightness. Some cold.* And then plunging into her with a latexed wand, probing the walls of her body, saying, *Just a moment, now, hold, right there*, as she waited, splayed open, her eyes on this clean white ceiling, wondering if everything was about to begin.

Dazed, I made my way back outside. The corridor lights shut off as I moved. The lobby door clanged closed behind me. I remembered one of Sanjena's captions on her social media: an ongoing project about community for pregnant people and intended parents currently in beta— more soon! This wasn't just Killian and Sanjena's temporary babymoon spot. This was *Sanjena's* business, like the IVF clinic Maneesha had gone to in Barbados a few years ago. Of course—a fertility influencer shilled not only her own pregnancy but also her ability to impregnate others.

I headed back to my room, but with my first shaky step onto the tiled path, I began to slide down its slick, slippery incline. That same uneven spot caught me and I rolled, just as my phone had, into the thrush. A rock scratched at my elbow. A tree root thwapped me in my lower back and thigh. Then I came to a rough stop. I'd been bowled eight feet down the steep hill.

"Fucking hello?" I yelled, trying to stand. "Killian?"

Silence. Then a crunching, like leaves or branches underfoot. A vague scraping in the distance, perhaps a tree limb bending beneath the weight of a swinging langur monkey or an alighting bulbul bird. And then: a pair of narrow yellow eyes met mine. When Maneesha and I were little, Ajji and Ajja had taken us on a safari in rural Maharashtra, not far from where I was now. I recalled the promise of wild dogs and tigers and panthers prowling the preserve at night. My mother had pressed her binoculars to her eyes for three days straight as we clattered through the jungle in a beige jeep. On our last night, she insisted she'd spotted a panther, sleek and shiny, lurking in some shrubbery before bolting away. She'd felt its yellow eyes on us, *hungry*, she maintained.

I took a step toward those eyes, but as soon as I did, they were gone, replaced only by an unyielding darkness.

"Killian!" I tried again. "Killian!" It felt horrible to call for him. I switched: "Mireille?!"

The last thing I remember: the sight of my borrowed nightgown, bright as a beacon, fluttering, then snagging on a root, as I willed one last person to come and help me: "Sanjena?"

And then a plunge, into blackness.

4

Gregor Samsa

For what might have been days, months, lifetimes, rain fell in sheafs and the air went viscous and I sweated myself out. My head throbbed, as though my brain wanted to leave my skull, ooze out of my temples, gather in a gray lump on the floor. My dreams were so lucid, they were more like waking funeral—my mother's?—squatting before a fire. A priest spoke at me in Sanskrit, and I kept saying, *I don't speak Sanskrit, no one speaks Sanskrit, it's a dead language, the language of the dead, stop speaking the language of the dead*, and then I discovered that I was not at my mother's funeral but my own. I was lying ashen, cloaked in white, as the crematory flames encroached on my skin. I woke and puked, certain that I really *was* dying, wondering who would find me, regretting through my fever that I had lived in such a way that no one would look for me; I could disappear unnoticed.

But I was not unnoticed. Shadowy figures swept in and out of my room, bearing wet washcloths, thermometers, turmeric milk. I remembered being sick like this on trips to India when I was a child, remembered, once, being bent over a toilet and lifting my eyes to find a syringe about to plunge into my arm, and my mother running into the bathroom shouting, *No, no, we don't do that in America, let her vomit, let her get it all out.*

"Ajji," I heard myself whisper. "Ajji, soup?"

The voices around me asked, what? What? I tried to explain: I wanted the rasamy tomato soup, thin and umami, that my grandmother made when I got sick on those childhood visits. Minuteshoursdays later someone brought me a crimson liquid in a mug. It was not Ajji's soup, but it stung pleasantly behind my sinuses.

"Mommy?" I asked, but someone said, "Shh."

"Kill?" I asked.

"No one's trying to kill you," said the someone, and padded out, but I sat up and shouted, *You*, you're making me sick, someone hit me on the head, someone tried to hurt me, and the person—a woman—shushed and cooed. No, no, she said. You're confused. You're jet-lagged. You ate something funny. You had a little accident. Calm down. This will pass.

My mouth opened—did I open it myself, or was that someone's hand on my jaw?—and I tongued a pill, swallowed, and the pain abated.

I woke after those fevered days to find myself trapped in a net. I had been metamorphosed, like Samsa, into a beast. Then I realized that I was in a bed and the net was a mosquito net and I was still, roughly, me. I glanced down. I was wearing something I did not recognize—an ankle-length cream garment, hemmed with lace at the wrists. An anachronistic piece of clothing.

Human noise resounded nearby. The rhythm of bare feet on wood, someone opening a drawer, and then—a face appeared. A dark-skinned, attractive Indian woman who spoke with a throaty timbre and deliberate, cosmopolitan vowels. She wore purple cat-eye glasses. Her hair sprung out in thick coils. "Something's paining?" The back of her palm on my brow. "Your fever's gone. Feeling any better?"

"Head," I said. "My head hurts. That light." I pointed to the fixture behind her. I examined myself with my hands. When I pressed on my neck and temples, a stabbing sensation set in. My brain felt amoebic and wet and full of air bubbles.

She went to dim the bulb, then returned to flutter her fingers in my sight line. "There. Now, can you tell me your name?" She spoke slowly, like she expected me to be dense.

"*You* don't know my name," I said. Stubbornness arrived before knowledge.

"I know all about you," she said. "Do *you*?"

"Samsa," I started. "I mean, Sahana."

"Hm," she said. "Can you try to spell your name?"

"S-A-N-J-E …" I trailed off, furious. I knew my name. I knew that I knew my name. And yet my name would not arrive on my lips.

"Mm," she said. "Are you dizzy?"

I tried to shake my head, but then I *was* dizzy. "I'm itchy." I seized my inner thigh—I had a nasty sensation of an organism crawling on me. "Something is eating me."

"That could be neurological, or it could be real, which is not to say that it's *not* real if it's real in your brain," the woman said.

"Huh?"

She'd thrust her hands into my armpits and was already hauling me up by the rib cage, sending spirals into my vision, when she thought to ask if it was okay to touch me.

"Who are you?" I asked, pulling back as she brushed my breasts.

She chuckled. Instinctively, I disliked her for her ability to laugh.

"I told you, but you've forgotten. I'm Omna. Omna Mirani. I'm a doctor, okay? I've been helping you with your concussion. You can call me Omna, though, not Dr. Mirani. We're all very familiar here. Show me where you're itching?"

I pointed to my crotch.

"May I lift your nightgown? I need to see if all the leeches fell off of their own accord."

"*Leeches?*"

"You went for a moonlit hike in monsoon season, dear. I found three on your arms the night we brought you in, but there may be more. They may even have latched on while you were sleeping, if someone left damp clothes around." She clicked her tongue, impatient, as though some peon had failed at their task, and pushed my nightgown up, bringing her face close to my legs. Her purple spectacles gave her the appearance of a child detective using a magnifying glass on a "clue." As I had that thought, I wondered how I could have *that* thought and not get my own name right. It seemed random, what my mind was willing to yield, and what it sought to withhold.

Omna was still talking. "Adjust your right knee, slightly? Yes. That's one little sucker."

I strained my neck to see. Omna was right. A plump black thing, like a smooth centipede or a tiny eel, nestled at the top of my thigh, was greedily feeding on me. I gagged.

Omna tutted again, reached out of the mosquito netting, and grabbed something. She tossed a fistful of white crystals onto the leech. "If you try without salt, it sticks harder," she explained, still tugging. The leech didn't give. "Fire it is."

She bustled around somewhere else in the room, and returned holding a large blue lighter. She flicked it on.

"Whoa," I said, eyeing the waggling flame. "You said you're ... a doctor. Like, a doctor-doctor? Not a ... ?" The phrase *witch-doctor* escaped me.

"*Yes*," she snapped. "I am an allopathic physician, though I also have training in Ayurveda and homeopathy. Do you have any other questions for me before you allow me to remove a bloodsucking parasite from your body?"

I squinted, which also produced further head pounding.

"Did you look at my brain?" I asked.

"Darling, it's inside your skull," she said wearily.

"With a machine. A catty machine. A kit machine."

Omna blinked, confused. "Oh! A CT scan! Americans." She sighed. "Everything needs some machine, some surgery, some pill, powder. You will be fine, okay? You only need to rest and recuperate."

Omna brought the lighter to my leg, and sure enough, the leech fell onto my sheets. Omna showered it with salt and it stopped wriggling.

"See? Now. How's everything else? The ankle?"

"I don't think I can walk."

"I wouldn't," she agreed. "You howled and howled when you tried. We all had to carry you in."

I saw now that someone had wrapped my right ankle.

"Where's ... Killian?" *Killian* came easily. Killian I could picture: his height, his stooped shoulders, his concave stomach.

"Kalyan is out."

It took me a second to clock how she'd pronounced Killian's name: with two syllables rather than three, and an *i* that sounded like an *a*. I wondered if I'd misheard.

"*Kill*-i-an." I drew it out. "My husband. Killian Bane. Irish giant. Black hair. Green eyes." Articulating his looks was calming. "He's my husband," I said again.

"You two haven't seen each other in about a year," she said, and this rang as truth, though I could not have said it myself. "Things have changed. He goes by Kalyan, now." Her decisive intonation reminded me of something—a French accent, saying *the privacy of the past*. "He's out. Ran to town for a call. With his manager, I think. The internet's being fiddly."

She rubbed her palms together with finality and turned to go. "Things may feel topsy-turvy for you, for a while. You need to rest. No reading. No screens. Minimal physical activity. And don't *think* too hard."

I was waking up from a nap when I was startled by a sudden noise on my bed. A black cat with yellow eyes and a single smear of white shot through its flank, like Killian's own stripe in his black hair, pounced onto my lap and sat, sphinx-like, judging me.

I thought of Omna, and her purple spectacles, and the phrase *witch-doctor*. Witches! I thought again. Omna and Mireille: witches, who had turned Killian into a black cat!

"Killian," I whispered.

I extended an index finger toward the cat. It sniffed me regally and then bounded off the bed, landing lightly on the floor. It took a few steps toward the door, then looked over its shoulder as though expecting me to follow. It seemed utterly natural to try to stand up, trailing in the cat's wake toward the darkness outside.

It was dusk. Though it wasn't raining, the air felt thick and wet. The sky was imbued with the blue of the distant hills, which were neon green and flush with rainwater. To my right, down a steep mud-slicked incline, lay a lagoon ringed with bright foliage.

Slightly dizzy, I walked toward the sinking sun, tracking the cat, who was slinking a few feet ahead of me, continuing to cast its yellow eyes back in my direction. An intelligent part of me knew that this creature was not literally Killian, but there was something human in the animal's gaze that compelled me. It occurred to me that this might have been the being that had watched me the night I fell, a tiny panther. The cat reached the edge of the hallway and paused. I did the same, just in time to see a column of figures—seven? twelve?—all wearing floaty, ankle-length garments like my own, amoeba-ing around a corridor like a great white jellyfish. They emerged from the lobby and made for a singlestory building across from me. They did not seem to see me. They paused at the mouth of a room, formed a circle, grabbed hands, kicked their heads back, and ... wailed. A miserable ululation; a squalling, emanating from their throats. They all keened that way for ten or more seconds before coalescing into a shared embrace and stepping into that room.

The cat's yellow eyes were glowering at me, ahead, as if to say, *Are you done?* Then it bounded toward the lobby and out of sight.

Inside, the same vacancy greeted me: the unstaffed reception desk, the furniture-bare space.

The hallway beckoned, so I kept limping that way until I heard the patter of cat paws on the other side of two swinging doors. I edged through them. A laundry room: a lustrous white machine, a ceramic sink, several huge hampers. On the ground lay a pile of linens, atop which the cat sat, curled into itself, looking pleased to have led me here. Its sheeny blackness contrasted with the garments, which were all white—or, no, once white. Amid the white sheets and towels and flowing dresses were streaks of an unsettling coppery crimson.

I leaned against the wall, catching my breath, and turned to find myself facing a large mirror. I took in my reflection. There was still some dirt on the side of my face. Drool was encrusted around my mouth. And then, in the looking glass, my eyes crossed. I was seeing double. Two glossy smiles. Two brown faces.

"Hi, Sanjana," said the Other.

I screamed, then she screamed, and then the noise mutated into a laugh. "Oh, my," she said, in an alto that seemed too deep for her frame. "You terrified me."

5

Regression

I had hoped that our likeness was a trick, that we appeared similar only because of the name thing, and that in person, our differences would be plain. But now that we were so close that I could smell her—lemongrass and rose—it was as though the distance between us had contracted. I glanced, instinctively, at her belly, which was concealed beneath another white flowing kaftan—no rounding, but the garment was very loose.

"*I?*" I managed to eke out. "*I* terrified *you*?"

Her mouth widened into an enormous, froglike smirk, and she became conspicuously *not* me. Where my eyes were incapable of concealing any feeling, mild or strong, hers had a darker, hooded quality. There was, within them, a discretion that I lack.

"Fair point." The alto seemed to be coming from elsewhere, as though a heftier person were ventriloquizing her.

"That looks like murder," I said, pointing at the copper-stained sheets. "Did someone … murder?" I was trying to sound snarky, in control, but everything came out thick.

"Do you remember where you are?" she asked.

"Baby hotel," I said.

A shadow crossed her face, as though she were disappointed, in either the simplicity of my language or the simplicity of my intellect. "Yes, that's the spirit of it. We try to help people make babies. But sometimes it doesn't work."

I rubbed my temples. I knew things, could feel and almost taste them, but I was having difficulty jigsawing them into speech. I understood that she was referencing a miscarriage, but I could not get a grip on the word *miscarriage*.

"Killian," I said. "You're Killian's baby. I mean, you're Killian's mother. I mean. Is it—you?" I pointed at the blood.

"No, honey, not me. Not this time," she said sadly.

"Where is he?" I asked. "He is my husband."

"Don't I know it." She smirked. "We'd all like to put an end to that, don't worry. He had to go to Bombay to meet with a producer. You've been unwell for a few days. You don't remember seeing him? He was sitting with you. He was *very* worried. He brought you soup. Oh, that must be so scary …"

"Can I talk to him? Where is my phone?"

"Your phone is gone, honey. It slid way down the mountain. It could be twenty feet deep in the lagoon. Not that you should be looking at screens right now. I'd call Kalyan on *my* phone but the service is out. We're in high monsoon."

"*You* were there," I said. "You were there when I … fell. You—*you* hit me?"

She bristled. "*Me?* Oh, no. You had a terrible dream. Look at you. You're … *stuck* in there." She pointed at her own head.

"I know the feeling. I had a bad concussion in high school. Car accident. I had to lie in a dark room for weeks. It's tragicomic, having your reality twisted like that. Feeling trapped, because you can't communicate with the world, because other people don't understand you. It's a bit like being a baby again."

I nodded, or something nodded me, and I felt like a marionette, being moved. But the feeling did not bother me. It was pleasant, that emptying out. I leaned on Sanjena while she helped me back to my room, murmuring encouragement all the way—*Good, just one more step*—taking as much of my weight as possible.

I slept fitfully that night, then spent the next morning testing myself—my reflexes (slow), my memory (mottled), my ability to read (minimal), and my ability to write (slightly better). I found a notebook in my nightstand and began jotting things down, trying to keep track of how I'd gotten to the compound, and what had happened since. As I worked, painstakingly slowly, two different women brought me breakfast (oatmeal) and then lunch—yogurt rice, prepared the Kannadiga way, scattered with halved grapes and pomegranate seeds. One, whose name escaped me, offered me a massage to help bring circulation back to my rolled ankle. I declined politely.

I'd just taken a hot shower when I emerged to find the black cat perched on my bed. It glanced up at me snootily, as though we had not already become acquainted. I approached and stroked it, and it purred, softening at my touch.

Then, a voice behind me: "She normally hides from new people." A woman was holding a pile of white linens in the doorway. When she set them down on the entryway table, I saw that she was tiny, with a childlike face, skin the color of unpeeled almonds, and luxuriant eyelashes. "You must be nurturing."

"She looks like my … husband," I said, cocking my head. "But she is a girl. I mean, a girl cat. Do you know my husband? He is my husband. He is an actor. He is white with black hair and has black hair with a white stripe."

"Kalyan is out," she said, in a manner I might have called *practiced* if I'd had my wits.

I had sat on the bed and stopped stroking the cat, who now nudged my hand, miffed. "Animals *never* like me," I said. I had proof in both Lia's cat, Sandra Day O'Connor, and Beef Jerky.

"Well, sometimes the right little creature can bring out the best in us." The woman smiled radiantly. Her hands dropped to her stomach, which bulged slightly. "Oh, sorry!" she said, her mouth making a little doughnut on the *o* in *sorry*—a Canadian accent. "I'm Reema. We haven't met properly. I, um, I found you, out there."

"Oh," I said. "Something hit me."

Her brow furrowed. "Yes. A rock hit you. You hit a rock." She took a seat on the edge of the bed, hoisting the cat out of my lap and onto her shoulder. "Come here, Kali baby." To me: "She's our little goddess of destruction, Kali."

Kali wriggled out of Reema's hands, bounded to me, and began kneading my belly. "She's making biscuits," Reema said, with a giggle. "It's a compliment."

Kali flipped to her back, exposing her stomach, and I obliged, scratching her.

"That is *weird*," Reema said. "She always hides from strangers. Maybe she thinks you're … well—" She cut herself off. "I wanted to see how you were feeling, because the banquet is starting soon. Keep resting if you like, but things might get loud. Omna said you looked better."

"A banquet," I repeated. I couldn't remember anyone telling me about a banquet, but I didn't want to keep broadcasting my newfound idiocy. "I don't have anything to wear to a party."

"Oh, you don't have to worry about that," Reema said, sweetly. "I brought something for you to wear. I'm *sure* it will work."

Moments later, she was gone, and a pink cotton dress was set out over my feet. I lifted it and was seized with recognition: Had I seen this before? I was sure I had. I slid it on. Reema had also left a pair of crutches, wrapped in thick plastic. I leaned on them and staggered to the mirror. The dress cinched me around the bust and waist and clung to my butt, giving me the illusion of curves.

Shaking off Kali, who was rubbing up against my ankles, I donned a pair of black rain boots that had been left by my door. They had a familiar air to them, and they also fit perfectly. I made my way out to the main area of the hotel, leaving Kali in my room, where she seemed to want to stay. Water sloshed to my heels in the open-air hallway. I turned the corner, heading toward the lobby, and walked right into a cluster of people wearing pink and blue, gathered beneath a thatch roof lit up by twinkle lights. I tried to count them, but numbers evaded me. More than ten, fewer than twenty? Some were helping themselves to a buffet, where steam rose from chafing dishes.

Then, a bright-eyed person with olive skin, a septum piercing, and purple hair stood before me.

"Helper, receiver, or ideator?" they asked efficiently.

"Excuse me?"

They waved a handful of wristbands at me. Three colors: pink, blue, and green.

"She's up!" someone called—the woman who had just been in my room. Ria. Ramya. Reshma. Reema. She stood from her spot at a round table and waved me over. "Sanjana!" "*Oh*," the person in front of me said, squinting. "Oh, I'm so sorry—I didn't realize—in the darkness." They raced off, and I crutched over to where Reema was sitting. Two cheery-looking brown women flanked her; across from her was the Frenchwoman, Mireille, who nodded curtly at me as I took my own seat.

"It's nice to see you up and about," Reema said, beaming.

"Who are all these people?" I asked.

Reema pointed around at the other tables. "These are the clients Sanjena admitted to the Shakti Center on a trial basis. Intended parents and such. *We're* the founding team." She gestured at our table and flicked her green bracelet. "We're the ideators. *We* work with Sanjena. Us, and Omna, who you met. And Dr. Joglekar, but she oversees the bigger fertility clinic and birthing center, in Pune." There was a glimmer of pride in her voice, which she seemed to want to bestow upon me, in turn. I had found myself at the popular girls' table, among the inner circle.

Mireille, who had slipped off to the buffet, now clanged a plate down in front of me, plus one at her own spot. I was starving. I began devouring the paratha and masala baingan. It was the best meal I'd eaten in months.

As I ate, I remembered that not long ago I had been researching intensely, trying to figure out where Sanjena and Killian were, and coming up with nothing. "I didn't know about this place," I said between bites. "I mean, I couldn't find it. On the internet."

"Of course you couldn't find us online. We haven't launched yet," said Mireille.

"And Sanjena wants things quiet, because a *big star* is coming," Reema added. "A *Bollywood* star. My guess is it's Bunny Arora. We're getting a whole VIP cottage ready for her." She pointed at the horizon line. I spotted an A-frame roof peeking through the trees, up a slight hill, the green of the mountainside ringed by the light of a pink sunset.

Mireille was spooning dal into her mouth delicately, like it was vichyssoise.

"Sanjena." I hesitated. "She's not a doctor."

"No, no," one of the other women, whose name I hadn't caught, said. "She's sort of … a counselor."

"What does she, like, *do*, though?"

Reema bit her lip, as though considering whether I would be able to follow. "She specializes in helping people visualize their ideal family situations, and then she goes about helping to make those families a reality. She does *emotional* work, and then helps connect people to clinical and legal help. Obviously all the medical stuff is more affordable in India, so people have come from all over for that. But they're—we're— not just here for cheap doctors. We're here for *her*."

I struggled to follow the rest of the dinner conversation, as though it were happening in a language I'd once spoken but had since forgotten. So I was relieved when, at the table next to us, Sanjena stood. A hush fell. She raised a flute filled with a boggy brown liquid.

She said something I didn't hear. Tinnitus was filling my head, but the next thing I knew, all heads had turned to me, and polite applause was rippling through the crowd. I lifted my hands to my ears.

"Shh," someone next to me said, and the group went silent. "Her head hurts."

Reema touched my shoulders tenderly. "Are you okay?"

I made a squeaking noise.

"Yes, let's be gentle," Sanjena was saying, softly. "Sanjana has been through an ordeal."

"Another Sanjena," someone said.

"Yes, about that," Sanjena said, her alto resonant. "I've been thinking that perhaps I should be *Sunny*—I used to go by Sunny, when I was younger. To avoid confusion. Sanjana certainly doesn't need *any* more mix-ups. You know, for weeks, people have been harassing her, thinking she's me!" The inner circle chuckled at that.

There were more murmurs, as though of dissent, but Sanjena—Sunny—cleared her throat with finality, and the disagreement was settled.

"What we are celebrating today," Sunny said, raising her voice, "is more important than names, or superficial identities, of course"

I turned to Reema. "I have to go," I said. "My head. I need darkness. Quiet."

"We are here to welcome *life*," Sunny was saying. "And possibility."

"Oh, of course," Reema whispered, sympathetically. "Can I walk you?"

"I know the way," I said.

She frowned, skeptical, but then her glance fell on Sunny. She clearly did not want to miss anything her leader said.

I crutched out of the dining area, feeling, once more, the eyes of the group on my retreating back.

I was headed for my room, but I felt antsy at the thought of locking myself up there like a fugitive. I decided to make a lap on my own. I hobbled around until I found myself standing before a black door, which was cracked open.

The light behind me was enough to clarify the strange contents of the room as I stepped inside: aggressive red walls, and a space empty but for a pink tube, perhaps three feet in diameter, stretching ahead, into the darkness.

It seemed the most natural thing in the world to drop to my knees and lie prone in the tube. It was fuzzy. I crawled deeper in, and as I moved, the tube expanded vertically, warping into bizarre proportions until suddenly I was in a round room. The floor was lined with a shag rug. A low light, as from a lava lamp, emanated from a nook to my right. To my left, I discovered a nest of pillows, and a furry pink blanket.

And then, a booming voice emerged from the floor and the ceiling. There must have been speakers mounted around the room—perhaps motion-activated, or perhaps I'd bumped some switch.

"Welcome. Focus, and listen to your breath," came the voice. "Seek out the most intuitive pattern of inhalations and exhalations. Not too fast, not too deep. Feel your tailbone root into the floor. This is your natural state of being."

The voice—that alto. Sanjena's—Sunny's—voice. I curled up in the pillow nest, pulling the blanket over me. My head was pounding. I let that voice reach me from a galactic distance. Sunny spoke leisurely, leaving long pauses between each sentence.

"As I speak to you, we're going to try to visualize some things. You're going to see images. Some may be 'real,' and others 'imagined.' Ready?"

I felt myself accepting the terms. I knew that some other Sanjana might disdain this place, this whole night, but, curiously, this version of me was untroubled.

"Picture the first place you can remember living.

"The body knows more than the rational, conscious mind. It remembers. Listen to it.

"Are you there, in your memory, as a little baby, or a toddler?

"Do you have a body there? Wait. Wait for your body and your mind to find each other there, in the past.

"Okay. Good. Now. What does the house look like?"

The voice slowed even further.

"Pick a room and wander into it.

"When were you last here?

"What sense memories await you here?

"What does your body know that your mind has forgotten?"

I don't know how long it took for me to be plunged into another world, but the next thing I remember is seeing the brown door of my parents' bedroom, in the Lexington house. Inside that room lay my mother, in bed, sheets tucked up to her chin. She looked dead.

Her expression, even in repose, was a scowl. I crawled to her and waited for her to open her eyes and see me. Her breathing shifted. She knew I was there. She did not open her eyes. I watched for a long time.

Sunny's voice, coming to me as though from underwater: "Keep looking through those child eyes. You can see things now that you could not see when you were there the first time. You understand it anew."

My mother, in this thing that was memory or invention or dream, shook the covers off and stared down at me and said my name, over and over, asked what I was doing up. It must have been the middle of the night. I must have been too young to understand time. I had only found my way to her bedside out of gravitational, biological pull. My mother was asking, *What do you need? What do you want from me?*

I saw her with my adult eyes: her unlined face, the same face that I wore around the world today, the face Sunny wore, too. I walked through the world wearing a mask of my mother's face—how grotesque for her.

She was saying, through my lips, with my face, *Please, please go to sleep*, and I recognized terror in the helpless gestures.

"Now breathe out of that memory," Sunny was saying. "Open your eyes. *That* is the past, yes. But this room is your deeper past. This place that was always your home. Can you feel the warmth? The darkness that does not mean you harm? The walls and ceiling and floor pulse, like muscles contracting and relaxing."

I was so tired. I had been doing nothing but resting for days, but I was still so tired.

"This was, and is, the most comforting room you've ever been in. Here, you are not scared. You are not hungry. You have no physical needs or wants."

I *wasn't* hungry. I was quite full from dinner.

"Here, you've made no mistakes," Sunny said. "No one has hurt or failed you. You are not afraid. The purpose of this womb regression is to bring you here, to your mother's womb, the home you've missed as long as you've been alive.

"When you come out of this womb, this time, you will be brand-new. New as the day you were born."

My eyes were filling. I had barely cried in a year, and now—

"Turn that off," someone whispered.

The crackling voice on the speakers was lowered. Someone lay down next to me.

"Sanjana." I felt breath on my ear and a palm petting my sweaty neck.

"Oh, honey," the person—Sunny—said, and I felt myself pulled to the heat of her body. "You scared us. We thought you'd fallen again. We thought you'd hurt yourself again. That you'd done something stupid—"

"Somebody hit me," I whispered.

"Oh, Sanjana," she said. "I didn't want to tell you. *You* hit yourself. You slammed your head into the rock. Over, and over. Reema had to pull you away."

As she said it, a hazy vision that had been hovering in my mind clarified, as though it had been waiting for someone to speak it into being: a vision of Nakusha's postulant Kamda, the woman who'd banged her own head into the wall, trying to knock something out of her brain.

"You were trying to kill yourself," Sunny said.

"No. No, I wasn't," I said, with certainty. "I was trying to get *her* out."

"Who?"

"*Her*," I said, insistent. "Her, me, her."

"*Oh.* I see," Sunny said in my ear. "All you're afraid of, darling, is you."

6

Washed Out

In the morning, outside my door, an inch of stagnant water licked the legs of a brown card table. Atop the table was a large navy blue raincoat, folded up. I didn't need to eye the label sewn into the inside pocket to know where it had come from, but I checked anyway. The lettering was weathered, but I could just make it out: *Killian Bane*. Mary had marked all his clothes this way years earlier. I donned the jacket and crutched to the dining area in the rain boots: my own left behind in my Bandra flat. I was piecing my world together, like the war veteran Killian had once played in that nixed pilot.

Everyone was gathered at breakfast, in the same thatch-roofed area where the banquet was held the night before. All wore white. I counted—numbers came more easily today— fifteen people.

I chose the table with Mireille and Reema. Members of the *inner circle*, I remembered. Without comment, Mireille stood, filled a plate with two flaky dosas and a bowl of sambar, and smacked it down in front of me.

"Eat," she said, in her surly manner.

"Is there coffee?"

There came a sharp, shared intake of breath.

"There's nothing caffeinated here," Reema whispered.

My eyes went out of focus before fastening onto something I hadn't seen in the daylight yet: the A-frame cottage peeking out of the trees. Someone in white was scrubbing the windows, their back to us. *Bollywood star*, I remembered, which made me think of Killian. Where was he? I frowned, then drew up the word *manager*—Killian taking a call with his manager; Killian heading to Bombay to meet with a producer. He had restarted his career.

Someone squeezed my shoulder. Sunny was lowering the hood of a clear poncho, which she wore over her white dress. "Kalyan said you would want coffee. I called our local kirana store to get you some Nescafé, but Vikram, our deliveryman, says the roads are completely washed out. At least that's what he managed to tell me before the line cut."

"We're *stranded*?"

A bout of merry, untroubled laughter, all around me.

"You've lost your monsoon hardiness," Sunny said, mock-reproving. "It's standard flooding. A tree might have come down, maybe a power line. They'll clear it soon. And don't worry, we have *plenty* of food."

"*Not* that you should be on screens at all," said someone, sitting down across from me. Purple glasses. Medusa hair. Doctor?

"Omna," she said, placing a palm on her chest, speaking slowly. "Remember me? Memory is okay?"

"I don't know," I said. "I don't know what I don't know. I just know I *don't* know things."

"Unknown unknowns. Very wise," Sunny said, amiably. "The same could be said for any of us. But Omna is right. Focus on getting better. Nothing to worry about."

The five women flashed five radiant white smiles. I flinched. And then I remembered what I had learned from Sunny the night before—how *I* had tried to hurt myself—and I thought how foolish it was of me, how typical, to fear something so gentle as a group of women smiling.

I smiled back, my mouth moving without me, and for the next few days, I tried to keep my face that way. It was unnatural, at first, like I was imitating someone, and then my expression changed more permanently into one of relatively unthinking cheer. That was how things worked at the Shakti Center, I learned. You pretended for a while until you became what, or who, you'd imagined yourself to be.

The roads weren't clear the next day, or the next, or the one after that. Rain continued to batter the mountain, and water pooled at ankle level. If the rest of the area looked like this, or worse—landslides or mudslides; felled trees and smashed power lines—it made sense that nothing could reach us.

No reason to worry, according to one of the guests I spoke to in passing, a coiffed South Bombay woman who was there with her husband, seeking counseling before committing to IVF. We, she said, were lucky. We were safe. Zoya, a woman in the inner circle who ran the kitchen, had thought to freeze some veg. Things were sustainable. The lack of consistent electricity and fresh sabzis was mere inconvenience. The hotel was also built into an incline, so our water could drain off. The structures were sturdy, responsibly constructed, on slabs of concrete that kept the water from seeping indoors.

As three days turned into four, then five, I rested in my dark room, popping painkillers for the nasty headaches that hadn't stopped. Kali the cat nestled into my side. People visited me in my suite, people whose names I could not always remember; they asked me friendly questions about my family and my work at Yale. I kept writing by hand, though I struggled to read back my own words, let alone any of the books I'd brought. Omna said that I would recover from the concussion, despite its severity; all I could do was wait myself out.

I tried to assemble a picture of the Shakti Center, setting everything down when I could, quizzing myself on basic facts every morning to test my short-term memory. I learned that the whole place had been a four-star eco-resort before Sunny purchased it with her savings from a prior business career (she'd been some sort of HR consultant); the owners had gone bankrupt and she'd bought it for a song. I learned that the inner circle affectionately called the compound not the Shakti Center but the God Complex—the GC for short.

I tracked routines. In the mornings, everyone breakfasted in the thatched area. Afterward, people peeled off, organized by their wristbands. Mireille and Reema and the team— green bracelets: *ideators*—busied themselves with business meetings, as well as with the day-to-day tasks of running the place. Reema and Zoya oversaw the kitchen, while Mireille and a woman called Evangeline managed cleaning and laundry. They were assisted by guests who signed up for work shifts at the start of each week. Most of the guests' wristbands were blue—*receivers*—and everyone in the inner circle except Mireille sported a blue bracelet, in addition to their green ones. Receivers hoped to become parents. They met with Omna for consults or with Sunny for counseling in her office; when the roads were cleared, they'd go to Pune for procedures at the larger fertility clinic. Some couples were struggling to conceive and sought emotional, spiritual, and medical advice. Some single people were freezing eggs. Only Mireille sported a pink *helper* bracelet, which she wore beneath her green one; she, I learned, was willing to donate her eggs or become a surrogate, not actively trying to have her own children.

I was not allowed to help with anything, nor was I given a wristband. My only role, Sunny said, was to recuperate.

Though I ate most meals with the inner circle—save Sunny, who spent most of her time out of view, in her private office or suite—they were sometimes called away to meetings, and I was left with guests. I met an American couple, a white woman named Bree and her husband Ravi, who had come in search of support on their "fertility journey"—after three IVF cycles, Ravi wanted to quit, while Bree wanted to double down, possibly using an egg donor, a sperm donor, or both. They were inquisitive, asking me more questions than I liked about how I'd come to be there. I also spent some time with one of the egg-freezing women, Ionie, a Jamaican British investment banker on "garden leave" between finance gigs; she had arrived about a week before me for the soft launch. Like the other guests, she'd heard of Sunny through whisper networks and had DMed her enthusiastically until she was invited to join. She mentioned that she had at first been given the wrong number, through the grapevine, and spent a while texting someone who was not Sunny at all. That this story rang familiar did not help me place it.

Ionie wasn't certain she wanted children, but believed in covering her bases. Egg freezing was a matter of practicality. "Until you try to use them, you've got, like, Schrödinger's eggs," she said one morning, shoveling tofu scramble into her mouth. "You know—they could be good or bad, and you'd never figure it out till you open yourself up to check. That's what's so *strange* about being young, don't you think? We spend our twenties feeling infinite and invulnerable and then, *bam*, you're finite, and your body is *so* vulnerable."

Ionie and I had been chatting freely when Mireille wafted by in her wraithlike fashion, and Ionie suddenly lowered her voice.

"So, did you grow up in London?" I asked.

"Shh," Ionie said. "We're actually not meant to talk much about our pasts here, outside of structured contexts. I didn't think they cared that much about it, but that French girl is a bit weird. Hey, I'm off. I've got a session with Sanjena— Sunny, sorry."

The *structured contexts* in which the past arose seemed to be the womb room regressions and the meetings with Sunny in her lair, which was situated up a winding, roped-off wooden staircase that led to something called the Treehouse Tier. Only Sunny and "Kaylan" stayed in the Treehouse Tier, it was said. I had not had any occasion to go up there, both because I wasn't in therapy and because my ankle and crutches made the staircase inaccessible.

I never mentioned outright that I was "Kalyan's" ex, here to divorce him, but at some point, word got out, despite the rules about the past. Guests began to give me a wide berth, as though they had been instructed to leave me alone. I was surprised to find myself stung. I had liked the brief, pleasant buzz around me—feeling as though I mattered.

On long, wet afternoons, I found myself wobbling into the womb regression room. It was the darkest space at the Shakti Center, and my headaches were eased there. I'd clamber into the pink cavern, wait for Sunny's voice to flip on, wait to be soothed. Each time, I was plunged into some visualization that, like a dream, was an anagram of real and unreal, things I'd lived and things I imagined. Yet unlike in a normal dream, I always had the sense that what I was seeing was fundamentally *true*, as though even if it had not happened literally, frame by frame, the way I was experiencing it, it had *happened*, or was *going to happen*, in some other quantum universe.

The specifics of those visualizations are now difficult to conjure up. I recall the part of the recording in which Sunny's voice instructed the listener to recast an old memory with new wisdom, to see one's child self as a mother, and one's mother as a child in need of compassion. Obediently, I drew up pictures of my mother, each time in a new, more tender light. *She did not know any more than you do*, I thought. I saw Killian, too, and he transformed in my mind until his presence seemed to loosen, cloud, and then disappear. *He desired what you could not give him*, I thought. I watched old resentments unlatch from me. It was intoxicating to retell myself to myself. When I emerged into the daylight after a session in the womb room, I felt purified.

This transformation was uneven. Every so often, as I curled into the blanket in the womb room, a flicker of my old self would appear, a phantom me. I blinked hard when she appeared, tried to shove her away. I did not want her back, that sour, mean woman.

There was one night, perhaps six days into my stay at the God Complex, when she accidentally reemerged. It happened because I tottered over to the womb room in the afternoon and found it occupied; a sign hung on the door that read (I managed to parse the lettering) *Meditation in Session: Please Come Back Later*. In the early evening, it was in use once more. At eleven p.m., it was still locked. I became annoyed. I'd spent the day without a single headache, and had been able to not only write but also read what I'd written. I was feeling better—and this *concerned* me. I had begun to fear reverting to who I'd been. I feared being possessed, once more, by whatever *me* had slammed my head over and over into a rock.

At a loss, I crutched out to the hallway. The rain had stopped for a spell. I was moved to try something. I had seen Sunny, Omna, and other members of the inner circle carry around keys on little leather shoelaces. Perhaps Sunny kept those keys in her office—in the Treehouse Tier. I still hadn't been up those winding stairs, but my ankle was now on the mend. Emboldened, I made my way to the foot of the staircase, leaned the crutches against the banister, reached into the pocket of Killian's raincoat, and pulled out a headlamp Reema had given me. I donned it, did one of Dharma's Kegels for courage, and took a hesitant step on my left foot, then my right. There was a twinge, but no shooting pain. I took another step. And another. The stairs were slick. Up I went, into the foliage, where all was mist, the stars obscured by silvery clouds.

The staircase looped to several landings, nestled in the trees and branching off to glass boxes in the sky. To the right of the first landing was Sunny's office. It was dark, and the blinds were drawn. It was also locked. Around me, the whirring chorus of insects twittered. And then, just as I took a step down the stairs, away from the office, I spotted something beneath me: a Coleman lantern, gripped by a skeletal figure I recognized as Mireille. The lantern bobbled; Mireille was coming up the stairs. *Following me?* On instinct, I began to run as fast as my ankle would allow—up, not down, away from Mireille.

Below me, the lantern was still rising. There was nowhere else to go. Operating on some deep instinct that told me to avoid Mireille at all costs, I ducked, soundlessly, inside the unlocked room at the top of the stairs.

It was a suite: wide, sparsely furnished, with high rafters, a wooden armoire, and an egg chair wedged against one of two windowed walls. In the moonlight, I spied a balcony overlooking the resort. There was someone sleeping on the bed. A body—tall, pale, with a mop of black hair streaked with white.

I clapped my hands to my mouth and took a horrified step toward the figure—Killian—

But of course, it was not Killian. It was a white duvet, flung off by Sunny, who was dozing with her back to me, orange earplugs in her ears, a pink satin sleeping mask over her eyes; the linens were piled like a lover spooning her. Atop the duvet, Kali curled into the headboard, dozing, one paw on her nose. I was still catching my breath when I saw, through the corner of my eye, that lantern continuing to rise through the trees.

I dropped under the bed and waited with bated breath. It was possible that Mireille had not seen me. I was not wearing the white kaftan that day, but some of my own clothing— black palazzos and a black tank top, other items that I'd left in Bombay, and that Killian and Sunny had apparently brought to the compound; I might have blended into the night. I waited, and waited, and then Mireille's footsteps were on the landing outside Sunny and Killian's suite.

"Sanjana," came Mireille's throaty, twisty voice. "Sanjana, you've gone where you should not be."

Above me, the mattress and slats creaked. Sunny, turning over.

I could not understand why Mireille was not entering, why she had not already flung the door open and hauled me out from under the bed. The only explanation I could think of was that no one was supposed to be in Sunny and Killian's room—not me, not even Mireille.

"Hey!" Mireille cried suddenly. "Get off of me! Stupid creature!"

A yowling, and then Mireille was running down the steps. I must have not shut the door completely; Kali had bounded outside and frightened Mireille away.

The bed groaned.

"Hello?" Sunny whispered into the darkness.

A pair of feet. Standing, walking to the door.

"Mireille?" Sunny called from her landing.

No one replied.

"So fucking *clingy*," Sunny muttered to herself. She began to tug the door shut, but there came a scratching on it—Kali trying to squeeze back through. "Oh, hello, darling," Sunny cooed. "You've been neglecting me, haven't you? For the Other one." She scooped Kali up, and I held my breath, certain Sunny would see me, but she didn't. "Oh, little princess, little goddess, little monster." Holding a purring Kali, she kept murmuring barbs and endearments.

Sunny lay down again. The bed slats juddered. I heard the sound of fluffy linen flapping over her.

I held completely still. I waited as Sunny's breath slowed and deepened—perhaps in her sleep, whispering things that might have been another language. When I heard snoring, I stood, as silently as I could.

You never see yourself sleeping, of course. Never know how vulnerable you look that way. Sunny's mouth was parted like she had just been kissed. Her breasts were gathered between her elbows. She lay right in the middle of the mattress, on her back. That struck me as bold: it had taken me months, even after my breakup with Killian, to occupy the center of a bed rather than my prescribed side. She had adjusted to his brief absence rather quickly.

Then I noticed something else. She wasn't wearing the usual kaftan, but instead, a blue T-shirt with white font. I'd seen that shirt many times: it was mine. It had come in the welcome package at grad school orientation, but I'd never worn it, because I preferred not to sport the name of a university on my chest. She shifted, rolling onto her stomach, then back to her side.

The movement nudged Kali, who stretched, clawing lightly at the headboard. Her yellow eyes surveyed Sunny and then me, as though she were trying to decide which of us deserved her. She pounced onto the hardwood, rubbed against my shins, and scampered to the doorway, urging me downstairs.

I paused on the landing, craving one last glance at Sunny before rushing after Kali into the cool night.

7

Mirror Stage

The next day, I found a piece of paper taped to the inside of my door, below the peephole. I could read the note with minimal headache. It said:

> *Would you join me before breakfast*
> *in my office? —S*

Someone with a key had helped themselves to my space, and they wanted me to know it. I was annoyed, until I remembered the way I'd stolen around last night.

Outside, a sliver of precious sunlight cracked through the clouds. The other guests and the inner circle were gathered at breakfast, and glanced at me inquiringly as I limped toward the stairs. I didn't meet anyone's eyes.

Sunny was in her office, cross-legged on a floor cushion, wearing her usual shapeless white kaftan and a toothy, knowing smile. Her hands cradled her belly. I knew from talk at meals that she was into her second trimester—about as far along as I'd been, before the abortion.

She gestured to the floor, inviting me to sit. I did as I was told. She had this way of conducting you with a flick of the hand; she never had to raise her voice.

"You found the place."

I fidgeted, trying to arrange myself comfortably on the pillow. "Yeah." I decided to cop to it. "I, uh. I came looking for you last night."

"Did you," Sunny said, her voice impassive.

"Did, um—did Mireille tell you?"

Sunny raised an eyebrow. "Mireille did not tell me anything," she said. "She is struggling with boundaries of late. She will be spending some time in the east wing. Dealing with a little *mold* problem we have there." Sunny waggled her eyebrows as though we were sharing an inside joke. "Anyway, I would not take her all that seriously on the subject of *you*. She is not your biggest fan."

"I've noticed."

"She finds our situation unhealthy," Sunny said, rising from her cushion and prancing over to her desk, where she began rustling through papers. "Tea, I think," she said. "Tea, yes."

She turned her back to me and opened one of the blue plastic water bottles behind her desk. She filled an electric kettle and then pulled a mahogany box from a drawer, extracting a handful of dark tea leaves—at least, that's what I thought they were. They were brownish and stringy.

While the water boiled, she dropped the tea into a teapot next to two black ceramic mugs, which were set out on a cane tray. As she worked, the sleeves of her kaftan slid, slightly. I noticed that she did not wear a wristband like the others.

"She thinks it is *strange*," Sunny went on, still talking about Mireille. She said *strange* with disdain, as my mother might have. "*Strange* that I am getting along so well with my partner's ex. His *wife*. *Strange* that you have been here over a week now. *Strange* that I have tried to host you well. She is not Kalyan's biggest fan, either, I will add."

"It *is* strange," I said. "To be fair. And Killian . . ." I swallowed. I had been on the verge of saying something biting about Killian, but I stopped myself. I did not feel much rage toward him now. After my week in the womb room, he was slipping from me, and my anger was dissolving.

Sunny hummed as the tea steeped. The melody sounded familiar, like an old bhajan I had heard during my childhood.

"*Kalyan*," she said pensively, interrupting herself. "I feel no animosity toward you, Sanjana, because I understand how you must feel toward Kalyan. Anyone would understand why you left him. From what I understand, he was unkind to you, especially near the end. I am not excusing the behavior, but I will tell you, Sanjana, that he regrets it. He is different these days."

She started humming again. I had the sense that she was using the song to count the time the tea needed to steep. When it was done, she served me ceremonially, setting the cane tray in front of me.

"Please," she said, and I took a sip. The room was cold— she'd left a window cracked, and the brief sunlight that had been warming the compound as I walked to her office had gone. Outside, gray clouds were roiling, wind was whipping, a storm brewing. I shivered. The tea was bitter, but warm.

"No, Sanjana, Mireille did not tell me anything about you," Sunny was saying. "No—*I* saw you last night. I *felt* you. In my room. Watching me."

I lowered my cup, mortified, prepared to apologize.

The perennial, almost laconic grin that Sunny usually wore was gone. It was as though a mask had slipped. It had happened the night I'd first met her, too, in the instant after I mixed her up with me. She was me, and then, violently, she was not; she was another kind of being, inhuman, passing for me. I inched away, my pillow curling at the edges, and hot tea splashed onto my shin. Then I blinked and she was back wearing my face, only more tender.

I thought of seeing that vision of Killian on the bed next to Sunny—how real it had been. If anyone was *strange*, it was me. I had tried to mortally wound myself. I was seeing things that were not real; my mind was conspiring against me.

"I—" I stuttered. "I'm sorry."

"Anyone else here, Sanjana, would immediately be asked to leave. But you are more than forgiven," she said, her voice dulcet again. "You were curious. For a week, you have been occupied with your own recovery. As you began to improve, you felt, 'I must know what Sunny, the Other, is up to.' You felt, 'She is not telling me everything,'" Sunny said huskily. She took a long drag from her own black mug. "So. What questions do you have for me?"

I drank, too. My head was starting to ache. I clenched my jaw, trying to focus. *Questions*—I had plenty. Rain began to pelt the glass. Sunny went to shut the cracked window. The sound of the storm muffled, and the rain sounded like a drum line pounding a faraway, militaristic, warmongering beat. *Questions*—what had Sunny and Killian been up to over the past year? Why had she pretended to be me to Mary? Had she or Killian mailed that letter to my mother? Why? What was happening with the road clearances? Why was Sunny sleeping in my shirt? When was Killian coming back? Would he grant me the divorce with no trouble? When would I leave? What would I do once I left? It all made my head hurt even more, and made me think of Omna telling me, the morning I woke from my sickness: *Don't* think *so hard*. Thinking hurt.

I swallowed the questions like hot bile.

"What do you do up here?" I asked, surprising myself. "With your clients?"

Sunny flashed a composed smile. A flicker of her too-white teeth; I winced.

"We do something," she said, "called *mirroring*. It's a kind of therapy. I help people who are struggling—with intimacy, with infertility, with their relationships to themselves—get on the same page." She raised one eyebrow. "I don't need to tell *you* how difficult it is, when you and your partner do not … overlap."

"Uh. Yeah. No." I pictured Killian, coming home from his *Touch My Trauma* workshop, reporting with that fervent new glimmer in his eyes that he had been *changed*: he was now in possession of new knowledge—parenthood as purpose!—and all he wanted was for me to see it, too. I thought of how, at Moksha Living, he seemed to always be scanning my face for signs of change, for proof that I was finally crossing over into his reality. I thought of how it had felt all year to know that I had been unable to meet him in that other realm. Perhaps I was too cold, too insistent on my own selfhood, to share a picture of the world with someone else.

"Oh," I said. "So, it's just for couples."

"No, not at all," she said. "Anyone can mirror you. Anyone can help you see yourself. It's especially important for couples to be on the same page, but all of us need to feel that we *can* be understood. Reema, on our team? She's pursuing single motherhood, so she mirrors with someone else who's also in her position, like Ionie, your new friend, the one freezing her eggs. Or I mirror with them. I more than know what they're going through. Why do you ask?" There was a canny upturn in her voice.

I glanced down at the tea and I did think—I *know* I thought, for a moment—*What's in this?* But I watched Sunny sip her own and I thought, *Don't be stupid, it's only tea.* I sat, downing the now lukewarm drink, failing to respond to Sunny—why *did* I ask? I couldn't stop thinking about all the things I'd been unable to see in Killian's reality—the things I couldn't quite grasp about my friends' evolving worlds. What made them want to change? What drew all these people to the other realm, the next stage of prescribed adult-hood, while I was being left behind?

I remembered standing before Rivka, beneath the banyan tree at Moksha Living, hoping she would reveal the source of her faith. I recalled all those women who told me that they had been transmuted, from the inside out, in a manner that defied language, how they had nearly drowned in the overpowering waves of their desire. When I was pregnant, I had waited to be changed. I was waiting for G. Waiting and waiting for purpose to set in. My whole life, I had been waiting for my life to begin.

I said: "Can I … can you … me? I mean, can you help *me*?"

"Help you … ?" Sunny asked.

"Change," I said, choking slightly on the word.

"Oh, darling," she said, doubtfully. "I wonder if that's ethical. To do anything therapeutic with you. With our unique relationship, you know, Kalyan and everything."

"Please," I said.

I pictured myself banging my head against the rock until I knocked myself out. I could not be trusted with myself. "I want to be someone else," I said.

"No. Not someone else. A better you," Sunny said, her dark, secretive eyes catching a spark. "You feel, 'I might be consumed by emptiness if I do not meet her.'"

…

"So," Sunny said, after we had arranged ourselves on two cushions, "I am your mirror." She chuckled. "The irony."

She raised her palms and indicated that I should do the same, but I flinched.

"Would it help you to know a bit more about the exercise?" She lowered her hands and folded them in her lap, brushing her belly once more. I nodded. "I warn you. It is *strange*. It is not for everyone."

This drew up in me an oddly defiant hope: I *wanted* something strange to work on me, for once.

Sunny adjusted herself. Her knee bumped against her black mug, and a bit of liquid sloshed over its lip. My own mug was empty.

I gulped. The headache was worsening, and I was starting to feel nauseated now, too.

"The truth is that I developed this practice with *you* in mind."

She waited to see if I would balk. I didn't.

"*Me?*" I pressed my hands to my stomach, trying to suppress the urge to vomit. My migraines of late had been accompanied by this vertiginous sensation, and the world skewed into Hitchcockian angles.

"Yes," she said. "Kalyan and I met in Goa, last year. You two had *just* split up. He was mourning you. He kept saying he wanted to understand why you hadn't been able to see eye to eye. How you could have diverged so violently."

I was surprised to find that this moved me. For the past year, I had imagined Killian's silent anger as a sort of protest, picturing him stubborn and unmoving. Somehow I had not imagined that he had spent any time trying to understand me.

"So," she went on. "I thought perhaps he and I should try to … channel you. In a way."

"Channel me," I echoed.

"I'm alarming you."

"No, no," I said. "Just . . . what do you mean?"

"Well. I told him I would be you. Like a role-play. He was, after all, an actor. I cast myself as you. It was not difficult. Not just because of our likenesses. You were easy for me to play. I could understand why you didn't want children with him. Or why you might not want them at all."

Her voice was growing more rapid and my vision was going kaleidoscopic, the storm outside escalating in intensity and my nausea rising. Sunny's voice reached me the way it did in the womb room—from afar, a god-voice. "*I* was uninterested in children for a long time. I did not trust my own ex-husband. I had the sense that he was . . . how shall I put it? Using children as a heuristic for meaning, and commitment. We had problems, and he believed we could solve them all with the creation of another human being. It struck me as irresponsible. Kalyan did the same to you. *Many* of us do that to our partners, Sanjana, and to ourselves.

"In Kalyan's defense, it is hard to give voice to these deep desires. And purpose, true purpose, is prelinguistic. It is pre-cognitive. It lives in the marrow, you see?"

I thought of my mother saying, *duty*. Saying, *You don't have to go on and on talking*. My mother, and her belief in a patterned life.

She continued: "So, we mirrored, several times, and our relationship evolved from friendship into a partnership born of mutual respect. And, Sanjana . . . I felt during those sessions that you, or my idea of you, or Kalyan's idea of you, *possessed me*. That is the only way I can describe it. I felt so close to you, Sanjana. I did things *as* you. I spoke to your landlady as you, I wore your clothing, I read your journals, I admit it. I have a vague memory of mailing a letter you wrote your mother. I talked to Mary, as you know. I believe that I was not being cruel, or at least not intentionally. I was simply consumed with the act of playing you, consumed by the role, as Kalyan put it. It *is* strange, but it is a strangeness born of love. Ask Kalyan: to inhabit a role, one must love one's character, in a way."

"Oh," I said. I raised my knees up and pressed my forehead to them. As far as I knew, Sunny was watching me, but she did not seem concerned by my physical discomfort. The things she was saying—*possessed* by me?—did not perturb me as they should have. I understood this otherworldly logic; my disbelief was suspended. "Yes," I agreed.

"Are you feeling a little sick?" Sunny whispered. Her fingers were in my hair, squeezing my temples. And my migraine lessened, as though she had taken it on her fingers.

"Yes," I said.

"Do you want to throw up?" she asked.

"Yes," I said.

"Here," she said, and a small aluminum bucket was in front of me.

I retched. Her hands remained on my back. First the heaves were dry, and then it splattered out of me—the tea I'd drunk, the khichdi I'd eaten the night before, a lump of partially digested brown rice and lentils, chunks of orange carrot, a sliver of green bean.

"The tea," I said. "The tea made me sick."

"No," Sunny said forcefully. "You think, 'The world has made me sick.' You think, 'I am worldsick.' You must think, Sanjana, '*I* make myself sick.' You must think, '*I* can heal myself.'"

A moment later, her smile filled my entire vision. "Or," she said, "*I* can heal you. Because, Sanjana, I am your mirror. I was you. I am you."

8

Crack an Egg on Your Head

The monsoon's ferocious slough abated, and though it still rained in violent bursts as late June slid into early July, the sun came more often, and cheekily. A jackal's wedding, my mother used to call those paradoxical days of sunshine and wetness, when the weather is both and neither, when the earth smells freshly tended, the soil loamy and moist.

I somnambulated through those days, time occasionally punctuated by an awareness of the outside world. News arrived that the roads were being tended to; trees cleared and power lines lifted. Service and wi-fi remained elusive, but anyone who wanted the internet could go to Pune with Vikram, the deliveryman. Personally, I wanted for nothing. Screens still made my head ache. Plus, I remembered too well what waited for me beyond the God Complex: nothing and no one. (Did Sunny say, at some point, *You will not look beyond this place*, or was that my own voice ordering me as much?) Even for the other guests, phones and screens were discouraged, as they made one less *present*. Sunny—an influencer, after all—was the exception; she had to be documented as she moved through her day. Someone was always tailing her with a camera, snapping photos that were later posted from a café in town. Sunny holding a pink lotus flower in her hand, offering it to her followers. Sunny with her arm around a client, in a posture of intense intimacy and confidence. All of us, our hands linked, blue bracelets nudging each other, looking over the lagoon, heads tilted up to the sky.

Sunny communicated with Killian on my behalf; he had left the country to shoot a film abroad, a Bollywood remake of *Dirty Dancing: Havana Nights* whose title translated roughly to *The Heart Wants to Sway in the Mountains*. It followed a wealthy Delhi girl traveling in Switzerland who falls in love with a half-Indian dance instructor, played by the man who had taken the stage name Kalyan Babar. He was contractually obligated, having signed on months ago, and unfortunately, since he'd been kept from the compound during the rains, he'd had to fly straight from Bombay. I did not ask to speak to him myself. Sunny assured me that he was looking forward to "wrapping up" our marriage when he returned, and this explanation sufficed. Hearing about the world beyond was like hearing about the plot of a novel I had never read.

Though my days were easy, I did not sleep peacefully. As I tossed and turned, I often felt eyes on me, the sensation of being examined. I would wake, certain that someone had been—was still—in my room, breathing on my face and my neck, but it was only ever Kali, who liked to prowl around my head in the middle of the night, scratching at the bed-post. Reema had named her correctly; she was destructive. Once, I rose in the night to find her decapitating a tiny mouse. She lifted her head to me and seemed to smile, her cat fangs drenched in blood. I shrieked, hid under the quilt. In the morning I got up, prepared to find a dead rodent on my floor. There was nothing there, but the floor was wet, as though someone had come in to clean it up. I kept a notebook by my bed, in which I tried to jot down my dreams, but whenever I began to put language to what I'd seen, clarity escaped me. The nightmares transformed into dark geometries. Another set of logics pressing on mine, trying to break through, but kept at bay.

In the daylight, if I looked shaken, someone in the inner circle—Mireille (relieved from her job scrubbing mold) or Reema—would come escort me to the womb room, or offer me a massage or some tea, and I would calm, shaking off the vise grip of the night. Sunny often summoned me if she had no other clients, and in her office, we talked long hours, as friends rather than therapist and client. Twice more, we drank the tea I now knew was infused with a mild psychedelic that helped (Sunny said) plummet one into one's deeper self, and we mirrored.

It was much like it had been that first, dreamlike time, which I still recall in fits and snatches: Sunny's palms kissing mine; her body the same temperature as mine. I remember that she asked me to describe my future, and I remember that the act of trying to speak about who I might one day be made me sick again, and I threw up more. I remember the sensation of inevitability I always felt in her company: biological, historical destiny, subsuming me; the relief of being told what I was *for*. I remember feeling it—that thing Sunny promised was pouring from her fingertips into me. I remember her saying, *I will choose to bring life into the world.* I remember saying, *Mirror*. Over and over again. I remember lying on the floor of Sunny's office, coming to. That first time, I'd lifted myself from the trip to find a blue band on my wrist, with an *R* on it. *Receiver*. The bracelet for intended parents, which I saw no need to remove. Indeed, after two more sessions, it seemed terribly natural, like I had always worn it.

I came to especially crave Sunny's touch at the end of those mirroring sessions, when she brushed my head, my back, the pressure points on my feet. Her gestures made me think of childhood sleepovers. My favorite part always came when those circles of girls stroked my shoulders and French braided my hair and intoned, *Crack an egg on your head, let the yolk run down*, and ran their hands along my scalp and spine, raising little goose bumps along my skin. More than once I'd lain awake after having an "egg" cracked on my head, feeling I was attracted to some of those girls individually, but even more, I was lusty for the collective, the mass, the way their voices chorused together so you couldn't distinguish one from another. I wanted my limbs and hair tangled in theirs. I wanted to feel the brush of their fingertips, to be enraptured in the cocoon of their attention. At some point, I had stopped speaking the language of those sleepover girls. They formed their own *we*s. Elsa and her gaggle of white art girls, ironically smoking cigarettes. Lia and her GirlBosses, swearing allegiance to one another as they battled corporate masculinity. Maneesha and her desi gal pals, dancing to Bollywood hits at each other's sangeets. The buzz of other women understanding each other; me, failing to hear their secret language. But now I belonged to a *we*—me, and my Other.

The day after our second mirroring session, as Sunny and I descended the treehouse stairs, I saw, beyond her billowing kaftan, the front gate of the Shakti Center, and beyond that, the road I had taken to get to the compound. A red bus, its roof peopled with young men, zoomed downhill. The roads were open. I remember an awareness that my life was branching in two directions. I remember acknowledging that I could leave. Then Sunny turned to me, calling my name, a little bell of welcome ringing in her voice: "Sanjana, aren't you coming?" and I trailed after her in the waning daylight, overtaken by a vision of my many possible selves assembled like dryads in the phosphorescent green forests. I skipped down from the foliage, where I could see everything so clearly, and wandered back toward my room, the gate growing smaller behind me, finally changed into an incontrovertibly new animal.

As midsummer slid by, many of the guests who'd come for the soft launch left, having decided to return to the GC when they were ready for embryo transfer. The ones who stayed on began going into town, at Omna's behest, for appointments and procedures at the big clinic with which the GC partnered.

Something happened about a fortnight after that first mirroring session with Sunny, in mid-July. It was afternoon, and I was dangling a ratty toy over Kali, who was batting it around, when Mireille knocked on my door to tell me I had to move.

I scooped Kali off the floor. She went floppy in my arms and began purring.

Mireille glared. "That cat is confused," she said tersely. "She thinks you're Sanjena."

"I *am* Sanjana," I said.

"Of *course* you are. Please come."

Her expression was acrid. I followed her, holding Kali. I did not know why Mireille did not like me. I understood that she found the situation—me being Killian's wife—distasteful. But that did not account for her overt hostility. Perhaps she disliked that she'd so often been sent to serve as an aide of mine, bringing me chai, or asking what I wanted from the kirana store delivery. Perhaps she was angry with me for getting her in trouble; I had, after all, lured her to Sunny and Killian's room, which led to her castigation, but she never spoke to me about that night, nor I her.

"*Sunny* wants you to move," she said, practically spitting the name Sunny, and beckoned me to follow. "Someone will pack and bring your things. Because of course they will."

"Why do you hate me?" I called after her. She was walking too quickly for me to keep up. My ankle was fine now, but I was still ginger with it.

"I don't hate you. I just think you are overhyped. You know, you don't really look like her," she said. "Your hair is much too curly. And you lack her grace."

"Where are we *going*?" I asked, panting. I was out of shape and the air was thin. Mireille kept tromping on, past the dining area and the lobby, past the winding staircase that led to the Treehouse Tier. We were almost at the front gate when she veered right toward a steep cobblestone path. We were heading for the A-frame cottage.

"Isn't this for the Bollywood star?" I asked.

Mireille snorted. "You are a fool," she said, turning on me viciously. The cobblestones were slippery from the rain. I could have sworn she was about to push me.

Suddenly: "Mireille!" Reema shouted, sternly, clutching my elbow and stabilizing me. "*I* was supposed to escort Sanjana!"

"I was taking initiative," Mireille said mutinously. Her skeletal face angled wistfully downhill.

Reema yanked Mireille up to the cottage, both of them moving briskly, Reema chiding her just out of my earshot.

Then, we arrived at the cottage and Reema, beaming, flung the doors open.

The first thought I had was that it resembled the houses I used to jerk off to on Zillow. It had that craftsman bungalow aesthetic—modern and airy—but was lusher and brighter than the cookie-cutter places you saw in the US. The walls were painted in daisy yellow and aquatic blue, and huge abstract Indian canvases were mounted throughout. The living room was outfitted with a plush orange sofa; a wicker swing topped with pink bolsters dangled from the ceiling. To my left was a small kitchen with an island and two barstools, and past it was a dining table. French doors led to a study with red tile floors and a blue settee and built-in bookshelves with a ladder propped against them. I couldn't make out the spines of the books. I spotted a few Moleskine notebooks on the desk. A ceramic cup held more pens. Outside sat a little garden.

"I had no idea all this was up here," I said. "It's incredible."

"It's yours," Reema said smoothly.

"You still have to go to the main resort for laundry," Mireille said, brusquely.

"Why *me*?" I asked.

"We hear a woman needs a room of her own," Reema said. "You have to write, don't you? Your dissertation?"

"I had a room down there," I said, stupidly. "And—my head. I can't work right now."

"Well, you have all this, for whenever you're ready."

They had already departed when I thought to ask them how long, exactly, they imagined I was staying.

Soon after I moved, Sunny arrived at the cottage to see me. I was poring over a book I'd found on the fully stocked shelf, which I recognized as one I had left in my old Bombay flat: Sarah Blaffer Hrdy's *Mother Nature*, one of my favorite anthro texts. It was still difficult to read for long stretches, but my headaches were diminishing in frequency and intensity. Omna had brought over a colleague from town, a neurologist she called Dr. Tarun, who had examined me with his black medical kit, testing my reflexes and having me squint at an eye chart. He confirmed that I had sustained a severe concussion and that recuperation in the clear mountain air was the best treatment he could prescribe. He added that he knew my *mental troubles* had contributed to the *injury*. "An American doctor would try to shove some horse pill antidepressant down your throat," he'd said, in his posh Oxfordian English. "But the natural world can heal us better than some synthetic chemicals. It's like an old-fashioned sanatorium up here." With a wink, he added, "The rest cure."

Dr. Tarun was right: the air on this mountain did me good. I had plumped up; I was dangerously thin when I arrived, having practically starved myself all year, as though I were seeking revenge against myself for swelling last summer. It helped, too, that I was well cared for. My linens were changed regularly, my clothes pressed, and the whole place cleaned and tidied every other day, though I never saw who was doing the work. The machinations of my new luxury were kept obscured.

"Hello," I said as Sunny rapped on the front door. "Come in!"

I hopped to my feet as she entered.

"Sanjana," she said, sounding grave. "May I come in?"

I said of course she could, and she settled in on the wicker swing.

"Do you want anything to drink?" I asked. "Nimbu pani? Smoothie?"

My fridge was stocked. There was a moka pot for me to make coffee and a full bar in the corner, with liquor and wine—the only booze at the GC, I was told. But I had found myself uninterested in drinking either coffee or alcohol, even discovered that when I tasted a little, both made me sick.

"Nothing for me, thank you," Sunny said, gesturing that I should sit; I sank onto the sofa. "But, well. I have some bad news."

"Oh!" I said. "Do you need the house back? For the actress? I can head out anytime, I mean, I'm not paying."

"Oh," Sunny said. "*The actress.* The funny thing about her is that Kalyan—oh, I might as well call him Killian. Killian was the connection to the actress. Bunny Arora." She smiled wryly, bitterly. "His costar in the dance movie? The one he was going to recruit to come *here*? She, it turns out, is his new girlfriend. It's in all the tabloids."

"Killian is dating Bunny Arora?" Even I had heard of her. She came from an esteemed Bollywood family. "He … *dumped* you?" My eyes fell to her belly. "*Now*, I mean, in your *condition*?"

"A funny thing about Killian," she said. "You were right. About everything. He was a terrible choice—for you, and for me. For us. He didn't really want a child, per se. He wanted something else. Fame, maybe. Power. Purpose. Whatever he wants, anyway, he can buy it now. Thanks to this dance movie, he is quite rich, and his picture is everywhere in Bombay and Delhi, on every hoarding and screen." She snorted. "He says he wants to remain involved with me as a *co-parent*, but that *she's* his soulmate. I've been suspicious for a while, Sanjana. But I was embarrassed to tell you."

"Embarrassed?"

She'd begun pumping her legs, swinging. The chain creaked. "I feared you would find me foolish."

"Of course I don't," I said. "But are you okay?"

"Well. I have an awkward request. It's a tad inappropriate."

"What do you need?"

She sighed. "I'm feeling very, very alone right now. And I wondered if *you* would consider mirroring with *me*. Kalyan—Killian used to do it." She busied herself examining the swing. Her eyes filled and she blinked hurriedly. "Therapeutically, it is perhaps unacceptable, but … see …"

"I do see."

"I knew you would." She dismounted from the swing with a little leap and sat on the rough jute carpet. Her kaftan clouded around her. I joined her there. Our palms touched. My eyelids drooped shut, heavily. Having done this a few times now, I knew the routine.

"What do you see?" I asked.

"I am afraid," she said.

"Mirror," I said. Neon fractals cartwheeled in my mind's eye. "I feel your fear."

She squeezed my palm. "I feel … I feel that I chose wrong."

"How?"

"With … him. K."

"Mirror," I said, emphatically.

"I fear I've made myself the wrong kind of life."

"Mirror."

"But—I was desperate." She was whispering now. "When I met him, you must understand, I was desperate."

"For love?" I asked.

"For the life I wanted for myself," she said. "I was in a hurry for everything to fall into place. I had been waiting. For so long. To finally become who I was meant to be."

"Mirror," I said.

"Because I knew what could happen. To the body. At my age. I'm thirty-nine. The things my clients have been through, Sanjana, you can't imagine. One day you wake up and you are not legible anymore. You are utterly ravaged by a physical need—not rational—a need that may even betray your sense of self. You start to hate everything you did before, every decision you made that led you to who you are now. You realize your past self has trapped your current and future self."

I opened one eye. Her features had gone waxy, frighteningly still.

I did not say *Mirror*. But my mouth was forming that *m*. "You start to lose hope," she rasped. "The medications and surgeries cost thousands of dollars. Your whole body is acne and depression and blood—so much blood. You feel so left behind. You realize that if you want to give yourself what you want, what you wish you didn't want, you'll have to rewrite everything. People tell you that you have a god complex, that all the fertility treatments and the hoping and lighting candles and wishing and praying make you a monster. You should accept the hand you've been dealt. But *you* know that the *only* way to make your life your own life is to have this complex. To be arrogant enough to make a whole new world for yourself. Because if you don't, no one else will. Because that's how it's always been for some people. Certain women."

"Okay," I said. I had heard this before—these things other women had been trying to tell me, to warn me about, for half a decade. I hesitated. "Mirror?" I said, hoping she would not hear my inflection.

"Sanjana," she said.

"You?" I asked. "Or me?"

She was shaking my hands, urgently, and I opened my eyes to find hers locked on me.

"We are the same," she said. "Don't have regrets. You have a choice, now. I don't want you to rue the day you failed to take advantage of your *choices*. You can do what almost no woman in the world has been able to do, in the history of time. You can control your body. I can help you, here. It would cost you nothing."

I shrank from her. My hands slackened in her insistent grip, and I tried to scoot away. My body mounted this last resistance, this final objection. I think that was why she added, "Only if you want. Only if it's what you choose. But I can't *not* tell you—I can't let you make my mistakes. Try to imagine, Sanjana. If you had not spent so much of your life with *him*, with that man. If he had not stolen nearly a decade from you. Who would you be? Is it possible that there is a whole other version of you, out there, who did not marry that *fool*, who did not get pregnant at the *wrong* time, who did not have to fight for her own life? Is it possible that *that* version of you might want *something else*? Might be some*one* else?"

As she spoke, she squeezed my fingers tighter. Her nails dug into my skin. My breath became shorter, panicked, and my vision went spotty.

"*What if,*" she said, "you gave yourself a chance? To let that other you into your life—in two years, in five, in ten—whenever you're ready?"

9

An Immodest Proposal

An egg-freezing cycle begins on the second day of your period and we—I—had been waiting several weeks for mine to start, weeks during which I had become prone to cracking jokes about being a werewolf, dependent on the moon to transform. Which is to say: I had participated in making my impending menses a matter of public concern, the shared body politic of the compound. So it should not have been that surprising that when I emerged from the cottage one morning, having just discovered blood in my underwear, I found the inner circle enclosing me.

Reema held out a little red cupcake. "A big day," she said sweetly.

"Ready, then, are we?" Omna asked. She was wearing a white coat.

My spine went rigid. "How did you know?"

"A lot of people are synced." Reema giggled. "And you ate, like, three brownies at dinner."

"Come along to the clinic now," Omna said.

"Ow." My abdomen convulsed. My periods had always been irregular and unpleasant, and no form of birth control ever eased the experience, not even the hormonal IUD I'd recently sprung for. I reliably bled, cramped, and groused for several days.

"Are you okay, Sanjana?" Omna asked. I grimaced.

"I used to be laid up in bed once a month," Reema said, sympathetically.

"I have … cramps," I said hurriedly, backing into my cottage.

The other women reacted with a start to my sudden movement.

"Why so jumpy, everyone?" Mireille asked, lazily. She was carrying a steel bowl that she apparently had brought up from breakfast. It was full of fruit. Plump imported strawberries and Amrapali mangoes. She shoved a berry in her mouth and flashed a rapacious smile, her teeth stained and pocked with juice and seeds.

"Omna, can I meet you in the clinic in a minute?" I asked.

"Okay, soon," she said grimly. "Given your irregularity, we have to—"

I had already shut the door.

I sat in the bathroom for a long while, feeling *off*. I was in a terrible mood, one I recognized as typical for my period, but there was something else, too: the women's arrival at my front door was rubbing me the wrong way. The freshly laundered towels hanging in my bathroom, which I had not seen anyone bring in, the newly lined trash bin—hadn't I tossed some bloody wadded-up toilet paper the day before?—the scrubbed bathtub porcelain … all these comforts felt, suddenly, like surveillance. The phantom me, the grouchy, scowling me, was reconstituting in my mind, asking, *What are you doing here?* My blood must have brought with it my old negativity, suspicion, and meanness. It made me a bitch again.

I thought I heard voices outside the cottage still, and I wanted to gather myself before everyone tried to escort me down to the clinic. So I took the back exit, through the private garden, and stood gazing up the mountain. Someone was burning trash in the distance, and a coil of smoke lifted above the lurid neon canopy, clearing out waste, making space for something new. I thought of Maneesha telling me, after she and Ajay got married, that she was now expected to have a guest room at the ready for her mother-in-law, all the time. That was family, she said; that was marriage, wifehood, womanhood. You are always a host, keeping yourself and your rooms ready for guests anytime. You make your world around the possibility of someone else arriving to need you, to use you.

I convulsed another blurt of blood. I needed a tampon. I wound around my cottage, onto the empty path, and toward the lobby. Near the kitchen was a small closet where the team stowed toilet paper and linens and cleaning solutions and sanitary pads and off-brand Tampax. I had almost reached that closet when I heard voices in the laundry room. Something about their tone—a husk and hush—made me pause.

"Wash hers separately," someone was saying. Mireille, I thought.

I sidled up to the door, which was propped half open. Two people stood with their backs to me, facing the machines: Mireille and Reema. On the floor was a basket of linens and white kaftans. Mireille was holding a stained piece of fabric. For a moment I clutched my stomach in embarrassment. Had someone stripped my bed and found that I'd stained my sheets like an adolescent?

"Why does she free-bleed like this?" asked Reema.

"Hush," Mireille said. "There are all sorts of benefits. Sanjena always says—"

I stiffened: Had they seen me? I readied my sheepish face. But no one went around the compound saying, *Sanjana always says* about *me*. Mireille meant Sanjena—with an *e*.

"—the pill was awful for her. She thinks it made her ignorant of her fertility."

"Well," Reema whispered. "She won't have to deal with this soon."

"She might. We don't know that it's going to work this cycle. *She's* not that young, either, and you don't know how many Omna and Dr. Joglekar will get," Mireille huffed. "And—"

"Wait," Reema said, pausing.

"What?" Mireille snapped, and then she squeaked a disgusted *eek*. Kali must have followed me from the cottage; she had slipped past me into the laundry room. "Stupid beast," Mireille said. "I hate this cat."

"No, wait," Reema said, and I could hear her stepping nearer.

I ran. The supply closet was too far. I only made it to the clinic.

The door was ajar, as though someone had just gone, and the room itself was empty. Panting, I shut myself in, attempting to make sense of what I had heard. We were all synced up. Sunny—Sanjena—having a period right now. Perhaps those bloodstained sheets I'd seen back in June—the miscarriage— had been hers. Sinking onto Omna's doctor stool, I rested my forehead on the medical bed, which had already been lined with paper. Prepared for me.

The thought made me panic. I rose and began rooting around the room. I needed to orient myself. Then my gaze fell on the metal Godrej cabinet, the one I'd first seen all those weeks ago, the night of my fall. I tugged it. It did not open. I'd seen Omna lock it when we met for an egg-freezing consult; she had recorded my blood pressure, height, weight, last period, and a flurry of other statistics I hadn't paid much attention to, then stowed the forms in a big brown accordion folder, which in turn went into the cabinet.

"Hello?" Someone knocked. The doorknob rattled. "Somebody's in there?"

I ducked behind the door as Omna swung it open. She did not shut it.

Omna tied her hair back, reached for the latex glove dispenser on the wall, and donned a pair. She was humming. From my hiding place, I caught the wink of something silver—the prong of a syringe. Something else, too: next to the sink, one of those shoelaces she and the inner circle carried around, strung with a set of keys. Suddenly her footsteps approached the door—where I was standing. Before I could be exposed, I shoved her into the hallway and—

A disembodied hand in the doorjamb. Its fingers, gray and purple, horribly askew.

"Sanjana!" Omna shouted. "What the fuck?"

In the hallway, she hunched into herself, her features contorted in pain, and then she turned that grotesque expression on me. She dropped her mangled hand, reached for me with the good one. As rapidly as I could, I locked myself in. I ignored her howls, the battering kicks, and turned my attention to the keys she had left by the sink: a few large bronze ones, one medium silver one, and a small gold one.

The silver key opened the cabinet. The gold opened a drawer, inside of which was the large brown accordion folder I'd seen Omna handle.

I hoisted the file out of the drawer. Each section was labeled, in sloping handwriting: *Zoya Ali. Ionie Bailey. Mireille Deveraux. Francine Dubois. Reema Kapadia. Arya and Eknath Sharma. Sanjana Satyananda. Evangeline Varghese. Bree Williams and Ravi Tripathi.*

Beneath the accordion file lay a separate, thick green folder labeled *Sanjena Sathian.*

Her file contained a hundred or more pages. I sifted through them, hypnotized by charts and graphs I couldn't understand, the occasional block of text, and tens of loopy signatures. They were health documents—physicians' charts, consent forms, pamphlets—

from multiple clinics and doctors, over many years. It took all my effort to parse the text; it was the most reading I'd attempted to do since my concussion.

November 15, 2013 | Patient name—Ramaswamy, Sanjena. (Preferred name: Sunny. Maiden name: Sathian.) DOB: 11/11/1979. Marital status: Married.

Is this your first pregnancy? No. (Prev: medical abortion at six weeks, 2004)

Is this pregnancy the result of receiving any procedures to enhance fertility, stimulate hormones, stimulate ovulation, or stimulate egg production or correct menstrual irregularities? No.

January 12, 2014 | Patient name—Ramaswamy, Sanjena. (Preferred name: Sunny. Maiden name: Sathian.) DOB: 11/11/1979. Marital status: Married.

Form B: EARLY PREGNANCY LOSS.

August 15, 2015 | Patient name—Ramaswamy, Sanjena. (Preferred name: Sunny. Maiden name: Sathian.) DOB: 11/11/1979. Marital status: Married.

Request for pregnancy test.

Pregnancy History: Indicate total number of prior pregnancies (not including this one) 2

Number of abortions 1

Number of spontaneous miscarriages 1

Number of pregnancies that resulted in a stillbirth 0

January 1, 2016 | Patient name—Sathian, Sanjena. (Preferred name: Sunny.) DOB: 11/11/1979. Marital status: Separated.

Dilation and Curettage (D&C) Consent Form

I hereby give my consent to Dr. Mark Hill to perform a Dilation and Curettage upon me …

June 5, 2016 | Client name—Sathian, Sanjena. DOB: 11/11/1979. Marital status: Divorced.

Consent for Supplemental Acupuncture for Fertility Treatments

August 8, 2016 | Patient name—Sathian, Sanjena. DOB: 11/11/1979. Marital status: Divorced.

In Vitro Fertilization: Process, Risk, and Consent

Informed Consent for Intracytoplasmic Sperm Injection

And so on. She had taken photos of every form she'd ever filled out in a doctor's office, made a copy of every faxed request for records. She'd jotted notes by hand in meeting after meeting with physicians and nurses and midwives, with chiropractors and homeopaths and Reiki masters. She'd kept eight-week sonograms from four pregnancies, stowed in plastic binder sheets, tenderly, next to the paperwork that declared those pregnancies over. I lost my breath at the sight of it all spelled out this way, in black-and-white. How the losses amassed. I remembered tumbling into her social media posts and discovering the vocabulary of her longing: rainbow babies and baby dust. Next to the frigid language of these forms—*recurrent pregnancy loss* and *unexplained infertility* and *menorrhagia* and *premature ovarian failure* and *blighted ovum*—all those new words made sense; I understood why one would craft another language, when the standard one talked about you this way.

The last pregnancy recorded was in March 2017—over a year earlier. In America. An IVF cycle with donor sperm, her second attempt. She had lost the pregnancy seven days after the transfer.

It was over well before I'd left Killian. Well before she'd come to India. Well before she'd insinuated herself into my life.

I thought of Sunny's voice intoning, in the womb room. The way she insisted memory worked, the way there was always another truth lurking at its edge. You can tell yourself whatever story you want to about yourself. You can tell another person a certain story about herself.

Across from me, a large window overlooked the lagoon; I could see the outline of myself in the glass, filled in hazily with the bombastic green foliage, the blue water, the graying sky. I was wearing the white kaftan, the same one as everyone else, and it flowed around me so that you could not have seen what kind of body it concealed.

I flung the clinic door open. Omna was convulsing on the ground. Blood ran down her knuckles; her face was flushed and furious.

"Sanjana!" she shouted. "What the fuck do you have those for?"

I glanced down at myself. In my left arm, I clutched the sheaf of health records to my chest—the accordion file and Sunny's fat green folder, too. I turned and ran.

It was the first time I'd seen Sunny's room in daylight. I noticed new things: how low the ceiling was, and that the walls needed a fresh coat of paint. There was something ascetic about it, so unlike the plush cottage she'd given me. Her armoire was cracked, and a line of white kaftans was visible through the opening, hanging like a row of dead angels. She was reclining in bed, with a heating pad over her belly.

Her eyes widened at the sight of me.

"Sanjana," she said, warily.

"Sanjena," I said. "In pain? Cramps? That's not a good sign. At five months along. Is it?"

She bit her lip, pouted. Her mouth was very persuasive. It always had been.

"You and I," I said. "We're synced up. Aren't we?"

She spared no moment for panic. She hoisted herself higher against her teak headboard. It seemed to darken when her dark hair met it. "That first night you saw those bloody sheets ... that was mine. My miscarriage. I didn't tell the other women, either. I felt like a fraud. It's my job to help them get and stay pregnant, and here I am—"

"No," I said. "There's no record of you being pregnant anytime this year."

I dumped the files over her bed. My blue *receiver* bracelet, which had marked me for several weeks now as an *intended parent*, slid down my wrist as I shook the papers out. Her files, and everyone else's, mingled over her legs, a black-and-white quilt of follicles and uterine linings and blood and consent and liability.

Her eyes were steady, but her mouth parted slightly, in shock. Bite marks indented her lower lip.

"Okay." In a dangerously cheery voice, she said, "Should we do some mirroring?"

I recoiled. "What? Now?"

"I want you to understand what I want. And why I want it."

"You want a baby," I said quickly. "And you don't have one."

Her tongue hung at the edge of her smile, little white bubbles of saliva forming and dissipating. She looked hungry, like Beef Jerky considering wet kibble.

"Slow down, Sanjana. Do me that kindness." She closed her eyes, pained, and massaged her stomach. "I did it for you. I took the time to understand you. I let myself be *possessed* by you. And for a month now, haven't I heard you out? I've listened to you regret things other people would kill for. A graduate degree from a prestigious university. A family that wants nothing from you except your presence and attention. A marriage to a handsome actor who loved you so much he wanted *more* of you. A *baby*. You had it all, Sanjana. You *have* it all. And look what you do with it. Look what you do to yourself. Look how you *waste* your life." She spat that last bit, unable now to conceal her loathing.

She breathed deeply. When she spoke again, it was in her normal, calmer tone. "Yes, I want a child. Is that so wrong? Why do you see that fundamental desire as so *base*? Why do you fight it so intensely?"

From the bed, she reached for me. I was over an arm's length away, but I felt myself pulled toward her. Two steps, then three. I stooped, let her palm touch my cheek. It was not exactly sexual, that touch, nor was it maternal. It was something more primordial. What had she said to me, once, about purpose and desire? They preceded language. They lived *in the marrow*. "You want a home. I gave you that. You want something like a family. You want meaning. *I can give you all of that.*"

I was close enough, now, that she could touch my blue bracelet. She rubbed her thumb on the band and smiled wryly at it. "This is not for you." She eased it off my wrist. Then she shifted awkwardly to her hip, and opened her nightstand. She pulled out a pink bracelet, enclosed in a plastic bag. *Pink—helper.* No one at the compound but Mireille had a pink bracelet. Everyone wanted their own babies. No one wanted to give their baby-making bits away. "*This* is for you."

She held it out to me.

"You're not using them," she went on. Her palm stayed flat; the pink ring beamed up at me. Her voice, usually that rich timbre, was rising in pitch. There was a new, fraught whistle in it. "Not right now. Your eggs. You could use some later. Until then, you … pass a few to me. I'm *out*." She closed her eyes. "It's like a grocery list. Mine are all rotten." She broke into cackles. "And you *throw* yours out. Every month, you bleed that life away."

"But your—" I pointed at her belly.

"Doctors have differing opinions on my womb. *Unexplained infertility*, they call it, and wash their hands of me. But Mireille, you know. Mireille's uterus is very good. A happy place. Hospitable. Not *hostile*, like mine. Her cervix is lovely, too. Not *incompetent*, like mine. And Mireille *loves* being pregnant. She's done it twice for other people, been a surrogate. And she loves me. Oh, yes, she does. I wish she didn't love me exactly the way she does—it's made her *rude* to you, hasn't it? But she's protective. And jealous. She's offered me her egg *and* her womb, many times. She wants to give me a baby. But I didn't want *her*. I wanted *you*."

My hand rose to my throat. It rested there like a choker.

"It's ... my face. You just want my face."

She quailed. "Sanjana. Don't insult me, after all we've been through. It *began* with your face. And your name. And your education and your healthy family. I had looked everywhere. I tried banks of egg donors. There aren't enough South Asian donors, you know, and of the ones I saw, well ... not the quality I sought. I looked at the social media of every brown woman who DMed me, and trust me, there were many. I'm not trying to flatter you; I'm being truthful. No one else made me feel what I wanted to feel. Yes, you're right, no one had my face. None of them could give me a child that would feel like mine. But it's more than *identity* that connects you and me, Sanjana. We're so close. You see that, right? It's as though the universe mixed up a few of our parts."

I pictured a plastic model of the V-shaped female reproductive system sitting inside me. I pictured giving birth and having not a baby burst forth but that plastic model covered in goo and blood, then finally—finally—being outside of me.

"You have the body I need. I have the body you want—the body that is female but can't betray you."

She opened her eyes. They were unfocused and cloudy. They reminded me of my grandmother's in her final days, cataracted and hazy. Ajji had faded like a photograph, her dark brown skin lightening, her black hair ebbing into an ethereal blond.

"One day," she said quietly, "there will be a different world. There will be self-cloning, in vitro gametogenesis, and artificial wombs. We will be able to do this without sex, without romance. But for now, we are all ... gloriously dependent on one another. I need you. We need each other. We *all* need you. Isn't it beautiful, Sanjana?"

In that moment, I did not immediately turn my back on her vision. In fact, the notion, for a swollen second, made sense. The promise of the end of worry, the end of uncertainty. A place in the world, tied to my very biology.

Behind me footsteps crescendoed, as the other women raced up the winding wooden staircase. They stood haloed in the doorway, all in their white kaftans, their heads cocked in unison. They paused, eerily, on the threshold. Kali swiped at their ankles.

"They won't come in unless they're invited," Sunny whispered. "Like vampires."

"Wait," I said. "You said *we*. You said you *all* needed me."

I glanced at the pile of papers I'd dumped over Sunny's bed. I dove for the pages, grabbing at random, scanning headers, tossing charts and consent forms. "None of them," I shouted. "Is anyone here actually pregnant? Was anyone? All those other guests! *They* wanted me! That's why you told them to stay away, that's why people stopped talking to me, and you sent me to that cottage—you were saving me ... for *you*."

"Don't be paranoid," Sunny said coolly, as though disappointed by my loss of composure. "Reema is very much pregnant. Zoya lost hers, a month ago. And the clients, they're fine, or they're going to be fine. But my inner circle—they love me. They want to have my babies. Who will also be their babies. Who could technically be your babies. Our babies."

"They helped you," I said. "They helped you *get* me."

"They helped *invite* you here, yes," she said. "Yes, they gave your number to a few people who wanted mine. Who wanted me. Yes, they toyed with you for a few weeks, to stimulate your interest. Yes, we wanted you to know how it felt to be needed. Yes, perhaps that's *strange*. But they also built you a house with their own hands. They cared for you. They made you a life when you forgot to make one for yourself."

Sunny dropped the pink bracelet onto the sheets next to her. She nudged it toward me.

In my periphery, I could see the other women holding hands on the landing, as though in prayer or protest. All except Omna, whose left hand hung limply. Her fingers jutted out at ugly angles, several clearly broken.

I turned back to the papers, avoiding Sunny's eyes. Sonograms. Pamphlets explaining miscarriage management and selective reduction. Page after page of losses and attempts. An archive of hopes and cravings and regrets. I could save these women, Sunny wanted me to believe, and save myself.

I paused on a piece of thick cream cardstock, tucked into a plastic sheet protector.

At first, I thought I was looking at a marriage certificate—*my* marriage certificate. It was an official document, with raised lettering and colored ink and a stamp. But it wasn't from the state of Connecticut. Hindi ran along the top. The text read:

This is to certify that *Killian Bane* passed away
on *the fourth of July, 2017*.
Attested to in *Goa, India* by his wife,
Sanjana Satyananda.

And there was my signature, the *s*'s slender and cramped, the *a*'s plump and clumsy. Well—not my signature, of course. Just a convincing forgery, written by a certain hand. A hand, I should add, that might have written me a letter, signed it *Killian*, and posted it in February from our Bombay flat.

The part of me that had been straining to be heard that month at the God Complex—the cynic, the skeptic, the selfpreservationist—found her way back into me then. She pulled the film of credulity from my eyes. And as she marshaled her strength and cruelty—the forces that both protected her and also made her lonely—the Sanjana I had been preparing for, the mother in me, the mother who might or might never come to pass, evaporated.

"Did you kill him?" I whispered.

Sunny—Sanjena—craned her neck to see what I was gripping so tensely. "Oh, no!" She laughed. "No, no, it's not what you think—it's actually a funny story!"

"You killed him," I said, with conviction. "You did."

"No, Sanjana. He *wanted* to reinvent himself. I helped him. It was a game—"

"You hit me, too," I said. "The night I fell and got hurt—that was you. You just had to keep me alive, like a specimen. But after I give you my eggs, you'd kill me, too. Wouldn't you?"

Sanjena shuddered. Wetness welled in her eyes; her mouth trembled. A convincing performance of deep offense. "You truly think I am capable of that," she said, quietly. "You think I am a monster. You, and the world."

She lifted herself from the bed. "Sanjana," she said, shuffling toward me. "Please, you know me better than that."

She lunged for me. I know she lunged for me. Surely I wouldn't have thrown myself onto her, closed my hands around her throat, begun to throttle, if she hadn't attacked first. Surely *I* was not the aggressor. Surely she was as dangerous to me as I perceived her to be right then. Surely I was right to trust the terror in my marrow, the voice that told me firmly, for the first time in weeks, that she was *not* me.

I cannot be sure. I just know that the instant I touched her, the other women burst into the suite in a flurry of white. Their arms lifted as they stumbled at me, zombielike. That sight of them—all of them one indistinct mass—sent me fleeing. Sometimes I revisit it all again in a nightmare and am certain I got it wrong. I find a possible truth hiding at the edge of the memory: another story I could have chosen to tell myself, that those women were converging to hold me, not harm me. I don't know. Perhaps it was all a horrible error of misinterpretation, the way the whole of womanhood is a like an optical illusion, defined by the way you squint at it.

As I rushed away, I reached for Kali, to try to take her with me, but she pounced, instead, into Sunny's lap, her severe yellow eyes boring into me. All had been revealed: I was not what she'd thought I was.

10

Your Own Worst Frenemy

Bombay was apocalyptically ashen with smog. As soon as I got off the train at Dadar, I was seized by a fit of coughing. I blew my nose on my kaftan sleeve; my snot was black. I transferred to one of the women's carriages on the intracity to Bandra West. Mahim whipped by, and the Western Suburbs, my former home, came into view. I smelled hot garbage, followed by a blast of salt and sea. I felt the torridness of forty or more women sweating on me, on each other. Ego obliteration; selfhoods sublimated into sweat and snorts and people expectorating out windows, saliva globules landing on shimmering metal tracks where they refracted and glittered like costume jewels.

As we approached my old neighborhood, one woman, wrinkled and leathery, squatting on her haunches, her long gray braid melding with the gray of her sari and the gray of the sky, called out, *Bandra? Bandra?* I nodded, as did a few others. I had forgotten this ritual of the women's car. Together we were pulled to the open doorway, and as the train slowed, some people began to take the stop at a run. I waited. I felt a hand on my lower back, giving me a shove. Someone was trying to make sure I didn't miss my station. It was not violent. It was the kindness of anonymity, a belonging that asks for nothing in return. The world was waiting.

I gathered myself on the platform, watching the blue carriages whistle out of view. I saw, as they departed, a regal and flinty face framed in a barred window: the spitting image of my mother, Frida Kahlo unibrow and all. The woman squinted, folding her features into an expression that undeniably resembled that of my mother right before she spat the word *strange*. Then she was gone. Strangers' shoulders knocked against mine, a pani puri vendor shouted, a child's palm brushed my hip and was tugged away.

After I walked halfway down the mountain with nothing on me, no passport, no phone, no money, after a vehicle carrying tittering schoolchildren picked me up and brought me to Koregaon Park, after I went to a café and borrowed a kindly man's laptop … I discovered several weeks' worth of messages. It took about thirty minutes to plow through them all. My mother had sent an email in early July saying she'd tried me on WhatsApp: Have not heard from you. Would be nice to get an update. Hope the money is enough. Then, a few weeks later, came a strange follow-up: I am seeing on social media that you are doing well, my mother wrote. Good.

Then there was a note from Lia, dated a few weeks after her Join Our Village blast. She said she hadn't seen my letter from June. I'd stuck it to the fridge, but the magnets had all fallen down shortly after I'd left—they were holding up six or seven sonograms—and my note had gotten lost. The housekeeper found it wedged between the fridge and the cabinet while Lia and Gor were in the Hamptons on their babymoon. Which was all to say: She was sorry for the radio silence. Was I okay?

After that note, there had been others from Lia—many, in fact, over the past month.

> Sanj, where are you? Call me?!
>
> Sanjana! I'm worried about you. I found that crazy profile via Tara. WTF are you doing? Is this like performance art? Are you anthro-ing those women or something?
>
> Sanjana, I got your DM, but I don't believe that's you. It didn't sound like you, and all the shit "you" said was fucking weird, so I'm not replying there. I think you need to GET OUT.
>
> If I don't hear from you soon I'm contacting your sister.

I, of course, did not have social media, and I had not looked at a screen in over a month. I opened another tab and searched my own name. I clicked on the second hit: a profile belonging to Sanjana Satyananda. "Sanjana Satyananda" had fourteen followers. Most appeared to be bots. One was my mother. One was Maneesha. One was Beef Jerky. One was Lia.

"Sanjana Satyananda" had been posting semi-regularly for a month. There were photos of her—me, the actual me—in the profile. There I was in meditation in Sunny's office, propped up on an orange pillow. There I was writing, painstakingly, in the red-tiled study of the cottage. There I was with my back to the camera, linking arms with four women, staring out at the lagoon.

This summer has been such a special time to connect with female friends, "I" wrote. There I was twirling beneath the thatched-roof hut, dancing with Reema and Zoya. Saturday night baby fever, "I" wrote.

At this point, my benefactor needed his laptop back. When I asked if he could spare some money for the train to Bombay, where I could pay him back digitally, he considered me with pity.

"I was in a cult once," he said, eyeing my white kaftan. "My advice: get a therapist and a job. And contact your family." He gave me two thousand rupees and said to call it a gift.

I had another email from a name I now knew: *Kalyan Babar*.

> It's K. My new email/stage name. Old email doesn't work, I got hacked—probably by that woman you're with. I'm worried about you. I don't know how she got to you but she's a *stalker.* I haven't had anything to do with her for a long time. Please, when you see this, call me here on my asst's number. Or better yet come see me in person.

He'd written out an address, where I now sat, in an idling auto-rickshaw. I knew the place well: the most famous studio in Bollywood, across from our old flat, a block from the sea. He had been here all along.

A supercilious security guard cracked the gate when my auto arrived. I spoke hesitantly: "Main guest hoon," I said. "Kalyan Babar?"

I was let into the leafy lane. Lush green fronds formed a canopy, shielding the stars from potential gawkers. The scent of dead pomfret baking in the sun at the nearby Chimbai Road fish market cut through the air. Film people dressed in black, wearing headsets and walkie-talkies, hustled down the cobblestone lane, looking harried.

A wiry girl with jaunty buck teeth greeted me warmly as I paid the rickshaw driver.

"Lavanya," she said, extending a hand. "Kalyan Sir's assistant. He has been very worried about you. Please follow me."

She led me to the end of the hallway, opening a door that read *Kalyan Babar*. This was, apparently, Killian's dressing room. The walls were papered with film posters—Killian's favorites. *Children of Men. A Clockwork Orange. Pierrot le Fou.* Directly across from me was a nearly life-size image of Killian and the woman I recognized as Bunny Arora dancing in the Swiss countryside. So, Killian had indeed done the *Dirty Dancing: Havana Nights* remake. "Kalyan Sir will be out in a moment," Lavanya said, gesturing with an open palm to a green couch and excusing herself.

I was examining the blown-up "Kalyan," who was dipping Bunny Arora with a seductive flourish, when I heard a flush, a tap running, and I saw Killian Bane, my husband, emerge from a bathroom. He was shirtless, still pale as a bone, wearing athleisure shorts. He had bulked up; there was more of him than there had been the last time I'd seen him, in seated meditation on a Goan beach. The world had fed him.

"*Kalyan*," I said.

"Jesus Christ," he said, enveloping me in a hug. He smelled the way he used to: woody and masculine, like a wet forest. "We were all so worried about you."

I pulled away, embarrassed to be touched. "We?" I pointed to his shiny new movie poster. "You mean you and Bunny?"

Killian's face cracked into a grin. "That was a tabloid rumor. You think Bunny Arora would go for *me*? Hey. Do you, um. Do you maybe want some new clothes?"

I glanced down at my kaftan. I had bled right through it.

Killian and I sat in his dressing room nursing cold coffees from the studio canteen. I had cleaned up and donned some clothing Lavanya scrounged from the costume department. She seemed to take a sadistic pleasure in the options she'd provided me: stuff worn by a middle-aged actress known for playing old maids and sassy aunties. A pair of drawstring palazzos and an oversize Fabindia tunic; the brown woman's Eileen Fisher. Killian had also covered up, and now sported a large black T-shirt that read *The Future of India Is Female.*

"New look," I observed, settling myself onto one end of the couch, while he took the other. It was strange to be so near him after all this time, and to be seized with neither affection nor fury, as though everything I had ever felt for him pertained to another epoch.

"I owe you an apology," he said.

"For what, exactly?"

"I made a major error," he said. "In how I related to you."

"Which was?"

"As a womb, first."

"And how should you have related to me?"

"As a clitoris, first," he said.

I tried not to spew my coffee all over the sofa. "Excuse me?"

"Kalyan has been spending a lot of time taking in Yaz," Lavanya, who'd been busying herself cleaning the bathroom mirror, offered.

"Like, the birth control?"

She giggled. "No, no, Yazmin."

"Yazmin who?"

Killian reached for the book on the coffee table between us. From the acclaimed author of *Touch My Trauma*, a second collection of "poems," *Womanspreading*.

"Oh, her," I said.

"I really missed her *thrust*, before," Killian said. "Yaz makes some compelling points about the orgasm gap as the foundational rift between people with penises and people with vaginas. It goes all the way back. She has a poem about her sex ed class, in middle school. How boys were taught about wet dreams and girls were taught about periods." He raised his eyebrows, impressively. "As though men are permitted pleasure and women are allowed only—"

"I understand," I said.

"Oh no," he said, glancing droopily at Lavanya, who was scrubbing the doorframe with a toothbrush, which was definitely not her job. "Was I mansplaining?"

She reddened, delighted to be asked. They were either fucking or about to begin fucking very soon.

"Your intentions are excellent," she said, loyally.

"So," I said. "You're apologizing for trying to get me pregnant?"

"Among other things," he said. "I've spent a lot of time just *listening* this year. Just learning. Just taking up a little less space. It was all part of my process."

"To be reborn as Kalyan Babar, Bollywood star?"

"Well, yes." His mouth sank into a frown, as though he were disappointed by what lay on the other side of his attempt at reparations.

"So," I said. "I have a bunch of questions. Number one, why you aren't dead."

The day I left Goa, Killian Bane enrolled in a guided ayahuasca session on Arambol Beach. He had gone for a run after discovering my absence, hoping an endorphin-and-sweat pump might expunge the wound of being left by his wife. Someone had pressed a flyer for the Mother Drug Journey into his hands. Attending such an event violated the laws of Moksha Living, he knew.

"But," he said, "I was feeling down." He inclined his unkempt black head toward me as if to acknowledge my small contribution to his depressive episode. Lavanya had excused herself to pick up Killian's dry cleaning, leaving us alone. ("She's a very talented playwright, actually—working for me is her side gig," Killian said defensively, in a manner that confirmed their romance.)

The session was led by a giant blond Swede named Jurgen, who began by distributing to all ten participants rather convincing mock-ups of blank Indian death certificates. They wrote in their names and the date. They were about to die. Well—their egos were, anyway. By the end of the session, they would all attest to one another's spiritual deaths.

"Every day we kill off our old selves and every day we can choose to be reborn," Jurgen told them.

There was a moment, while Killian was barfing into a wicker basket, when he looked up to find the looming face of a demon staring down at him. The demon was me … except it wasn't. It was a girl named Sunny, on her own journey to expel the demon that possessed her—the unexplained infertility, the thing without a name.

When they came down, Sunny served as witness to Killian's ego death; he asked her to sign the death certificate as me. Jurgen then instructed everyone to choose new names. Killian chose Kalyan. Somewhere in this very dressing room was a birth certificate commemorating the arrival of a brand-new baby boy, Kalyan Babar, born the same day that Killian Bane died. He glanced around as if to offer to locate it for me.

I recalled Sunny's expression as I left her behind in her room in the trees—the bewilderment that I could think her capable of murder. I thought of that often, in the months and years after: the fact that the thing that sent me running from her was a lie. Sometimes I answer myself: the thing that drew me to her was a lie, too. I lived in fiction that summer, but the fiction concealed truths.

"What then?" I pressed.

She helped him clean up that night and let him crash with her. She had a room in a guesthouse in Morjim and was taking a yoga course at a local Ayurvedic institute. She did not tell Killian, at the time, that this was a Yogic fertility course.

"She came off as … thirsty," Killian said. "Like, totally rank with need—a need to fuck, a need for *more*. I own this: I took advantage of her, but I think she also took advantage of me. It's so easy to substitute one person for another."

I could feel, as his cadence slowed, that he was trying to impress me with this reflection.

Sunny claimed to be on a kind of spiritual walkabout to get in touch with her roots. She was, herself, a recent divorcée. This was all he learned about her, because she just kept asking *him* questions. Obligingly, he spilled himself into her ear.

"I guess I said everything to her in one night that I'd never said to you. I was reenacting our relationship. And she wanted to help me understand you, better, with this thing—"

"The mirroring," I said.

"Yes." Killian reached for a rosewater electrolyte infusion that Lavanya had left on the coffee table, instructing him to drink it all by the time she got back.

He told her about his dead brother, and about his desire to track down his Indian father. He told her he barely spoke to his mother these days. He told her how the loss of his own family had made him want a new, better family with me. He told Sunny things he had never told me; he wondered, as he talked, whether I would have wanted his child if he'd shared himself more, as he was now sharing himself with her.

They had sex. He tried to put on a condom, but he hadn't worn one in years, and he couldn't get hard. He took the risk. He meant to pull out. But it happened so quickly. And, anyway, she was kind of old. What were the chances? He left Goa the next morning and signed up for a ninety-day silent retreat—a purge—in Dharamshala.

"So who ... who *is* she? *Was* she?"

Killian pointed at a small bookshelf beneath the *Pierrot le Fou* poster. It held all of his favorite plays, and his beloved performance bible, *The Actor and the Target*.

"I was curious, too," he said. "So I looked her up."

Her name ran down the spine of a thin book, which I pulled from the shelf. *You're Your Own Worst Frenemy*, by Sunny Sathian. The jacket was bright yellow, and Sunny was posed on the cover, wearing a pink floral blazer and a low-cut black top emphasizing her considerable bosom. She'd wrangled blurbs from business names even I recognized. The brown CEO of a soft drink company. The brown COO of a social media company. The Asian CFO of an e-commerce company. The praise was gratuitous. Genius and ground-breaking and illuminating. All hailed Sunny Sathian, feminist corporate messiah.

"That's who she was, until she wasn't," Killian said. "She preached leaning in, et cetera, until I guess at some point, she burned out. The story is she had a miscarriage in the middle of a meeting. And she just kept pitching."

I couldn't help it: I was disappointed. It was so plain. She was not a guru. She was a finite woman, a product of a particular moment in history.

I set the book aside.

"So where were you for the rest of the year?" I asked. "You just shot this whole Swiss thing, right?" I pointed at the poster.

After Dharamshala, Killian had gone in search of his father, like the war veteran in the show that never aired. Mary had finally given him some details—a cousin his dad had stayed with in Delhi before coming to Rishikesh. The Delhi lead took him to Darjeeling. Here Killian paused and took a dramatic, ragged inhale, as though this were the part of the story I had been waiting for. The revelation of his paternity.

"My father," he said with disdain, "was named Frank Hatton. He was a drunk. He'd been dead for ten years by the time I got there."

"So, he *wasn't* Indian?"

"Well," Killian hedged. "He was . . . part."

"How much?"

"Um," he said. "An eighth."

"The other seven eighths?"

He wrinkled his nose. "English."

I gripped my stomach to keep from laughing. "You *are* a colonizer."

"But I was also colonized. The *majority* of me was colonized."

Lavanya knocked on the door and entered, bearing a steel tray with three tall, cloudy glasses, and lime quarters wedged onto their rims.

"Nimbu pani," she said, and hung Killian's dry cleaning on a door hook. She hesitated, trying to decide whether to stay or go. Finally, she sat, letting her knee bump his.

I accepted the drink. "So," I said. "That was why Mary never told you his name. Because he was English."

"She was embarrassed. I mean, her brothers were in the feckin' IRA." He adopted the accent he used to use to mock Mary, but there was tenderness. Learning the details of his mother's biography had softened his attitude toward her. He understood this part of Mary—the instinct to confabulate, the desire to spin a story that made your world more bearable, more impressive, to play a different role.

"But at some point, you came back to Bombay," I said, snapping my fingers.

"I signed up for this language immersion school in Uttar Pradesh," he said. "You're cut off from everything, and you're only allowed to communicate in Hindi. This guy I met there also helped me finally learn to dance, or kind of. It's all in the hips, you know. Anyway, when I was done, I came back to Bombay, started auditioning again, and things finally clicked."

"Kalyan is *very* talented," Lavanya said, loyally.

"Where did the photos of you on Sunny's social media come from, though?" I asked.

"She took a bunch of pictures when we were tripping. And, my guess is that she found some in my email. I think she went to Moksha after we met—I'd told her I was staying there. She probably got into my email via the Moksha desktop, which I'd been using to see if you'd contacted me." Killian conjectured that Sunny, signed in as him, had forwarded his inbox to hers and changed his passwords, locking him out. That, he added, was probably also how she got Mary's info, and all our mutual friends'.

"Someone texted me a photo of you two on Carter Road, though," I said. "And Shazia called me, and Miranda—everyone seemed to think *I* was pregnant."

"Well yes," he went on. "She and I did meet here, briefly. I got in from Darjeeling and came back here and she was *squatting* in our house." He pointed in the direction of our old Mount Mary flat. Probably she had just shown up at the building—our address was on Jurgen's forms—claiming to have lost her key, telling the guard to call Miranda Madam, to get the spare. "You always walked past those men so quickly," he said. "And Miranda only met you in person that one time. The Other Sanjena probably passed for you. Or maybe she said she was your sister. I don't know."

Here, in Bombay, Sunny said he had gotten her pregnant and that she planned to keep it; she said that she had been in touch with his mother, who was so happy to hear about her grandchild, and didn't he hope to not be an absentee father, like his own?

"I told her I wanted to go to a doctor with her, to see proof," he said. "She showed me a sonogram and claimed it was hers. She tried to make us a couple, but when it was clear I wasn't into it, she claimed she had lost the baby."

Killian told Sunny never to talk to his mother again. He accused her of playing with a heartbroken woman's emotions. That stung Sunny. She did not like to think of herself as cruel, especially not to other females. He kicked her out. That was the last he heard from her. He was only too happy to leave for Switzerland when the role came his way.

"So, you two," I said. My eyes fell on Lavanya. "It's new."

"Sanj is discreet," Killian said to Lavanya, soothingly.

I snorted and glared at Lavanya. "You know he's still married, right?"

She bit her lower lip coquettishly. "Kalyan fully admits that it was immature to freeze you out. Now, you two can take care of that. You should do it soon. The press would have a field day if they found out."

"*The press*," I echoed.

"I'm not *so* big," Killian said. "No one cares about me like that, Lavanya."

"They *will*," she said, and Killian glowed, basking in the warmth of her adulation.

I put my face in my hands. "You're definitely going to give me the divorce with no issues?" I asked, my voice muffled by my sweaty palms. "I don't want your money or anything."

"You can have money," he said magnanimously. "In fact, we can get started right now. If you want … Lavanya, is my laptop here?"

She pointed out the laptop, on the coffee table, under *Womanspreading*.

In the end, it was terribly simple. There were a few buttons to click on the Connecticut government website, some forms to fill out, an appointment to make with a judge when I got back to town. Killian said he would fly in if necessary. Then we were done, for the time being. I made to leave; outside, the scents of Bombay were calling—jeera and browning onions, the sour pucker of fish at the market, the bonfire scent of smog. Beyond the gates, the gray churning sea met the haze of the sky. I wanted, suddenly, to be there, in the ruck, to be alone in that kind of city where you're never truly alone.

My hand on the doorknob, I spoke over one shoulder to Lavanya. "Congrats," I said. "I hope he's everything you want."

She nodded, dignified, fiddling with her black walkie-talkie.

Then I turned to Killian. I wanted one final look to firmly lodge him in my past before I left.

"I'm free?" I asked.

He glanced askance at Lavanya, then met my eyes again, with the kind of blaze that always overtook him when he was seized by a role.

"If being alone means you're free, Sanj, then sure, I guess, you're free."

11

Who's Afraid of Sanjena Sathian?

One day that following January, when I was on my way home from visiting Lia, Gor, and the baby, Luc, I was startled by a display in a bookstore window. There she was— or, more accurately, there was her likeness: a cardboard cutout of Sanjena Sathian teetered next to a table stacked with hardbacks. She wore a bright mustard blouse and held up a new book: *A Lie of Love: My Fake Pregnancy and My Broken Heart*. By Sunny Sathian. She had returned to her old self after all, leaving me my name.

I went inside and cracked open a copy to an early page.

> I told myself I would never write about this until I was on the other side of my fertility journey. I shared it on social media, though, because that was my work.

> Telling the story to the public gave me purpose. But it also made me feel like I had to tell my Huge Lie. The one that made me the Crazy Lady. I was a pregnancy influencer, but I wasn't really pregnant.
>
> I am not writing to you with a baby crying in the background. No, I'm just surrounded by my friends, and my cat, and hope, for now. This is not a memoir of vanquishing my own body. It is a memoir of submitting to desire, being ravaged by it, and still not knowing whether the desire will ever love you back.

I looked up from the book and blinked at her giant cardboard face. A redheaded woman making for the section labeled *As Seen on #Bookstagram* did a double take, glancing between me and the cutout. She said, "Whoa, congrats, I loved your book," and took a tentative, confiding step toward me. "I don't have a baby, either," she whispered. "People forget: it's not a choice for everyone."

"Oh," I said. "I'm sorry."

She scowled and skulked away. I didn't realize until I read the rest of the memoir, later, that Sunny had a whole bit about not saying sorry when someone loses a pregnancy. *Sorry*, she wrote, *implies that the loss will only ever be a loss. That it won't, in some way, transform into something else. Sorry is a wall between sadness and hope. Try "May the world blossom for you." Try "May joy enter your heart space."*

I saw her all over the place for a month after that. On a billboard in Times Square; at the front of an airport stall when I hopped my flight to California, where I'd decided to study a couple of fertility-technology companies. Alisandra had agreed to let me use the God Complex as a colorful vignette to begin a dissertation largely consisting of cyber ethnography. I spent a lot of time parsing online forums where people trying to conceive gathered to support one another. It was a more manageable project than the one about Nakusha. Most important, I could finish it without much funding or time. And it might even get me a job—digital ethnography was hot.

The people I was studying in the TTC world knew of Sunny, of course, and they saw her as an embarrassing oddity. She was the hysterical example who made them all look bad. I tried to convey to them that I did not think Sunny was foolish, nor did I find her desire grotesque. She was, as she wrote in her book, a person transformed by the miasma of need. The way she described yearning, and her lie itself—the fact that it did not feel like a lie, because she had lived versions of it so many times before—confirmed for me that even in her unreality, there had been something true. It was the role she had been born to play.

Soon after *A Lie of Love* debuted on the bestseller list, a video journalist called me to discuss a documentary on the Shakti Center, which had boomed in popularity since the book launch. Sunny's follower count was up and people were flying to Pune to seek her counsel in droves. The journalist had found me on her social media and wondered if I would be willing to speak to him. He thought there was something fishy about this Sanjena Sathian figure. We spoke briefly. He wanted to know why I'd been there, and I said I went as an anthropologist—a detached observer. He wanted to know if I worried for the other women at the compound. Was fertility technology feminist liberation or patriarchy crossed with capitalism? Was Sunny a pathbreaking entrepreneur or something more nefarious? He hoped for the latter. Cult documentaries were very *in*.

I told the reporter that Sunny may have used tactics one might identify as cultish, but that she had also been something else: a storyteller who had left some indelible mark on me, despite the irreality of the *me* she'd conjured up.

He guffawed. "Could you dumb that down if you went on the record?" A toddler howled somewhere near him, and he hushed the child. "Tyler, Daddy's on the phone. Harriet? One second." A scuffling, as he passed his son to a woman.

"You still there?" I said I was. "The thing is," he said, lowering his voice, "my wife turned me onto this Sunny person. She thinks it's interesting that for all the talk about babies, there aren't any kids in her photos or her book. What's the deal with that?"

"I don't think it was entirely about children," I said. "It was more about imagination."

The untitled God Complex documentary fizzled out. Execs said it had no stakes; no one had died or been abused. I told the producer, "It should count, though." A few months had passed since we first talked. "The idea of the thing, not just the thing it becomes."

"What?" the guy said on the other end. He was whipping down a freeway in LA. "Look. If we find out she, like, killed someone. Or at least defrauded investors. Then I can probably make something happen. But I think what you said, uh … it's too nascent."

I visited Lia on the third Friday of every month. I squeezed her son Luc's fat little thighs and kissed him on the cheeks, but I never offered to babysit. Instead, I made her leave the apartment; Gor could handle Luc solo for a few hours. One night I got us tickets to a show: a contemporary reinterpretation of *Who's Afraid of Virginia Woolf?*, in which the bickering couple was two gay men and their guests, lesbians, which struck me as not all that much of a reinterpretation, since Edward Albee had been gay. But I couldn't resist. The play was still my favorite thing Killian had ever done. When I first saw it, I'd thought of it as vicious satire; more recently, I'd been considering it as a tragicomedy about the entrapments of aging, the way life forecloses everyone.

Before the show, we got Greek food in the theater district. Lia was a shadow of herself. Her labor had been traumatic—twenty hours, failed epidural, emergency Cesarean. She'd felt betrayed by her body. "All you have to do is *push*," she said. "And I couldn't do that." Even now, the breastfeeding was impossibly painful. My subletter, the nipple poet, could have written half a chapbook just on Lia's raw tits. To Gor's chagrin, Lia was opting for formula.

"Motherhood isn't, like, *noble*," she said. "It's really undignified. And I'm so anxious, all the time. I see death everywhere. Ways Luc could die, or Gor could die, or I could die. Not that I'm making the best pitch for it, and I don't mean to *trigger* you, but ..." She hesitated. "Would you still freeze your eggs? After everything with *her*?"

I'd thought about it endlessly, of course, after returning to the US. I still understood the appeal of not having to decide my whole future now, of lingering in bothness, not opening the lid to see whether those Schrödinger's eggs were good or rotted, in case I one day wanted them. But I didn't like the idea of living my life apocalyptically, prepping for every version of me. I didn't want to feel like I was waiting—for G, for some other Sanjana to appear. Perhaps Sunny was right, and one day I would regret my choices. But I was starting to suspect that there was no way to avoid regret, that all you had to do was find a way to live with it.

These were the moments when I took an odd comfort in the fact that Sunny had gone on as her and I had gone on as me. It was better when women did not mix ourselves up with each other, when we did not act as though our bodies belonged to each other.

"That shit is expensive," I said finally, settling on the insufficient but simple excuse.

Lia and I talked for a while longer, and at some point, we landed on Maneesha. After I got back to town, she had called me to make amends. The impetus for reconciliation: Beef Jerky had run away from Ajay's sister's house. Maneesha cried on the phone. The dog's disappearance was a reminder that people could vanish from your life at any moment, she said. I'd resisted pointing out that Beef Jerky wasn't a person. She'd shared a few updates: in Greece, away from job stress and American forever chemicals, she'd gotten pregnant *the old-fashioned way*. She would be taking some more time off work. Xerox was an obsolete company, anyway, and she was starting to have some questions about the way the corporate workforce treated women. The advent of a new baby had clearly inspired Maneesha to tie up loose familial ends, so everything could be *in order* for her perfect home. Perhaps at Maneesha's behest, my parents were also calling me once a month, and my mother had gone so far as to say that she looked forward to seeing me when she came to New Haven next—for Maneesha's baby shower.

I expected Lia to assert, in some essentializing way, that Maneesha was a mom who had to do right by her daughter, and I would never *get* what I'd put her through with the HomeSafe.

"Your sister is such a bitch," Lia said. "She should have gaslighted Naina."

"What?" I slopped tzatziki down my front and hurriedly took a napkin to it.

"That's what I'd do, like, 'You didn't see what you thought you saw!' Or if she were older, I'd say adults sometimes kiss each other's privates, but you wouldn't talk about going potty in front of other people, so it's best not to talk about this, either."

Another patron walked by, glaring at Lia.

"I guess she could have done that," I said. "Hey. I think you're going to be a good parent. I'm sorry I never said that before."

"Why?"

"I don't know if I have the imaginative capacity to make a life for a whole other human being. It takes so much for me to picture my own life. Your imagination might be … bigger than mine. In some ways. I never even thought of the idea that you could talk to a kid about sex without making it seem awful."

"Republicans don't think so," Lia said. "Republicans think that makes you a pedo. Is Maneesha a Republican?"

"She votes red in local races," I said. "Taxes."

Lia mimed vomiting. "Those are the ones that count."

Halfway through the play, Lia fell asleep. When she woke, she said it had been a bad choice: she'd thought the play was about the novelist, the crazy British one who put all the stones in her pockets? She didn't know it was about a *dead baby*. Why hadn't I warned her? I apologized. I didn't tell her the twist: that it wasn't about a dead baby, that George and Martha had made everything up. They were only ever with themselves, and their inner lives. That was the point: they had to create for themselves now.

I left Lia on her doorstep and walked to the train. As I descended into the subway at High Street, a window caught my eye. It was a little shop I'd spotted before. It sold expensive decorative home goods—ceramics and kilims and chandeliers. There was always something lush on display that I noticed (and resented), because it looked so appealing, like it belonged in one of my Zillow-porn listings, because I wanted not to want that domestic decadence myself. Tonight, the display was minimalist. I walked back up the subway steps and crossed the street to peer in. Inside, a blown-glass vase sat atop a white plinth. The vase was vibrant blue, streaked with autumnal hues of red and green, like the November sky. A couple of glass flowers poked out, one a gleaming imitation of a red daffodil, the other a fake pink carnation. I loved the vase, but I found the flowers dishonest. I could never have afforded either, but I wondered if they were sold separately— if I could leave the store with an empty vessel, then decide for myself if I wanted to fill it, or keep it just as it was.

A Note on Research

My research for this book was wide-ranging. Several people helped by discussing their fields with me. Thanks to Imran Jamal, Nile Davies, and Sophie Schrago for talking anthropology, to Roxana Moussavian and Imani Franklin for fielding questions about the law, and to Michael Solotke and Sonia Taneja, who counseled on medical matters.

I relied on the following texts in constructing Sanjana's anthropology research: *Shamans, Mystics, and Doctors: A Psychological Inquiry Into India and Its Healing Traditions* by Sudhir Kakar; *Possessed by the Virgin: Hinduism, Roman Catholicism, and Marian Possession in South India* by Kristin C. Bloomer; *The Self Possessed: Deity and Spirit Possession in South Asian Literature and Civilization* by Frederick M. Smith; and *When God Talks Back: Understanding the American Evangelical Relationship with God* by T. M. Luhrmann.

On sexuality, gender, reproductive technology, bioethics, surrogacy, and much more, I learned from *Full Surrogacy Now:*

Feminism Against Family by Sophie Lewis; *Mother Nature: A History of Mothers, Infants, and Natural Selection* by Sarah Blaffer Hrdy; *Motherhood, Rescheduled: Egg Freezing and the Frontier of Women Who Tried It* by Sarah Elizabeth Richards; and *The Art of Waiting: On Fertility, Medicine, and Motherhood* by Belle Boggs.

I borrowed the idea of a concussive experiencing "ghost" selves from Clark Elliott's *The Ghost in My Brain: How a Concussion Stole My Life and How the New Science of Brain Plasticity Helped Me Get It Back.*

Several other people's ideas found their way into these pages. Dan Chaon and Lynda Barry led me in hypnotic "X-page" exercises at the Clarion Writers' Workshop, which helped me write the "womb regression." Peter Wilczynski used the phrase "dark matter" to describe the way children explain adulthood. Rajesh Jegadeesh gifted me "broom dog."

Acknowledgments

Thank you to my agent Susan Golomb for being such a fierce advocate on my behalf, to my editor Ginny Smith Younce for asking generous questions that invite me back into my own pages, and to Caroline Sydney for the indispensable and keen-eyed reads. Thank you also to Peggy Boulos Smith, Madeleine Ticknor, and Sasha Landauer for the support from Writers

House; to Ann Godoff, Scott Moyers, Juliana Kiyan, Mollie Reid, Jessie Stratton, Katie Hurley, Janine Barlow, and all at Penguin Press; and to Jason Richman and my team at United Talent Agency.

To my other readers and conversation partners: I can make nothing without you. Andrew Ridker, my first interlocutor, always found time and never broke anything. Pooja Bhatia sharpened every sentence she touched. Lee Cole read with an eye not just to plot or pacing but to the ethics of fiction. Ariel Katz heard some of these characters when I could not. Shivani Radhakrishnan helped make this a novel of ideas. Janelle Effiwatt informed me that I was writing a gothic novel. Roshani Chokshi turned the book feral. Ted McCombs advised me to "literalize the metaphor." Ren Arcamone was gentle with a very early version of this project. Diana Saverin also tended to that iteration, and, along with Charley Locke, is eternally willing to turn over the dilemmas of choice, regret, and aging. Ginny Fahs has lived these ideas with me.

I'm grateful to my colleagues and students at Emory University, where I was teaching as I completed this novel. Thank you also to others who kept me company in Atlanta, indulging many rambles about cults and reproduction while this book came to be, especially Ishita Chordia, Kartik Shastri, Aliyya Swaby, Mary Callaway, Angela Tharpe, Poy Winichakul, and Ryan Head.

Thank you to my family for listening, and for understanding.

Finally, above all, thank you to Bill Kelson, for whom a dedication is insufficient. William, B, etc.: your wit, compassion, extraordinary patience, and instincts as writer, reader, and art-boy co-created this book. More importantly, you nourished our shared life outside these pages, making it funnier, vaster, and happier every day.

About the Author

Sanjena Sathian is the author of the critically acclaimed novel *Gold Diggers*, which was named a Top 10 Best Book of 2021 by the *Washington Post* and longlisted for the Center for Fiction's First Novel Prize. It won the Townsend Prize for Fiction. Her short fiction appears in *The Best American Short Stories*, *The Atlantic*, *Conjunctions*, *One Story*, *Boulevard*, and more. She's written nonfiction for *The New York Times*, *New York Magazine*, *The Drift*, *The Yale Review*, and NewYorker.com, among other outlets. She's an alumna of the Iowa Writers' Workshop and has taught at Emory University, the University of Iowa, and Victoria University of Wellington in New Zealand. In spring 2025, she will serve as the Ferrol A. Sams Jr. Distinguished Chair of English at Mercer University. *Goddess Complex* is her second novel.

Also by Sanjena Sathian

Gold Diggers: A Novel

A magical realist coming-of-age story, *Gold Diggers* skewers the model minority myth to tell a hilarious and moving story about immigrant identity, community, and the underside of ambition.

A floundering second-generation teenager growing up in the Bush-era Atlanta suburbs, Neil Narayan is funny and smart but struggles to bear the weight of expectations of his family and their Asian American enclave. He tries to want their version of success, but mostly, Neil just wants his neighbor across the cul-de-sac, Anita Dayal.

When he discovers that Anita is the beneficiary of an ancient, alchemical potion made from stolen gold—a "lemonade" that harnesses the ambition of the gold's original owner—Neil sees his chance to get ahead. But events spiral into a tragedy that rips their community apart. Years later in the Bay Area, Neil still bristles against his community's expectations—and finds he might need one more hit of that lemonade, no matter the cost.

Sanjena Sathian's astonishing debut offers a fine-grained, profoundly intelligent, and bitingly funny investigation into what's required to make it in America.